The *VOYAGES* *of*
DOCTOR DOLITTLE

THE YEARLING DOCTOR DOLITTLE BOOKS

YEARLING BOOKS/YOUNG YEARLINGS/YEARLING CLASSICS are designed especially to entertain and enlighten young people. Charles F. Reasoner, Professor Emeritus of Children's Literature and Reading, New York University, is consultant to this series.

For a complete listing of all Yearling titles, write to Dell Readers Service, P.O. Box 1045, South Holland, Illinois 60473.

The VOYAGES of DOCTOR DOLITTLE

ILLUSTRATED BY THE AUTHOR

BY HUGH LOFTING

THE CENTENARY EDITION
A YEARLING BOOK

Published by
Dell Publishing
a division of
The Bantam Doubleday Dell Publishing Group, Inc.
666 Fifth Avenue
New York, New York 10103

ISBN: 0-440-70014-0

Printed in the United States of America

One previous Dell edition 40002
Book Club edition
New Dell edition
September 1988

10 9 8 7 6 5 4 3 2
OPM

TO
COLIN AND ELIZABETH

· Contents ·

CONTENTS

PART FIVE

PART SIX

· Illustrations ·

The *VOYAGES* of
DOCTOR DOLITTLE

· Prologue ·

ALL that I have written so far about Doctor Dolittle I heard long after it happened from those who had known him—indeed a great deal of it took place before I was born. But I now come to set down that part of the great man's life which I myself saw and took part in.

Many years ago the Doctor gave me permission to do this. But we were both of us so busy then voyaging around the world, having adventures and filling notebooks full of natural history that I never seemed to get time to sit down and write of our doings.

Now, of course, when I am quite an old man, my memory isn't so good anymore. But whenever I am in doubt and have to hesitate and think, I always ask Polynesia, the parrot.

That wonderful bird (she is now nearly two hundred and fifty years old) sits on the top of my desk, usually humming sailor songs to herself while I write this book. And, as everyone who ever met her knows, Polynesia's memory is the most marvelous memory in the world.

First of all, I must tell you something about myself and how I came to meet the Doctor.

PART I

"I would sit on the river wall with my feet dangling over the water"

· The First Chapter ·
THE COBBLER'S SON

MY name is Tommy Stubbins, son of Jacob Stubbins, the cobbler of Puddleby-on-the-Marsh; I was nine and a half years old. At that time Puddleby was only quite a small town. A river ran through the middle of it, and over this river there was a very old stone bridge called Kingsbridge, which led you from the marketplace on one side to the churchyard on the other.

Sailing ships came up this river from the sea and anchored near the bridge. I used to go down and watch the sailors unloading the ships upon the river wall. The sailors sang strange songs as they pulled upon the ropes, and I learned these songs by heart. And I would sit on the river wall with my feet dangling over the water and sing with the men, pretending to myself that I, too, was a sailor.

For I longed always to sail away with those brave ships when they turned their backs on Puddleby Church and went creeping down the river again, across the wide, lonely marshes to the sea. I longed to go with them out into the world to seek my fortune in foreign lands—Africa, India, China, and Peru! When they got around the bend in the river and the water was hidden from view, you could still see their huge brown sails towering over the roofs of the town, moving onward slowly—like some gentle giants that walked among the houses without noise. What strange things would they have seen, I wondered, when next they came back to anchor at Kingsbridge! And, dreaming of the lands I had never seen, I'd sit on there, watching till they were out of sight.

Three great friends I had in Puddleby in those days. One was Joe, the mussel man, who lived in a tiny hut by the edge of the water under the bridge. This old man was simply marvelous at making things. I never saw a man so clever with his hands. He used to mend my toy ships for me, which I sailed upon the river; he built windmills out of packing cases and barrel staves, and he could make the most wonderful kites from old umbrellas.

Joe would sometimes take me in his mussel boat, and when the tide was running out we would paddle down the river as far as the edge of the sea to get mussels and lobsters to sell. And out there on the cold, lonely marshes we would see wild geese flying, and curlews and redshanks and many other kinds of seabirds that live among the samfire and the long grass of the great salt fen. And as we crept up the river in the evening when the tide had turned, we would see the lights on Kingsbridge twinkle in the dusk, reminding us of teatime and warm fires.

Another friend I had was Matthew Mugg, the cat's-meat man. He was a funny old person with a bad squint. He looked rather awful, but he was really quite nice to talk to. He knew everybody in Puddleby, and he knew all the dogs and all the cats. In those times, being a cat's-meat man was a regular business. And you could see one nearly any day going through the streets with a wooden tray full of pieces of meat stuck on skewers crying, "Meat! M-E-A-T!" People paid him to give this meat to their cats and dogs instead of feeding them on dog biscuits or the scraps from the table.

I enjoyed going around with old Matthew and seeing the cats and dogs come running to the garden gates whenever they heard his call. Sometimes he let me give the meat to the animals myself, and I thought this was great fun. He knew a lot about dogs and he would tell me the names of the different kinds as we went through the town. He had several dogs of his own; one, a whippet, was a very fast runner, and Matthew used to win prizes with her at the Saturday coursing races; another, a terrier, was a fine ratter. The cat's-meat man used to make a business of rat-catching for the millers and farmers as well as his other trade of selling cat's meat.

My third great friend was Luke the Hermit. But of him I will tell you more later on.

I did not go to school, because my father was not rich enough to send me. But I was extremely fond of animals. So I used to spend my time collecting birds' eggs and butterflies, fishing in the river, rambling through the countryside after blackberries and mushrooms, and helping the mussel man mend his nets.

Yes, it was a very pleasant life I lived in those days long ago —though of course I did not think so then. I was nine and a half years old, and, like all boys, I wanted to grow up—not knowing how well off I was with no cares and nothing to worry me. Always I longed for the time when I should be allowed to leave my father's house, to take passage in one of those brave ships, to sail down the river through the misty marshes to the sea—out into the world to seek my fortune.

· The Second Chapter ·
I HEAR OF THE GREAT NATURALIST

NE early morning in the springtime, when I wa
wandering among the hills at the back of the town, I hap
pened to come upon a hawk with a squirrel in its claws. I
was standing on a rock, and the squirrel was fighting ver
hard for its life. The hawk was so frightened when I cam
upon it suddenly like this, that it dropped the poor creatur
and flew away. I picked the squirrel up and found that two o
its legs were badly hurt. So I carried it in my arms back to th
town.

When I came to the bridge I went into the mussel man'
hut and asked him if he could do anything for it. Joe put o
his spectacles and examined it carefully. Then he shook hi
head.

"Yon crittur's got a broken leg," he said, "and another badl
cut an' all. I can mend you your boats, Tom, but I haven't th
tools nor the learning to make a broken squirrel seaworth
This is a job for a surgeon—and for a right smart one an' a
There be only one man I know who could save yon crittur
life. And that's John Dolittle."

"Who is John Dolittle?" I asked. "Is he a vet?"

HUGH LOFTING

"I came upon a hawk with a squirrel in its claws"

"No," said the mussel man. "He's no vet. Doctor Dolittle is a nacheralist."

"What's a nacheralist?"

"A nacheralist," said Joe, putting away his glasses and starting to fill his pipe, "is a man who knows all about animals and butterflies and plants and rocks an' all. John Dolittle is a very great nacheralist. I'm surprised you never heard of him —and you daft over animals. He knows a whole lot about shellfish—that I know from my own knowledge. He's a quiet man and don't talk much, but there's folks who do say he's the greatest nacheralist in the world."

"Where does he live?" I asked.

"Over on the Oxenthorpe Road, t'other side the town. Don't know just which house it is, but 'most anyone 'cross there could tell you, I reckon. Go and see him. He's a great man."

So I thanked the mussel man, took up my squirrel again and started off toward the Oxenthorpe Road.

The first thing I heard as I came into the marketplace was someone calling "Meat! M-E-A-T!"

"There's Matthew Mugg," I said to myself. "He'll know where this Doctor lives. Matthew knows everyone."

So I hurried across the marketplace and caught up with him.

"Matthew," I said, "do you know Doctor Dolittle?"

"Do I know John Dolittle!" said he. "Well, I should think I do! I know him as well as I know my own wife—better, I sometimes think. He's a great man—a very great man."

"Can you show me where he lives?" I asked. "I want to take this squirrel to him. It has a broken leg."

"Certainly," said the cat's-meat man. "I'll be going right by his house directly. Come along and I'll show you."

So off we went together.

"Oh, I've known John Dolittle for years and years," said Matthew as we made our way out of the marketplace. "But I'm pretty sure he ain't home just now. He's away on a voyage. But he's liable to be back any day. I'll show you his house and then you'll know where to find him."

All the way down the Oxenthorpe Road, Matthew hardly stopped talking about his great friend, Doctor John Dolittle . . . "M.D." He talked so much that he forgot all about calling out "Meat!" until we both suddenly noticed that we had a whole procession of dogs following us patiently.

"Where did the Doctor go to on this voyage?" I asked as Matthew handed around the meat to them.

"I couldn't tell you," he answered. "Nobody never knows where he goes, nor when he's going, nor when he's coming back. He lives all alone except for his pets. He's made some great voyages and some wonderful discoveries. Last time he came back he told me he'd found a tribe of Indians in the Pacific Ocean—lived on two islands, they did. The husbands lived on one island and the wives lived on the other. Sensible people, some of them Indians. They met only once a year, when the husbands came over to visit the wives for a great feast—Christmastime, most likely. Yes, he's a wonderful man is the Doctor. And as for animals, well, there ain't no one knows as much about 'em as what he does."

"How did he get to know so much about animals?" I asked.

The cat's-meat man stopped and leaned down to whisper in my ear.

"He talks their language," he said in a hoarse, mysterious voice.

"The animals' language?" I cried.

"Why, certainly," said Matthew. "All animals have some kind of a language. Some sorts talk more than others; some speak only in sign language. But the Doctor, he understands them all—birds as well as animals. We keep it a secret though, him and me, because folks only laugh at you when you speak of it. Why, he can even write animal language. He reads aloud to his pets. He's wrote history books in monkey talk, poetry in canary language, and comic songs for magpies to sing. It's a fact. He's now busy learning the language of the shellfish. But he says it's hard work—and he has caught some terrible colds, holding his head under water so much. He's a great man."

"He certainly must be," I said. "I do wish he were home so I could meet him."

"Well, there's his house," said the cat's-meat man. "Look, that little one at the bend in the road there—the one high up —like it was sitting on the wall above the street."

We were now come beyond the edge of the town. And the house that Matthew pointed out was quite a small one standing by itself. There seemed to be a big garden around it; and this garden was much higher than the road, so you had to go up a flight of steps in the wall before you reached the front gate at the top. I could see that there were many fine fruit trees in the garden, for their branches hung down over the wall in places. But the wall was so high I could not see anything else.

When we reached the house Matthew went up the steps to the front gate and I followed him. I thought he was going to go into the garden, but the gate was locked. A dog came running down from the house and he took several pieces of meat, which the cat's-meat man pushed through the bars of the gate, and some paper bags full of corn and bran. I noticed that this dog did not stop to eat the meat, as any ordinary dog would have done, but he took all the things back to the house and disappeared. He had a curious wide collar around his neck that looked as though it were made of brass or something. Then we came away.

"The Doctor isn't back yet," said Matthew, "or the gate wouldn't be locked."

"What were all those things in paper bags you gave the dog?" I asked.

"Oh, those were provisions," said Matthew, "things for the

animals to eat. The Doctor's house is simply full of pets. I give the things to the dog while the Doctor's away, and the dog gives them to the other animals."

"And what was that curious collar he was wearing around his neck?"

"That's a solid gold dog collar," said Matthew. "It was given to him when he was with the Doctor on one of his voyages long ago. He saved a man's life."

"How long has the Doctor had him?" I asked.

"Oh, a long time. Jip's getting pretty old now. That's why the Doctor doesn't take him on his voyages anymore. He leaves him behind to take care of the house. Every Monday and Thursday I bring the food to the gate here and give it him through the bars. He never lets anyone come inside the garden while the Doctor's away—not even me, though he knows me well. But you'll always be able to tell if the Doctor's back or not—because if he is, the gate will surely be open."

So I went off home to my father's house and put my squirrel to bed in an old wooden box full of straw. And there I nursed him myself and took care of him as best I could till the time should come when the Doctor would return. And every day I went to the little house with the big garden on the edge of the town and tried the gate to see if it was locked. Sometimes the dog, Jip, would come down to the gate to meet me. But though he always wagged his tail and seemed glad to see me, he never let me come inside the garden.

· The Third Chapter ·
THE DOCTOR'S HOME

ONE Monday afternoon toward the end of April my father asked me to take some shoes that he had mended to a house on the other side of the town. They were for a Colonel Bellowes, who was very particular.

I found the house and rang the bell at the front door. The Colonel opened it, stuck out a very red face, and said, "Go around to the tradesmen's entrance—go to the back door." Then he slammed the door shut.

I felt inclined to throw the shoes into the middle of his flower bed. But I thought my father might be angry, so I didn't. I went around to the back door, and there the Colonel's wife met me and took the shoes from me. She seemed to be terribly afraid of her husband, whom I could still hear stumping around the house somewhere, grunting indignantly because I had come to the front door. Then she asked me in a whisper if I would have a bun and a glass of milk. And I said, "Yes, please."

After I had eaten the bun and milk and thanked the Colonel's wife, I thought that I would see if the Doctor had come back yet. My squirrel wasn't getting any better, and I was beginning to be worried about him.

So I started off toward the Doctor's house. On the way I noticed that the sky was clouding over and that it looked as though it might rain.

I reached the gate and found it locked. I felt very discouraged. I had been coming here every day for a week now. The dog, Jip, came to the gate and wagged his tail as usual, and then sat down and watched me closely to see that I didn't get in.

I began to fear that my squirrel would die before the Doctor came back. I turned away sadly, went down the steps on to the road, and turned toward home again.

I wondered if it was suppertime yet. Of course I had no watch of my own, but I noticed a gentleman coming toward me down the road; and when he got nearer, I saw it was the Colonel out for a walk. He was all wrapped up in smart overcoats and mufflers and bright-colored gloves. It was not a very cold day, but he had so many clothes on he looked like a pillow inside a roll of blankets. I asked him if he would please tell me the time.

He stopped, grunted, and glared down at me—his red face growing redder still; and when he spoke it sounded like the cork coming out of a gingerbeer bottle.

"Do you imagine for one moment," he spluttered, "that I am going to get myself all unbuttoned just to tell a little boy like you *the time!*" And he went stumping down the street, grunting harder than ever.

I stood still a moment looking after him and wondering how old I would have to be, to have him go to the trouble of getting his watch out. And then, all of a sudden, the rain came down in torrents.

I have never seen it rain so hard. It got dark, almost like night. The wind began to blow; the thunder rolled; the lightning flashed; and in a moment, the gutters of the road were flowing like a river. There was no place handy to take shelter, so I put my head down against the driving wind and started to run toward home.

I hadn't gone very far when my head bumped into something soft, and I sat down suddenly on the pavement. I looked up to see whom I had run into. And there in front of me, sitting on the wet pavement like myself, was a little round man with a very kind face. He wore a shabby high hat and in his hand he had a small black bag.

"I'm very sorry," I said. "I had my head down and I didn't see you coming."

To my great surprise, instead of getting angry at being knocked down, the little man began to laugh.

"It was just as much my fault as it was yours, you know," said the little man. "I had my head down too—but look here, we mustn't sit talking like this. You must be soaked. I know I am. How far have you got to go?"

"My home is on the other side of the town," I said as we picked ourselves up.

"My goodness, but that *was* a wet pavement!" said he. "And, I declare, it's coming down worse than ever. Come along to my house and get dried. A storm like this can't last."

He took hold of my hand and we started running back down the road together. As we ran I began to wonder who this funny little man could be and where he lived. I was a perfect stranger to him, and yet he was taking me to his own home to get dried. Such a change, after the old red-faced Colonel who had refused even to tell me the time! Presently we stopped.

"Here we are," he said.

I looked up to see where we were and found myself back at the foot of the steps leading to the little house with the big garden! My new friend was already running up the steps and opening the gate with some keys he took from his pocket.

Surely, I thought, this cannot be the great Doctor Dolittle himself!

I suppose after hearing so much about him I had expected someone very tall and strong and marvelous. It was hard to believe that this funny little man with the kind smiling face could really be he. Yet here he was, opening the very gate which I had been watching for so many days!

The dog, Jip, came rushing out and started jumping up on him and barking with happiness. The rain was splashing down heavier than ever.

"Are you Doctor Dolittle?" I shouted as we sped up the short garden path to the house.

"Yes, I'm Doctor Dolittle," said he, opening the front door with the same bunch of keys. "Get in! Don't bother about wiping your feet. Never mind the mud. Take it in with you. Get in out of the rain!"

I popped in, he and Jip following. Then he slammed the door to behind us.

The storm had made it dark enough outside, but inside the house, with the door closed, it was as black as night. Then began the most extraordinary noise that I have ever heard. It sounded like all sorts and kinds of animals and birds calling and squeaking and screeching at the same time. I could hear things trundling down the stairs and hurrying along passages. Somewhere in the dark a duck was quacking, a cock was crowing, a dove was cooing, an owl was hooting, a lamb was bleating, and Jip was barking. I felt birds' wings fluttering and fanning near my face. Things kept bumping into my legs and nearly upsetting me. The whole front hall seemed to be filling up with animals. The noise, together with the roaring of the rain, was tremendous; and I was beginning to grow a little bit scared when I felt the Doctor take hold of my arm and shout into my ear.

"Don't be alarmed. Don't be frightened. These are just some of my pets. I've been away three months and they are glad to see me home again. Stand still where you are till I strike a light. My gracious, what a storm! Just listen to that thunder!"

So there I stood in the pitch-black dark, while all kinds of animals that I couldn't see chattered and jostled around me. It all seemed like some queer dream and I was beginning to wonder if I was really awake, when I heard the Doctor speaking again: "My blessed matches are all wet. They won't strike. Have you got any?"

"No, I'm afraid I haven't," I called back.

"Never mind," said he. "Perhaps Dab-Dab can raise us a light somewhere."

Then the Doctor made some funny clicking noises with his tongue and I heard someone trundle up the stairs again and start moving about in the rooms above.

Then we waited quite a while without anything happening.

"Will the light be long in coming?" I asked. "Some animal is sitting on my foot and my toes are going to sleep."

"No, only a minute," said the Doctor. "She'll be back in a minute."

And just then I saw the first glimmerings of a light around the landing above. At once all the animals kept quiet.

"I thought you lived alone," I said to the Doctor.

"So I do," said he. "It is Dab-Dab who is bringing the light."

I looked up the stairs trying to make out who was coming. I

could not see around the landing, but I heard the most curious footstep on the upper flight. It sounded like someone hopping down from one step to the other, as though he were using only one leg.

As the light came lower, it grew brighter and began to throw strange jumping shadows on the walls.

"Ah—at last!" said the Doctor. "Good old Dab-Dab!"

And then I thought I *really* must be dreaming. For there, craning her neck around the bend of the landing, hopping down the stairs on one leg, came a spotless white duck. And in her right foot she carried a lighted candle!

"And in her right foot she carried a lighted candle!"

· The Fourth Chapter ·
THE WIFF-WAFF

WHEN at last I could look around me I found that the hall was indeed simply full of animals. It seemed to me that almost every kind of creature from the countryside must be there: a pigeon, a white rat, an owl, a badger, a jackdaw—there was even a small pig, just in from the rainy garden, carefully wiping his feet on the mat while the light from the candle glistened on his wet pink back.

The Doctor took the candlestick from the duck and turned to me.

"Look here," he said, "you must get those wet clothes off— by the way, what is your name?"

"Tommy Stubbins," I said.

"Oh, are you the son of Jacob Stubbins, the shoemaker?"

"Yes," I said.

"Excellent bootmaker, your father," said the Doctor. "You see these?" and he held up his right foot to show me the enormous boots he was wearing. "Your father made me those boots four years ago, and I've been wearing them ever since —perfectly wonderful boots. Well now, look here, Stubbins, you've got to change those wet things—and quick. Wait a moment till I get some more candles lit, and then we'll go upstairs and find some dry clothes. You'll have to wear an old suit of mine till we can get yours dry again by the kitchen fire."

So presently when more candles had been lighted around different parts of the house, we went upstairs; and when we had come into a bedroom the Doctor opened a big wardrobe and took out two suits of old clothes. These we put on. Then we carried our wet ones down to the kitchen and started a fire in the big chimney. The coat of the Doctor's that I was wearing was so large for me that I kept treading on my own coattails while I was helping to fetch the wood up from the cellar. But very soon we had a huge big fire blazing up the chimney and we hung our wet clothes around on chairs.

"Now let's cook some supper," said the Doctor. "You'll stay and have supper with me, Stubbins, of course?"

Already I was beginning to be very fond of this funny little man who called me "Stubbins" instead of "Tommy" or "little lad" (I did so hate to be called "little lad"!). This man seemed to begin right away treating me as though I were a grown-up friend of his. And when he asked me to stop and have supper with him I felt terribly proud and happy. But I suddenly remembered that I had not told my mother that I would be out late. So very sadly I answered, "Thank you very much. I would like to stay, but I am afraid that my mother will begin to worry and wonder where I am if I don't get back."

"Oh, but my dear Stubbins," said the Doctor, throwing another log of wood on the fire, "your clothes aren't dry yet. You'll have to wait for them, won't you? By the time they are ready to put on, we will have supper cooked and eaten. . . . Did you see where I put my bag?"

"I think it is still in the hall," I said. "I'll go and see."

I found the bag near the front door. It was made of black leather and looked very, very old. One of its latches was broken and it was tied up around the middle with a piece of string.

"Thank you," said the Doctor when I brought it to him.

"Was that bag all the luggage you had for your voyage?" I asked.

"Yes," said the Doctor, as he undid the piece of string. "I don't believe in a lot of baggage. It's such a nuisance. Life's too short to fuss with it. And it isn't really necessary, you know. . . . Where *did* I put those sausages?"

The Doctor was feeling about inside the bag. First he brought out a loaf of new bread. Next came a glass jar with a curious metal top to it. He held this up to the light very carefully before he set it down upon the table, and I could see that there was some strange little water-creature swimming about inside. At last the Doctor brought out a pound of sausages.

"Now," he said, "all we want is a frying pan."

We went into the scullery and there we found some pots and pans hanging against the wall. The Doctor took down the frying pan.

While the Doctor was busy cooking I went and took another look at the funny little creature swimming about in the glass jar.

"What is this animal?" I asked.

"Oh that," said the Doctor, turning around, "that's a Wiff-Waff. Its full name is *hippocampus pippitopitus.* But the natives just call it a Wiff-Waff—on account of the way it waves its tail, swimming, I imagine. That's what I went on this last voyage for, to get that. You see I'm very busy just now trying to learn the language of the shellfish. They *have* language, of that I feel sure. I can talk a little shark language and porpoise dialect myself. But what I particularly want to learn now is shellfish."

"Why?" I asked.

"Well, you see, some of the shellfish are the oldest kind of animals in the world that we know of. We find their shells in the rocks—turned to stone—thousands of years old. So I feel quite sure that if I could only get to talk their language, I should be able to learn a whole lot about what the world was like ages ago. You see?"

"But couldn't some of the other animals tell you as well?"

"I don't think so," said the Doctor, prodding the sausages with a fork. "To be sure, the monkeys I knew in Africa some time ago were very helpful in telling me about bygone days, but they only went back a thousand years or so. No, I am certain that the oldest history in the world is to be had from the shellfish—and from them only. You see, most of the other animals that were alive in those very ancient times have now become extinct."

"Have you learned any shellfish language yet?" I asked.

"No. I've only just begun. I wanted this particular kind of a pipefish because he is half shellfish and half ordinary fish. I went all the way to the Eastern Mediterranean after him. But I'm very much afraid he isn't going to be a great deal of help to me. To tell you the truth, I'm rather disappointed in his appearance. He doesn't *look* very intelligent, does he?"

"No, he doesn't," I agreed.

"Ah," said the Doctor. "The sausages are done to a turn. Come along—hold your plate near and let me give you some."

Then we sat down at the kitchen table and started a hearty meal.

It was a wonderful kitchen, that. I had many meals there

afterward and I found it a better place to eat in than the grandest dining room in the world. It was so cozy and home-like and warm. It was so handy for the food, too. You took it right off the fire, hot, and put it on the table and ate it. And you could watch your toast toasting at the fender and see it didn't burn while you drank your soup. And if you had for-gotten to put the salt on the table, you didn't have to get up and go into another room to fetch it; you just reached around and took the big wooden box off the dresser behind you. Then the fireplace—the biggest fireplace you ever saw—was like a room in itself. You could get right inside it, even when the logs were burning, and sit on the wide seats at either side and roast chestnuts after the meal was over—or listen to the kettle singing, or tell stories, or look at picture books by the light of the fire. It was a marvelous kitchen. It was like the Doctor, comfortable, sensible, friendly, and solid.

While we were gobbling away, the door suddenly opened and in marched the duck, Dab-Dab, and the dog, Jip, drag-ging sheets and pillowcases behind them over the clean tiled floor. The Doctor, seeing how surprised I was, explained: "They're just going to air the bedding for me in front of the fire. Dab-Dab is a perfect treasure of a housekeeper; she never forgets anything. I had a sister once who used to keep house for me (poor, dear Sarah! I wonder how she's getting on—I haven't seen her in many years). But she wasn't nearly as good as Dab-Dab. Have another sausage?"

The Doctor turned and said a few words to the dog and duck in some strange talk and signs. They seemed to under-stand him perfectly.

"Can you talk in squirrel language?" I asked.

"Oh yes. That's quite an easy language," said the Doctor.

"You could learn that yourself without a great deal of trouble. But why do you ask?"

"Because I have a sick squirrel at home," I said. "I took it away from a hawk. But two of its legs are badly hurt and I wanted very much to have you see it, if you would. Shall I bring it tomorrow?"

"Well, if its leg is badly broken I think I had better see it tonight. It may be too late to do much, but I'll come home with you and take a look at it."

So presently we felt the clothes by the fire and mine were found to be quite dry. I took them upstairs to the bedroom and changed, and when I came down the Doctor was all ready waiting for me with his little black bag full of medicines and bandages.

"Come along," he said. "The rain has stopped now."

Outside it had grown bright again and the evening sky was all red with the setting sun; and thrushes were singing in the garden as we opened the gate to go down onto the road.

· The Fifth Chapter ·
POLYNESIA

I THINK your house is the most interesting house I was ever in," I said as we set off in the direction of the town. "May I come and see you again tomorrow?"

"Certainly," said the Doctor. "Come any day you like. Tomorrow I'll show you the garden and my private zoo."

"Oh, have you a zoo?" I asked.

"Yes," said he. "The larger animals are too big for the house, so I keep them in a zoo in the garden. It is not a very big collection, but it is interesting in its way."

"It must be splendid," I said, "to be able to talk all the languages of the different animals. Do you think I could ever learn to do it?"

"Oh surely," said the Doctor, ". . . with practice. You have to be very patient, you know. You really ought to have Polynesia to start you. It was she who gave me my first lessons."

"Who is Polynesia?" I asked.

"Polynesia was a West African parrot I had. She isn't with me anymore now," said the Doctor sadly.

"Why? Is she dead?"

"Oh, no," said the Doctor. "She is still living, I hope. But when we reached Africa she seemed so glad to get back to her own country. She wept for joy. And when the time came for me to come back here, I had not the heart to take her away from that sunny land—although, it is true, she did offer to come. I left her in Africa. Ah, well! I have missed her terribly. She wept again when we left. But I think I did the right thing. She was one of the best friends I ever had. It was she who first gave me the idea of learning the animal languages and becoming an animal doctor. I often wonder if she remained happy in Africa, and whether I shall ever see her funny old solemn face again. Good old Polynesia!. A most extraordinary bird—well, well!"

Just at that moment we heard the noise of someone running behind us and, turning around, we saw Jip, the dog, rushing down the road after us as fast as his legs could bring him. He seemed very excited about something, and as soon as he came up to us he started barking and whining to the Doctor in a peculiar way. Then the Doctor, too, seemed to get all worked up and began talking and making queer signs to the dog.

At length he turned to me, his face shining with happiness. "Polynesia has come back!" he cried. "Imagine it! Jip says she has just arrived at the house. My! And it's five years since I saw her. . . . excuse me a minute."

He turned as if to go back home. But the parrot, Polynesia, was already flying toward us. The Doctor clapped his hands like a child getting a new toy, while the swarm of sparrows in the roadway fluttered, gossiping, up onto the fences, highly scandalized to see a gray and scarlet parrot skimming down an English lane.

On she came, straight onto the Doctor's shoulder, where she immediately began talking a steady stream in a language

I could not understand. She seemed to have a terrible lot to say. And very soon the Doctor had forgotten all about me and my squirrel and Jip and everything else, till at length the bird clearly asked him something about me.

"Oh, excuse me, Stubbins!" said the Doctor. "I was so interested listening to my old friend here. We must get on and see this squirrel of yours. . . . Polynesia, this is Thomas Stubbins."

The parrot, on the Doctor's shoulder, nodded gravely toward me and then, to my great surprise, said quite plainly in English, "How do you do? I remember the night you were born. It was a terribly cold winter. You were a very ugly baby."

"Stubbins is anxious to learn animal language," said the Doctor. "I was just telling him about you and the lessons you gave me, when Jip ran up and told us you had arrived."

"Well," said the parrot, turning to me, "I may have started the Doctor learning, but I never could have done even that if he hadn't first taught me to understand what *I* was saying when I spoke English. You see, many parrots can talk like a person, but very few of them understand what they are saying. They just say it because . . . well, because they fancy it is smart or because they know they will get crackers given them."

By this time we had turned and were going toward my home with Jip running in front and Polynesia still perched on the Doctor's shoulder. The bird chattered incessantly, mostly about Africa, but now she spoke in English out of politeness to me.

"How is Prince Bumpo getting on?" asked the Doctor.

"Oh, I'm glad you asked me," said Polynesia. "I almost forgot to tell you. What do you think? *Bumpo is in England!*"

"In England! You don't say!" cried the Doctor. "What on earth is he doing here?"

"His father, the king, sent him here to a place called, er, Bullford, I think it was, to study lessons."

"Bullford . . . Bullford," muttered the Doctor. "I never heard of the place . . . oh, you mean Oxford."

"Yes, that's the place—Oxford," said Polynesia. "I knew it had cattle in it somewhere. Oxford—that's the place he's gone to."

"Well, well," murmured the Doctor. "Fancy Bumpo studying at Oxford. Well, well!"

"There were great doings in Jolliginki when he left. He was scared to death to come. He was the first man from that country to go abroad. But his father made him come. He said that all the African kings were sending their sons to Oxford now. It was the fashion, and he would have to go. Poor Bumpo went off in tears—and everybody in the palace was crying too. You never heard such a hullabaloo."

"And how is Chee-Chee getting on? Chee-Chee," added the Doctor in explanation to me, "was a pet monkey I had years ago. I left him, too, in Africa when I came away."

"Well," said Polynesia frowning, "Chee-Chee is not entirely happy. I saw a good deal of him the last few years. He got dreadfully homesick for you and the house and the garden. It's funny, but I was just the same way myself. I just couldn't seem to settle down. Well, one night I made up my mind that I'd come back here and find you. So I hunted up old Chee-Chee and told him about it. He said he didn't blame me a bit —felt exactly the same way himself. Africa was so deadly quiet after the life we had led with you. He missed the stories you used to tell us and the chats we used to have sitting around the kitchen fire on winter nights. The animals out there were very nice to us, and all that. But somehow the dear, kind creatures seemed a bit stupid. Chee-Chee said he had noticed it too. But I suppose it wasn't they who had changed; it was we who were different. When I left, poor old Chee-Chee broke down and cried. He said he felt as though his only friend were leaving him—though, as you know, he has simply millions of relatives there. He said it didn't seem fair that I should have wings to fly over here anytime I liked, and him with no way to follow me. But mark my words, I wouldn't be a bit surprised if he found a way to come—some day. He's a smart lad, is Chee-Chee."

At this point we arrived at my home. My father's shop was closed and the shutters were up, but my mother was standing at the door looking down the street.

"Good evening, Mrs. Stubbins," said the Doctor. "It is my fault your son is so late. I made him stay to supper while his clothes were drying. He was soaked to the skin and so was I. We ran into one another in the storm and I insisted on his coming into my house for shelter."

"I was beginning to get worried about him," said my mother. "I am thankful to you, sir, for looking after him so well and bringing him home."

"Don't mention it, don't mention it," said the Doctor. "We have had a very interesting chat."

"Who might it be that I have the honor of addressing?" asked my mother, staring at the gray parrot perched on the Doctor's shoulder.

"Oh, I'm John Dolittle. I daresay your husband will remember me. He made me some very excellent boots about four years ago. They really are splendid," added the Doctor, gazing down at his feet with great satisfaction.

"The Doctor has come to cure my squirrel, Mother," said I. "He knows all about animals."

"Oh, no," said the Doctor, "not all, Stubbins, not all about them by any means."

"It is very kind of you to come so far to look after his pet," said my mother. "Tom is always bringing home strange creatures from the woods and the fields."

"Is he?" said the Doctor. "Perhaps he will grow up to be a naturalist some day. Who knows?"

"Won't you come in?" asked my mother. "The place is a little untidy because I haven't finished the spring cleaning yet. But there's a nice fire burning in the parlor."

"Thank you!" said the Doctor. "What a charming home you have!"

And after wiping his enormous boots very, very carefully on the mat, the great man passed into the house.

· The Sixth Chapter ·
THE WOUNDED SQUIRREL

INSIDE we found my father busy practicing on the flute beside the fire. This he always did, every evening, after his work was over.

The Doctor immediately began talking to him about flutes and piccolos and bassoons, and presently my father said, "Perhaps you perform upon the flute yourself, sir. Won't you play us a tune?"

"Well," said the Doctor, "it is a long time since I touched the instrument. But I would like to try. May I?"

Then the Doctor took the flute from my father and played and played and played. It was wonderful. My mother and father sat as still as statues, staring up at the ceiling as though they were in church; and even I, who didn't bother much about music except on the mouth organ—even I felt all sad and cold and creepy and wished I had been a better boy.

"Oh, I think that was just beautiful!" sighed my mother when at length the Doctor stopped.

"You are a great musician, sir," said my father, "a very great musician. Won't you please play us something else?"

"Why certainly," said the Doctor ". . . oh, but look here, I've forgotten all about the squirrel."

"I'll show him to you," I said. "He is upstairs in my room."

So I led the Doctor to my bedroom at the top of the house and showed him the squirrel in the packing case filled with straw.

The animal, who had always seemed very much afraid of me—though I had tried hard to make him feel at home—sat up at once when the Doctor came into the room and started to chatter. The Doctor chattered back in the same way and the squirrel, when he was lifted up to have his leg examined, appeared to be rather pleased than frightened.

I held a candle while the Doctor tied the leg up in what he called "splints," which he made out of matchsticks with his penknife.

"I think you will find that his leg will get better now in a very short time," said the Doctor, closing up his bag. "Don't let him run about for at least two weeks yet, but keep him in the open air and cover him up with dry leaves if the nights get cool. He tells me he is rather lonely here all by himself and is wondering how his wife and children are getting on. I have assured him you are a man to be trusted, and I will send a squirrel who lives in my garden to find out how his family is and to bring him news of them. He must be kept cheerful at all costs. Squirrels are naturally a very cheerful, active race. It is very hard for them to lie still doing nothing. But you needn't worry about him. He will be all right."

Then we went back again to the parlor, and my mother and father kept him playing the flute till after ten o'clock.

I often look back upon that night long, long ago. And if I close my eyes and think hard, I can see that parlor just as it was then: a funny little man in coattails, with a round kind face, playing away on the flute in front of the fire; my mother on one side of him and my father on the other, holding their breath and listening with their eyes shut; myself, with Jip, squatting on the carpet at his feet, staring into the coals; and Polynesia perched on the mantelpiece beside his shabby high hat, gravely swinging her head from side to side in time to the music. I see it all, just as though it were before me now.

And then I remember how, after we had seen the Doctor out at the front door, we all came back into the parlor and talked about him till it was still later, and even after I did go to bed (I had never stayed up so late in my life before) I dreamed about him and a band of strange, clever animals that played flutes and fiddles and drums the whole night through.

· The Seventh Chapter ·
SHELLFISH TALK

THE next morning, although I had gone to bed so late the night before, I was up frightfully early. The first sparrows were just beginning to chirp sleepily on the slates outside my attic window when I jumped out of bed and scrambled into my clothes.

I could hardly wait to get back to the little house with the big garden—to see the Doctor and his private zoo. For the first time in my life I forgot all about breakfast; and creeping down the stairs on tiptoe, so as not to wake my mother and father, I opened the front door and popped out into the empty, silent street.

When I got to the Doctor's gate I suddenly thought that perhaps it was too early to call on anyone, and I began to wonder if the Doctor would be up yet. I looked into the garden. No one seemed to be about. So I opened the gate quietly and went inside.

As I turned to the left to go down a path between some hedges, I heard a voice quite close to me say, "Good morning. How early you are!"

I turned around, and there, sitting on the top of a privet hedge, was the gray parrot, Polynesia.

"Good morning," I said. "I suppose I am rather early. Is the Doctor still in bed?"

"Oh, no," said Polynesia. "He has been up an hour and a half. You'll find him in the house somewhere. The front door is open. Just push it and go in. He is sure to be in the kitchen cooking breakfast—or working in his study. Walk right in. I am waiting to see the sun rise. But, upon my word, I believe it's forgotten to rise. It is an awful climate, this. Now if we were in Africa, the world would be blazing with sunlight at this hour of the morning. Just see that mist rolling over those cabbages. It is enough to give you rheumatism to look at it. Beastly climate—beastly! Really, I don't know why anything but frogs ever stay in England. Well, don't let me keep you. Run along and see the Doctor."

"Thank you," I said. "I'll go and look for him."

When I opened the front door I could smell bacon frying, so I made my way to the kitchen. There I discovered a large kettle boiling away over the fire and some bacon and eggs in a dish upon the hearth. It seemed to me that the bacon was getting all dried up with the heat. So I pulled the dish a little farther away from the fire and went on through the house looking for the Doctor.

I found him at last in the study. I did not know then that it was called the study. It was certainly a very interesting room, with telescopes and microscopes and all sorts of other strange things that I did not understand but wished I did. Hanging on the walls were pictures of animals and fishes and strange plants and collections of birds' eggs and seashells in glass cases.

The Doctor was standing at the main table in his dressing

gown. At first I thought he was washing his face. He had a square glass box before him full of water. He was holding one ear under the water, while he covered the other with his left hand. As I came in he stood up.

"Good morning, Stubbins," said he. "Going to be a nice day, don't you think? I've just been listening to the Wiff-Waff. But he is very disappointing—very."

"Why?" I said. "Didn't you find that he has any language at all?"

"Oh, yes," said the Doctor, "he has a language. But it is such a poor language—only a few words, like 'yes' and 'no,' 'hot' and 'cold.' That's all he can say. It's very disappointing. You see, he really belongs to two different families of fishes. I thought he was going to be tremendously helpful . . . well, well!"

"I suppose," said I, "that means he hasn't very much sense —if his language is only two or three words?"

"Yes, I suppose it does. Possibly it is the kind of life he leads. You see, they are very rare now, these Wiff-Waffs, very rare and very solitary. They swim around in the deepest parts of the ocean entirely by themselves—always alone. So I presume they really don't need to talk much."

"Perhaps some kind of a bigger shellfish would talk more," I said. "After all, he is very small, isn't he?"

"Yes," said the Doctor, "that's true. Oh, I have no doubt that there are shellfish who are good talkers—not the least doubt. But the big shellfish—the biggest of them are so hard to catch. They are to be found only in the deep parts of the sea; and as they don't swim very much, but just crawl along the floor of the ocean most of the time, they are very seldom taken in nets. I do wish I could find some way of going down to the bottom of the sea. I could learn a lot if I could only do that. But we are forgetting all about breakfast. . . . Have you had breakfast yet, Stubbins?"

I told the Doctor that I had forgotten all about it and he at once led the way into the kitchen.

"Yes," he said, as he poured the hot water from the kettle into the teapot, "if a man could only manage to get right down to the bottom of the sea and live there a while, he would discover some wonderful things—things that people have never dreamed of."

"But men do go down, don't they?" I asked, ". . . divers and people like that?"

"Oh, yes, to be sure," said the Doctor. "Divers go down. I've been down myself in a diving suit, for that matter. But, my!— they go only where the sea is shallow. Divers can't go down where it is really deep. What I would like to do is to go down to the great depths—where it is miles deep. Well, well, I daresay I shall manage it some day. Let me give you another cup of tea."

· The Eighth Chapter ·
ARE YOU A GOOD NOTICER?

JUST at that moment Polynesia came into the room and said something to the Doctor in bird language. Of course I did not understand what it was. But the Doctor at once put down his knife and fork and left the room.

"You know, it is an awful shame," said the parrot as soon as the Doctor had closed the door. "Directly he comes back home, all the animals over the whole countryside get to hear of it and every sick cat and mangy rabbit for miles around comes to see him and ask his advice. Now there's a big fat hare outside at the back door with a squawking baby. Can she see the Doctor, please! Thinks it's going to have convulsions. Stupid little thing's been eating deadly nightshade again, I suppose. The animals are *so* inconsiderate at times—especially the mothers. They come around and call the Doctor away from his meals and wake him out of his bed at all hours of the night. I don't know how he stands it—really, I don't. Why, the poor man never gets any peace at all! I've told him time and again to have special hours for the animals to come. But he is so frightfully kind and considerate. He never refuses to see them if there is anything really wrong with them. He says the urgent cases must be seen at once."

"Why don't some of the animals go and see the other doctors?" I asked.

"Oh, good gracious!" exclaimed the parrot, tossing her head scornfully. "Why, there aren't any other animal doctors—not real doctors. Oh, of course there *are* those vet persons, to be sure. But, bless you, they're no good. You see, they can't understand the animals' language, so how can you expect them to be any use? Imagine yourself, or your father, going to see a doctor who could not understand a word you say—nor even tell you in your own language what you must do to get well! Poof!—those vets! They're that stupid, you've no idea! . . . put the Doctor's bacon down by the fire, will you, to keep hot till he comes back."

"Do you think I would ever be able to learn the language of the animals?" I asked, laying the plate upon the hearth.

"Well, it all depends," said Polynesia. "Are you clever at lessons?"

"I don't know," I answered, feeling rather ashamed. "You see, I've never been to school. My father is too poor to send me."

"Well," said the parrot, "I don't suppose you have really missed much—to judge from what *I* have seen of schoolboys. But listen: Are you a good noticer? Do you notice things well? I mean, for instance, supposing you saw two cock starlings on an apple tree, and you took only one good look at them—would you be able to tell one from the other if you saw them again the next day?"

"I don't know," I said. "I've never tried."

"Well, that . . ." said Polynesia, brushing some crumbs off the corner of the table with her left foot, "that is what you

" 'Being a good noticer is terribly important' "

call powers of observation—noticing the small things about birds and animals: the way they walk and move their heads and flip their wings, the way they sniff the air and twitch their whiskers and wiggle their tails. You have to notice all those little things if you want to learn animal language. For, you see, lots of the animals hardly talk at all with their tongues; they use their breath or their tails or their feet, instead. That is because many of them, in the olden days when lions and tigers were more plentiful, were afraid to make a noise for fear the savage creatures would hear them. Birds, of course, didn't care, for they always had wings to fly away with. But that is the first thing to remember: Being a good noticer is terribly important in learning animal language."

"It sounds pretty hard," I said.

"You'll have to be very patient," said Polynesia. "It takes a long time to say even a few words properly. But if you come here often, I'll give you a few lessons myself. And once you get started, you'll be surprised how fast you get on. It would indeed be a good thing if you could learn. Because then you could do some of the work for the Doctor—I mean the easier work, like bandaging and giving pills. Yes, yes, that's a good idea of mine. 'Twould be a great thing if the poor man could get some help—and some rest. It is a scandal the way he works. I see no reason why you shouldn't be able to help him a great deal—that is, if you are really interested in animals."

"Oh, I'd love that!" I cried. "Do you think the Doctor would let me?"

"Certainly," said Polynesia, "as soon as you have learned something about doctoring. I'll speak of it to him myself—sh! I hear him coming. Quick—bring his bacon back to the table."

· The Ninth Chapter ·
THE GARDEN OF DREAMS

WHEN breakfast was over the Doctor took me out to show me the garden. Well, if the house had been interesting, the garden was a hundred times more so. At first, you did not realize how big it was. When you were sure that you had seen it all, you would peer over a hedge or turn a corner or look up some steps, and there was a whole new part.

It had everything. There were wide lawns with carved stone seats, green with moss. Over the lawns hung weeping willows, and their feathery bough tips brushed the velvet grass when they swung with the wind. The old flagged paths had high clipped yew hedges on either side of them, so that they looked like the narrow streets of some old town; and through the hedges, doorways had been made; and over the doorways were shapes like vases and peacocks and half-moons all trimmed out of the living trees. There was a lovely marble fishpond with golden carp and blue water lilies in it and big green frogs. A high brick wall alongside the kitchen garden was all covered with pink and yellow peaches ripening in the sun. There was a wonderful great oak, hollow in

44

the trunk, big enough for four men to hide inside. Many summerhouses there were, too—some of wood and some of stone—and one of them was full of books to read. In a corner, among some rocks and ferns, was an outdoor fireplace, where the Doctor used to fry liver and bacon when he had a notion to take his meals in the open air. There was a couch, as well, on which he used to sleep, it seems, on warm summer nights when the nightingales were singing at their best; it had wheels on it so it could be moved about under any tree they sang in. But the thing that fascinated me most of all was a tiny little tree house high up in the top branches of a great elm, with a long rope ladder leading to it. The Doctor told me he used it for looking at the moon and the stars through a telescope.

It was the kind of a garden where you could wander and explore for days and days—always coming upon something new, always glad to find the old spots over again. That first time that I saw the Doctor's garden I was so charmed by it that I felt I would like to live in it and never go outside of it again. For it had everything within its walls to make living pleasant—to keep the heart at peace. It was the garden of dreams.

There were a lot of birds about. Every tree seemed to have two or three nests in it. And heaps of other wild creatures appeared to be making themselves at home there, too. Stoats and tortoises and dormice seemed to be quite common, and not in the least shy. Toads of different colors and sizes hopped about the lawn as though it belonged to them. Green lizards (which were very rare in Puddleby) sat up on the stones in the sunlight and blinked at us. Even snakes were to be seen.

"You need not be afraid of them," said the Doctor, noticing

that I started somewhat when a large black snake wiggled across the path right in front of us. "These fellows are not poisonous. They do a great deal of good in keeping down many kinds of garden pests. I play the flute to them sometimes in the evening. They love it. Stand right up on their tails and carry on no end. Funny thing, their taste for music."

"Why do all these animals come and live here?" I asked. "I never saw a garden with so many creatures in it."

"Well, I suppose it's because they get the kind of food they like, and nobody worries or disturbs them. And then, of course, they know me. And if they or their children get sick, I presume they find it handy to be living in a doctor's garden. Look! You see that sparrow on the sundial, swearing at the blackbird down below? Well, he has been coming here every summer for years. He comes from London. The country sparrows round about here are always laughing at him. They say he chirps with such a cockney accent. He is a most amusing bird—very brave but very cheeky. He loves nothing better than an argument, but he always ends it by getting rude. He is a real city bird. In London he lives around St. Paul's Cathedral. 'Cheapside,' we call him."

"Are all these birds from the country around here?" I asked.

"Most of them," said the Doctor. "But a few rare ones visit me every year who ordinarily never come near England at all. For instance, that handsome little fellow hovering over the snapdragon there, he's a ruby-throated hummingbird. Comes from America. Strictly speaking, he has no business in this climate at all. It is too cool. I make him sleep in the kitchen at night. Then every August, about the last week of the month, I have a purple bird of paradise come all the way from Brazil to see me. She is a very great swell. Hasn't arrived yet, of course. And there are a few others, foreign birds from the tropics, mostly, who drop in on me in the course of the summer months. But come, I must show you the zoo."

· The Tenth Chapter ·
THE PRIVATE ZOO

I DID not think there could be anything left in that garden that we had not seen. But the Doctor took me by the arm and we soon found ourselves before a small door in a high stone wall. The Doctor pushed it open.

Inside was still another garden. I had expected to find cages with animals inside them. But there were none to be seen. Instead there were little stone houses all over the garden, and each house had a window and a door. As we walked in, many of these doors opened and animals came running out to us, evidently expecting food.

"Haven't the doors any locks on them?" I asked the Doctor.

"Oh, yes," he said, "every door has a lock. But in my zoo the doors open from the inside, not from the out. The locks are there only so the animals can go and shut themselves *in* any time they want to get away from the annoyance of other animals or from people who might come here. Every animal in this zoo stays here because he likes it, not because he is made to."

"They all look very happy and clean," I said. "Would you mind telling me the names of some of them?"

"Certainly. Well, now, that funny-looking thing with plates on his back, nosing under the brick over there, is a South American armadillo. The little chap talking to him is a Canadian woodchuck. They both live in those holes you see at the foot of the wall. The two little beasts doing antics in the pond are a pair of Russian minks. . . . And that reminds me, I must go and get them some herring from the town before noon—it is early closing today. That animal just stepping out of his house is an antelope, one of the smaller South African kinds. Now let us move to the other side of those bushes there and I will show you some more."

"Are those deer over there?" I asked.

"*Deer!*" said the Doctor. "Where do you mean?"

"Over there," I said, pointing, "nibbling the grass border of the bed. There are two of them."

"Oh, that," said the Doctor with a smile. "That isn't two animals: That's one animal with two heads—the only two-headed animal in the world. It's called the pushmi-pullyu. I brought him from Africa. He's very tame—acts as a kind of night watchman for my zoo. He sleeps with only one head at a time, you see—very handy. The other head stays awake all night."

"Have you any lions or tigers?" I asked as we moved on.

"No," said the Doctor. "It wouldn't be possible to keep them here—and I wouldn't keep them even if I could. If I had my way, Stubbins, there wouldn't be a single lion or tiger in captivity anywhere in the world. They're never happy. They never settle down. They are always thinking of the big countries they have left behind. You can see it in their eyes, dreaming always of the great open spaces, dreaming of the dark jungles where their mothers first taught them how to scent and track the deer. And what are they given in exchange for all this?" asked the Doctor, stopping in his walk and growing all red and angry. "For the glory of an African sunrise, for the twilight breeze whispering through the palms, for the green shade of the matted, tangled vines, for the cool, big-starred nights of the desert, for the patter of the waterfall after a hard day's hunt? Why, a bare cage with iron bars, an ugly piece of dead meat thrust in to them once a day, and a crowd of fools to come and stare at them with open mouths! No, Stubbins, lions and tigers, the big hunters, should never, never be seen in zoos."

The Doctor seemed to have grown terribly serious—almost sad. But suddenly his manner changed again and he took me by the arm with his same old cheerful smile.

"But we haven't seen the butterfly houses yet—nor the aquariums. Come along. I am very proud of my butterfly houses."

Off we went again and came presently into a hedged enclosure. Here I saw several big huts made of fine wire netting, like cages. Inside the netting all sorts of beautiful flowers were growing in the sun, with butterflies skimming over them. The Doctor pointed to the end of one of the huts, where little boxes with holes in them stood in a row.

"Those are the hatching boxes," said he. "There I put the different kinds of caterpillars. And as soon as they turn into butterflies and moths, they come out into these flower-gardens to feed."

"Do butterflies have a language?" I asked.

"Oh, I fancy they have," said the Doctor, "—and the beetles, too. But so far I haven't succeeded in learning much about insect languages. I have been too busy lately trying to master the shellfish talk. I mean to take it up, though."

At that moment Polynesia joined us and said, "Doctor,

there are two guinea pigs at the back door. They say they have run away from the boy who kept them because they didn't get the right stuff to eat. They want to know if you will take them in."

"All right," said the Doctor. "Show them the way to the zoo. Give them the house on the left, near the gate—the one the black fox had. Tell them what the rules are and give them a square meal. Now, Stubbins, we will go on to the aquarium. And first of all I must show you my big glass sea-water tank, where I keep the shellfish."

· The Eleventh Chapter ·
MY SCHOOLMASTER, POLYNESIA

WELL, there were not many days after that, when I did not come to see my new friend. Indeed I was at his house practically all day and every day. So that one evening my mother asked me jokingly why I did not take my bed over there and live at the Doctor's house altogether.

After a while I think I got to be quite useful to the Doctor, feeding his pets for him, helping to make new houses and fences for the zoo, assisting with the sick animals that came, doing odd jobs about the place. So that although I enjoyed it all very much, I really think the Doctor would have missed me if I had not come so often.

And all this time Polynesia came with me wherever I went, teaching me bird language and showing me how to understand the talking signs of the animals. At first I thought I would never be able to learn at all—it seemed so difficult. But the old parrot was wonderfully patient with me—though I could see that occasionally she had hard work to keep her temper.

Soon I began to pick up the strange chatter of the birds and to understand the funny talking antics of the dogs. I used to practice listening to the mice behind the wainscot after I went to bed.

And the days passed very quickly and turned into weeks, and weeks into months, and soon the roses in the Doctor's garden were losing their petals and yellow leaves lay upon the wide green lawn. For the summer was nearly gone.

One day Polynesia and I were talking in the library. Polynesia was showing me the books about animals that John Dolittle had written himself.

"My!" I said, "what a lot of books the Doctor has—all the way around the room! Goodness! I wish I could read! It must be tremendously interesting. Can you read, Polynesia?"

"Only a little," said she. "Be careful how you turn those pages—don't tear them. No, I really don't get time enough for reading much. That letter there is a *k* and this is a *b.*"

"What does this word under the picture mean?" I asked.

"Let me see," she said and started spelling it out. "B-A-B-O-O-N—that's *monkey*. Reading isn't nearly as hard as it looks, once you know the letters."

"Polynesia," I said, "I want to ask you something very important."

"What is it, my boy?" said she, smoothing down the feathers of her right wing. Polynesia often spoke to me in a very patronizing way. But I did not mind it from her. After all, she was nearly two hundred years old, and I was only ten.

"Listen," I said, "my mother doesn't think it is right that I come here for so many meals. And I was going to ask you: Supposing I did a whole lot more work for the Doctor—why couldn't I come and live here, altogether? You see, instead of being paid like a regular gardener or workman, I would get my bed and meals in exchange for the work I did. What do you think?"

"You mean you want to be a proper assistant to the Doctor, is that it?"

"Yes. I suppose that's what you call it," I answered. "You know, you said yourself that you thought I could be very useful to him."

"Well"—she thought a moment—"I really don't see why not. But is this what you want to be when you grow up, a naturalist?"

"Yes," I said, "I have made up my mind. I would sooner be a naturalist than anything else in the world."

"Humph! Let's go and speak to the Doctor about it," said Polynesia. "He's in the next room—in the study. Open the door very gently—he may be working and not want to be disturbed."

I opened the door quietly and peeped in. The first thing I saw was an enormous black retriever dog sitting in the middle of the hearthrug with his ears cocked up, listening to the Doctor who was reading aloud to him from a letter.

"What *is* the Doctor doing?" I asked Polynesia in a whisper.

"Oh, the dog has had a letter from his mistress and he has brought it to the Doctor to read for him, that's all. He belongs to a funny little girl called Minnie Dooley, who lives on the other side of the town. She has pigtails down her back. She and her brother have gone away to the seaside for the summer, and the old retriever is heartbroken while the children are gone. So they write letters to him—in English, of course. And as the old dog doesn't understand them, he brings them here and the Doctor turns them into dog language for him. I think Minnie must have written that she is coming back—to judge from the dog's excitement. Just look at him carrying on!"

Indeed the retriever seemed to be suddenly overcome with

joy. As the Doctor finished the letter the old dog started barking at the top of his voice, wagging his tail wildly and jumping about the study. He took the letter in his mouth and ran out of the room snorting hard and mumbling to himself.

"He's going down to meet the coach," whispered Polynesia. "That dog's devotion to those children is more than I can understand. You should see Minnie! She's the most conceited little minx that ever walked. She squints, too."

· The Twelfth Chapter ·
MY GREAT IDEA

RESENTLY the Doctor looked up and saw us at the door.

"Oh, come in, Stubbins," said he. "Did you wish to speak to me? Come in and take a chair."

"Doctor," I said, "I want to be a naturalist—like you—when I grow up."

"Oh, you do, do you?" murmured the Doctor. "Humph! . . . well! . . . dear me! . . . you don't say! . . . well, well! Have you, er, have you spoken to your mother and father about it?"

"No, not yet," I said. "I want you to speak to them for me. You would do it better. I want to be your helper—your assistant, if you'll have me. Last night my mother was saying that she didn't consider it right for me to come here so often for meals. And I've been thinking about it a good deal since. Couldn't we make some arrangement—couldn't I work for my meals and sleep here?"

"But my dear Stubbins," said the Doctor, laughing, "you are quite welcome to come here for three meals a day all year round. I'm only too glad to have you. Besides, you do do a lot

56

of work, as it is. I've often felt that I ought to pay you for what you do. . . . But what arrangement was it that you thought of?"

"Well, I thought," said I, "that perhaps you would come and see my mother and father and tell them that if they let me live here with you and work hard, that you will teach me to read and write. You see, my mother is awfully anxious to have me learn reading and writing. And besides, I couldn't be a proper naturalist without, could I?"

"Oh, I don't know so much about that," said the Doctor. "It is nice, I admit, to be able to read and write. But the greatest naturalist of them all doesn't even know how to write his own name or to read the ABC's."

"Who is he?" I asked.

"He is a mysterious person," said the Doctor, "—a very mysterious person. His name is Long Arrow, the son of Golden Arrow. He is an Indian."

"Have you ever seen him?" I asked.

"No," said the Doctor, "I've never seen him. No European has ever met him. He lives almost entirely with the animals and with the different tribes of Indians—usually somewhere among the mountains of Peru. Never stays long in one place. Goes from tribe to tribe, like a sort of tramp."

"How do you know so much about him?" I asked, "if you've never even seen him?"

"The purple bird of paradise," said the Doctor, "she told me all about him. She says he is a perfectly marvelous naturalist. I got her to take a message to him for me last time she was here. I am expecting her back any day now. I can hardly wait to see what answer she has brought from him. It is already almost the last week of August. I do hope nothing has happened to her on the way."

"But why do the animals and birds come to you when they are sick?" I said. "Why don't they go to him, if he is so very wonderful?"

"It seems that my methods are more up-to-date," said the Doctor. "But from what the purple bird of paradise tells me, Long Arrow's knowledge of natural history must be positively tremendous. His specialty is botany—plants and all that sort of thing. But he knows a lot about birds and animals, too. He's very good on bees and beetles. . . . But now, tell me, Stubbins, are you quite sure that you really want to be a naturalist?"

"Yes," said I, "my mind is made up."

"Well, you know, it isn't a very good profession for making money. Most of the good naturalists don't make any money whatever. All they do is *spend* money, buying butterfly nets and cases for birds' eggs and things. It is only now, after I have been a naturalist for many years, that I am beginning to make a little money from the books I write."

"I don't care about money," I said. "I want to be a naturalist. Won't you please come and have dinner with my mother and father next Thursday? I told them I was going to ask you —and then you can talk to them about it. You see, there's another thing: If I'm living with you and sort of belong to your house and business, I shall be able to come with you next time you go on a voyage."

"Oh, I see," said he, smiling. "So you want to come on a voyage with me, do you? Aha!"

"I want to go on all your voyages with you. It would be much easier for you if you had someone to carry the butterfly nets and notebooks, wouldn't it now?"

For a long time the Doctor sat thinking, drumming on the

desk with his fingers while I waited, terribly impatiently, to see what he was going to say.

At last he shrugged his shoulders and stood up.

"Well, Stubbins," said he, "I'll come and talk it over with you and your parents next Thursday. And . . . well, we'll see. We'll see. Give your mother and father my compliments and thank them for their invitation, will you?"

Then I tore home like the wind to tell my mother that the Doctor had promised to come.

· The Thirteenth Chapter ·
A TRAVELER ARRIVES

THE next day I was sitting on the wall of the Doctor's garden after tea, talking to Dab-Dab. I had now learned so much from Polynesia that I could talk to most birds and some animals without a great deal of difficulty. I found Dab-Dab a very nice old motherly bird—though not nearly so clever and interesting as Polynesia. She had been housekeeper for the Doctor many years now.

Well, as I was saying, the old duck and I were sitting on the flat top of the garden wall that evening, looking down on the Oxenthorpe Road below. We were watching some sheep being driven to market in Puddleby, and Dab-Dab had just been telling me about the Doctor's adventures in Africa. For she had gone on a voyage there with him long ago.

Suddenly I heard a curious distant noise down the street, toward the town. It sounded like a lot of people cheering. I stood up on the wall to see if I could make out what was coming. Presently there appeared around a bend a great crowd of schoolchildren following a very ragged, curious-looking woman.

"What in the world can it be?" cried Dab-Dab.

The children were all laughing and shouting. And certainly the woman they were following was most extraordinary. She had very long arms and the most stooping shoulders I have ever seen. She wore a straw hat on the side of her head with poppies on it, and her skirt was so long for her it dragged on the ground like a ball gown's train. I could not see anything of her face because of the wide hat pulled over her eyes. But as she got nearer to us and the laughing of the children grew louder, I noticed that her hands were very dark in color and hairy, like a witch's.

Then all of a sudden Dab-Dab at my side startled me by crying out in a loud voice, "Why, it's Chee-Chee! Chee-Chee come back at last! How dare those children tease him! I'll give the little imps something to laugh at!"

And she flew right off the wall down to the street and made straight for the children, squawking away in a most terrifying fashion and pecking at their feet and legs. The children made off down the street back to the town as hard as they could run.

The strange-looking figure in the straw hat stood gazing after them a moment and then came wearily up to the gate. It didn't bother to undo the latch but just climbed right over the gate as though it were something in the way. And then I noticed that it took hold of the bars with its feet, so that it really had four hands to climb with. But it was only when I at last got a glimpse of the face under the hat that I could be really sure it was a monkey.

Chee-Chee—for it was he—frowned at me suspiciously from the top of the gate, as though he thought I was going to laugh at him like the other boys and girls. Then he dropped into the garden on the inside and immediately started taking off his clothes. He tore the straw hat in two and threw it

"A traveler arrives"

down into the street. Then he took off his bodice and skirt, jumped on them savagely, and began kicking them around the front garden.

Presently I heard a screech from the house, and out flew Polynesia, followed by the Doctor and Jip.

"Chee-Chee! Chee-Chee!" shouted the parrot. "You've come at last! I always told the Doctor you'd find a way. How ever did you do it?"

They all gathered around him, shaking him by his four hands, laughing and asking him a million questions at once. Then they all started back for the house.

"Run up to my bedroom, Stubbins," said the Doctor, turning to me. "You'll find a bag of peanuts in the small left-hand drawer of the bureau. I have always kept them there in case he might come back unexpectedly some day. And wait a minute—see if Dab-Dab has any bananas in the pantry. Chee-Chee hasn't had a banana, he tells me, in two months."

When I came down again to the kitchen I found everybody listening attentively to the monkey, who was telling the story of his journey from Africa.

· The Fourteenth Chapter ·
CHEE-CHEE'S VOYAGE

IT seems that after Polynesia had left, Chee-Chee had grown more homesick than ever for the Doctor and the little house in Puddleby. At last he had made up his mind that, by hook or crook, he would follow her. And one day, going down to the seashore, he saw a lot of people getting onto a ship that was coming to England. He tried to get on too. But they turned him back and drove him away. And presently he noticed a whole big family of people passing onto the ship. And one of the children in this family reminded Chee-Chee of a cousin of his with whom he had once been in love. So he said to himself, "That girl looks just as much like a monkey as I look like a girl. If I could only get some clothes to wear I might easily slip onto the ship among these families, and people would take me for a girl. Good idea!"

So he went off to a house that was quite close, and hopping in through an open window he found a skirt and bodice lying on a chair. They belonged to a fashionable lady who was taking a bath. Chee-Chee put them on. Next he went back to the seashore, mingled with the crowd there, and at last sneaked safely onto the big ship. Then he thought he had better hide, for fear people might look at him too closely. And he stayed hidden all the time the ship was sailing to England—only coming out at night, when everybody was asleep, to find food.

When he reached England and tried to get off the ship, the sailors saw at last that he was only a monkey dressed up in girl's clothes, and they wanted to keep him for a pet. But he managed to give them the slip; and once he was on shore, he dived into the crowd and got away. But he was still a long distance from Puddleby and had to come right across the whole breadth of England.

He had a terrible time of it. Whenever he passed through a town all the children ran after him in a crowd, laughing; and often silly people caught hold of him and tried to stop him, so that he had to run up lampposts and climb to chimney pots to escape from them. At night he used to sleep in ditches or barns or anywhere he could hide, and he lived on the berries he picked from the hedges and the cobnuts that grew in the copses. At length, after many adventures and narrow squeaks, he saw the tower of Puddleby Church and he knew that at last he was near his old home.

When Chee-Chee had finished his story he ate six bananas without stopping and drank a whole bowlful of milk.

"My!" he said. "Why wasn't I born with wings, like Polynesia, so I could fly here? You've no idea how I grew to hate that hat and skirt. I've never been so uncomfortable in my life. All the way from Bristol here, if the wretched hat wasn't falling off my head or catching in the trees, those beastly skirts were tripping me up and getting wound around everything. What on earth do women wear those things for? Goodness, I was glad to see old Puddleby this morning when I climbed over the hill by Bellaby's farm!"

"Your bed on top of the plate rack in the scullery is all ready for you," said the Doctor. "We never had it disturbed, in case you might come back."

"Yes," said Dab-Dab, "and you can have the old smoking jacket of the Doctor's, which you used to use as a blanket, in case it is cold in the night."

"Thanks," said Chee-Chee. "It's good to be back in the old house again. Everything's just the same as when I left, except the clean roller towel on the back of the door there—that's new. Well, I think I'll go to bed now. I need sleep."

Then we all went out of the kitchen into the scullery and watched Chee-Chee climb the plate rack like a sailor going up a mast. On the top, he curled himself up, pulled the old smoking jacket over him, and in a minute he was snoring peacefully.

"Good old Chee-Chee!" whispered the Doctor. "I'm glad he's back."

"Yes, good old Chee-Chee!" echoed Dab-Dab and Polynesia.

Then we all tiptoed out of the scullery and closed the door very gently behind us.

· The Fifteenth Chapter ·

I BECOME A
DOCTOR'S ASSISTANT

WHEN Thursday evening came, there was great excitement at our house. My mother had asked me what were the Doctor's favorite dishes, and I had told her: spare ribs, sliced beetroot, fried bread, shrimps, and treacle tart. Tonight she had them all on the table waiting for him, and she was now fussing around the house to see if everything was tidy and in readiness for his coming.

At last we heard a knock upon the door, and of course it was I who got there first to let him in.

The Doctor had brought his own flute with him this time. And after supper was over, the table was cleared away and the Doctor and my father started playing duets.

They got so interested in this that I began to be afraid that they would never come to talking over my business. But at last the Doctor said, "Your son tells me that he is anxious to become a naturalist."

And then began a long talk, which lasted far into the night. At first both my mother and father were rather against the idea—as they had been from the beginning. They said it was only a boyish whim, and that I would get tired of it very soon.

But after the matter had been talked over from every side, the Doctor turned to my father and said, "Well, now, supposing, Mr. Stubbins, that your son came to me for two years—that is, until he is twelve years old. During those two years he will have time to see if he is going to grow tired of it or not. Also, during that time, I will promise to teach him reading and writing and perhaps a little arithmetic as well. What do you say to that?"

"I don't know," said my father, shaking his head. "You are very kind and it is a handsome offer you make, Doctor. But I feel that Tommy ought to be learning some trade by which he can earn his living later on."

Then my mother spoke up. Although she was nearly in tears at the prospect of my leaving her house while I was still so young, she pointed out to my father that this was a grand chance for me to get learning.

"Now, Jacob," she said, "you know that many lads in the town have been to the grammar school till they were fourteen or fifteen years old. Tommy can easily spare these two years for his education; and if he learns no more than to read and write, the time will not be lost. Though goodness knows," she added, getting out her handkerchief to cry, "the house will seem terribly empty when he's gone."

"I will take care that he comes to see you, Mrs. Stubbins," said the Doctor, "every day, if you like. After all, he will not be very far away."

Well, at length my father gave in, and it was agreed that I was to live with the Doctor and work for him for two years in exchange for learning to read and write and for my board and lodging.

"Of course," added the Doctor, "while I have money I will keep Tommy in clothes as well. But money is a very irregular thing with me; sometimes I have some, and then sometimes I haven't."

"You are very good, Doctor," said my mother, drying her tears. "It seems to me that Tommy is a very fortunate boy."

And then, thoughtless, selfish little imp that I was, I leaned over and whispered in the Doctor's ear, "Please don't forget to say something about the voyages."

"Oh, by the way," said John Dolittle, "of course occasionally my work requires me to travel. You will have no objection, I take it, to your son's coming with me?"

My poor mother looked up sharply, more unhappy and anxious than ever at this new turn, while I stood behind the Doctor's chair, my heart thumping with excitement, waiting for my father's answer.

"No," he said slowly after a while. "If we agree to the other arrangement, I don't see that we've the right to make any objection to that."

Well, there surely was never a happier boy in the world than I was at that moment. At last the dream of my life was to come true! For I knew perfectly well that it was now almost time for the Doctor to start upon another voyage. Polynesia had told me that he hardly ever stayed at home for more than six months at a stretch. Therefore he would be surely going again within a fortnight. And I—I, Tommy Stubbins, would go with him—just to think of it!—to cross the sea, to walk on foreign shores, to roam the world!

PART II

· The First Chapter ·
THE CREW OF *THE CURLEW*

ROM that time on, of course, my position in the town was very different. I was no longer a poor cobbler's son. I carried my nose in the air as I went down the High Street with Jip in his gold collar at my side; and snobbish little boys who had despised me before because I was not rich enough to go to school now pointed me out to their friends and whispered, "You see him? He's a doctor's assistant—and only ten years old!"

Two days after the Doctor had been to our house to dinner he told me very sadly that he was afraid that he would have to give up trying to learn the language of the shellfish—in any event, for the present.

"I'm very discouraged, Stubbins, very. I've tried the mussels and the clams, the oysters and the whelks, cockles and scallops, seven different kinds of crabs, and all the lobster family. I think I'll leave it for the present and go at it again later on."

"What will you turn to now?" I asked.

"Well, I rather thought of going on a voyage, Stubbins. It's quite a time now since I've been away. And there is a great deal of work waiting for me abroad."

"When shall we start?" I asked.

"Well, first I shall have to wait till the purple bird of paradise gets here. I must see if she has any message for me from Long Arrow. She's late. She should have been here ten days ago. I hope to goodness she's all right."

"Well, hadn't we better be seeing about getting a boat?" I said. "She is sure to be here in a day or so, and there will be lots of things to do to get ready in the meantime, won't there?"

"Yes, indeed," said the Doctor. "Suppose we go down and see your friend Joe, the mussel man. He will know about boats."

"I'd like to come too," said Jip.

"All right, come along," said the Doctor, and off we went.

Joe said, yes, he had a boat—one he had just bought—but it needed three people to sail her. We told him we would like to see it anyway.

So the mussel man took us off a little way down the river and showed us the neatest, prettiest little vessel that ever was built. She was called *The Curlew*. Joe said he would sell her to us cheap. But the trouble was that the boat needed three people, while we were only two.

"Of course I shall be taking Chee-Chee," said the Doctor. "But although he is very quick and clever, he is not as strong as a man. We really ought to have another person to sail a boat as big as that."

"I know of a good sailor, Doctor," said Joe, "a first-class seaman who would be glad of the job."

"No, thank you, Joe," said Doctor Dolittle. "I don't want any seamen. I couldn't afford to hire them. And then they hamper me so, seamen do, when I'm at sea. They're always wanting to do things the proper way, and I like to do them *my* way. Now let me see: Who could we take with us?"

"There's Matthew Mugg, the cat's-meat man," I said.

"No, he wouldn't do. Matthew's a very nice fellow, but he talks too much—mostly about his rheumatism. You have to be frightfully particular whom you take with you on long voyages."

"How about Luke the Hermit?" I asked.

"That's a good idea—splendid—if he'll come. Let's go and ask him right away."

· The Second Chapter ·
LUKE THE HERMIT

THE Hermit was an old friend of ours. He was a very peculiar person. Far out on the marshes he lived in a little bit of a shack—all alone except for his brindle bulldog. He never came into the town, never seemed to want to see or talk to people. His dog, Bob, drove them away if they came near his hut. When you asked anyone in Puddleby who he was or why he lived out in that lonely place by himself, the only answer you got was "Oh, Luke the Hermit? Well, there's some mystery about him. Nobody knows what it is. But there's a mystery. Don't go near him. He'll set the dog on you."

Nevertheless there were two people who often went out to that little shack on the fens: the Doctor and myself. And Bob, the bulldog, never barked when he heard us coming. For we liked Luke, and Luke liked us.

This afternoon, crossing the marshes we faced a cold wind blowing from the east. As we approached the hut Jip put up his ears and said, "That's funny!"

"What's funny?" asked the Doctor.

"That Bob hasn't come out to meet us. He should have heard us long ago—or smelled us. What's that queer noise?"

"Sounds to me like a gate creaking," said the Doctor. "Maybe it's Luke's door, only we can't see the door from here; it's on the far side of the shack."

"I hope Bob isn't sick," said Jip, and he let out a bark to see if that would call him. But the only answer he got was the wailing of the wind across the wide salt fen.

We hurried forward, all three of us thinking hard.

When we reached the front of the shack we found the door open, swinging and creaking dismally in the wind. We looked inside. There was no one there.

"Isn't Luke at home, then?" said I. "Perhaps he's out for a walk."

"He is *always* at home," said the Doctor, frowning in a peculiar sort of way. "And even if he were out for a walk, he wouldn't leave his door banging in the wind behind him. There is something queer about this. . . . What are you doing in there, Jip?"

"Nothing much—nothing worth speaking of," said Jip, examining the floor of the hut extremely carefully.

"Come here, Jip," said the Doctor in a stern voice. "You are hiding something from me. You see signs and you know something—or you guess it. What has happened? Tell me. Where is the Hermit?"

"I don't know," said Jip, looking very guilty and uncomfortable. "I don't know where he is."

"Well, you know something. I can tell it from the look in your eye. What is it?"

But Jip didn't answer.

For ten minutes the Doctor kept questioning him. But not a word would the dog say.

"Well," said the Doctor at last, "it is no use our standing around here in the cold. The Hermit's gone. That's all. We might as well go home to luncheon."

As we buttoned up our coats and started back across the marsh, Jip ran ahead pretending he was looking for water rats.

"He knows something, all right," whispered the Doctor. "And I think he knows what has happened, too. It's funny, his not wanting to tell me. He has never done that before—not in eleven years. He has always told me everything. Strange! Very strange!"

"Do you mean you think he knows all about the Hermit, the big mystery about him that folks hint at and all that?"

"I shouldn't wonder if he did," the Doctor answered slowly. "I noticed something in his expression the moment we found that door open and the hut empty. And the way he sniffed the floor too—it told him something, that floor did. He saw signs we couldn't see. I wonder why he won't tell me. I'll try him again. Here, Jip! Jip! Where is the dog? I thought he went on in front."

"So did I," I said. "He was there a moment ago. I saw him as large as life. Jip . . . Jip . . . Jip . . . JIP!"

But he was gone. We called and called. We even walked back to the hut. But Jip had disappeared.

"Oh, well," I said, "most likely he has just run home ahead of us. He often does that, you know. We'll find him there when we get back to the house."

But the Doctor just closed his coat collar tighter against the wind and strode on muttering, "Odd . . . very odd!"

· The Third Chapter ·
JIP AND THE SECRET

HEN we reached the house, the first question the Doctor asked of Dab-Dab in the hall was, "Is Jip home yet?"

"No," said Dab-Dab, "I haven't seen him."

"Let me know the moment he comes in, will you, please?" said the Doctor, hanging up his hat.

"Certainly I will," said Dab-Dab. "Don't be long over washing your hands; the lunch is on the table."

Just as we were sitting down to luncheon in the kitchen we heard a great racket at the front door. I ran and opened it. In bounded Jip.

"Doctor!" he cried, "come into the library quick. I've got something to tell you. . . . No, Dab-Dab, the luncheon must wait. Please hurry, Doctor. There's not a moment to be lost. Don't let any of the animals come—just you and Tommy."

"Now," he said, when we were inside the library and the door was closed, "turn the key in the lock and make sure there's no one listening under the windows."

"It's all right," said the Doctor. "Nobody can hear you here. Now, what is it?"

"Well, Doctor," said Jip (he was badly out of breath from running), "I know all about the Hermit—I have known for years. But I couldn't tell you."

"Why?" asked the Doctor.

"Because I'd promised not to tell anyone. It was Bob, his dog, that told me. And I swore to him that I would keep the secret."

"Well, and are you going to tell me now?"

"Yes," said Jip, "we've got to save him. I followed Bob's scent just now when I left you out there on the marshes. And I found him. And I said to him, 'Is it all right,' I said, 'for me to tell the Doctor now? Maybe he can do something.' And Bob says to me, 'Yes,' says he, 'it's all right because—'"

"Oh, for heaven's sake, go on, go on!" cried the Doctor. "Tell us what the mystery is—not what you said to Bob and what Bob said to you. What has happened? Where *is* the Hermit?"

"He's in Puddleby Jail," said Jip. "He's in prison."

"In prison!"

"Yes."

"What for? What's he done?"

Jip went over to the door and smelled at the bottom of it to see if anyone was listening outside. Then he came back to the Doctor on tiptoe and whispered, *"He killed a man!"*

"Lord preserve us!" cried the Doctor, sitting down heavily in a chair and mopping his forehead with a handkerchief. "When did he do it?"

"Fifteen years ago—in a Mexican gold mine. That's why he has been a hermit ever since. He shaved off his beard and kept away from people out there on the marshes so he wouldn't be recognized. But last week, it seems these newfangled policemen came to town, and they heard there was a strange man who kept to himself all alone in a shack on the fen. And they got suspicious. For a long time people had been hunting all over the world for the man that did that killing in the Mexican gold mine fifteen years ago. So these policemen went out to the shack, and they recognized Luke by a mole on his arm. And they took him to prison."

"Well, well!" murmured the Doctor. "Who would have thought it? Luke, the philosopher! Killed a man! I can hardly believe it."

"It's true enough—unfortunately," said Jip. "Luke did it. But it wasn't his fault. Bob says so. And he was there and saw it all. He was scarcely more than a puppy at the time. Bob says Luke couldn't help it. He *had* to do it."

"Where is Bob now?" asked the Doctor.

"Down at the prison. I wanted him to come with me here to see you, but he won't leave the prison while Luke is there. He just sits outside the door of the prison cell and won't move. He doesn't even eat the food they give him. Won't you please come down there, Doctor, and see if there is anything you can do? The trial is to be this afternoon at two o'clock. What time is it now?"

"It's ten minutes past one."

"Bob says he thinks they are going to kill Luke for a punishment if they can prove that he did it—or certainly keep him in prison for the rest of his life. Won't you please come? Perhaps if you spoke to the judge and told him what a good man Luke really is, they'd let him off."

"Of course I'll come," said the Doctor, getting up and moving to go. "But I'm very much afraid that I shan't be of any real help." He turned at the door and hesitated thoughtfully.

"And yet . . . I wonder . . ."

Then he opened the door and passed out with Jip and me close at his heels.

· The Fourth Chapter ·
BOB

AB-DAB was terribly upset when she found we were going away again without luncheon, and she made us take some cold pork pies in our pockets to eat on the way.

When we got to Puddleby Courthouse (it was next door to the prison), we found a great crowd gathered around the building.

The news had run through the countryside that Luke the Hermit was to be tried for killing a man and that the great mystery, which had hung over him so long, was to be cleared up at last. The butcher and the baker had closed their shops and taken a holiday. All the farmers from round about and all the townsfolk were there. I had never seen the quiet old town in such a state of excitement before.

If I hadn't had the Doctor with me I am sure I would never have been able to make my way through the mob packed around the courthouse door. But I just followed behind him, hanging on to his coattails, and at last we got safely into the jail.

"I want to see Luke," said the Doctor to a very grand person in a blue coat with brass buttons standing at the door.

"Ask at the superintendent's office," said the man. "Third door on the left down the corridor."

From there another policeman was sent with us to show us the way.

Outside the door of Luke's cell we found Bob, the bulldog, who wagged his tail sadly when he saw us. The man who was guiding us took a large bunch of keys from his pocket and opened the door.

I had never been inside a real prison cell before; and I felt quite a thrill when the policeman went out and locked the door after him, leaving us shut in the dimly-lighted little stone room. Before he went, he said that as soon as we had finished talking with our friend we should knock upon the door and he would come and let us out.

At first I could hardly see anything, it was so dim inside. But after a little I made out a low bed against the wall, under a small barred window. On the bed, staring down at the floor between his feet, sat the Hermit, his head resting in his hands.

"Well, Luke," said the Doctor in a kindly voice, "they don't give you much light in here, do they?"

Very slowly the Hermit looked up from the floor.

"Hulloa, John Dolittle. What brings you here?"

"I've come to see you. I would have been here sooner, only I didn't hear about all this till a few minutes ago. I went to your hut to ask you if you would join me on a voyage, and when I found it empty I had no idea where you could be. I am dreadfully sorry to hear about your bad luck. I've come to see if there is anything I can do."

Luke shook his head.

"No, I don't imagine there is anything can be done. They've caught me at last. That's the end of it, I suppose."

"On the bed sat the Hermit"

He got up stiffly and started walking up and down the little room.

"In a way, I'm glad it's over," said he. "I never got any peace, always thinking they were after me—afraid to speak to anyone. They were bound to get me in the end. . . . Yes, I'm glad it's over."

Then the Doctor talked to Luke for more than half an hour, trying to cheer him up, while I sat around wondering what I ought to say and wishing I could do something.

At last the Doctor said he wanted to see Bob, and we knocked upon the door and were let out by the policeman.

"Bob," said the Doctor to the big bulldog in the passage, "come out with me to the porch. I want to ask you something."

"How is he, Doctor?" asked Bob as we walked down the corridor into the courthouse porch.

"Oh, Luke's all right. Very miserable of course, but he's all right. Now tell me, Bob: You saw this business happen, didn't you? You were there when the man was killed, eh?"

"I was, Doctor," said Bob, "and I tell you—"

"All right," the Doctor interrupted, "that's all I want to know for the present. There isn't time to tell me more now. The trial is just going to begin. There are the judge and the lawyers coming up the steps. Now listen, Bob: I want you to stay with me when I go into the courtroom. And whatever I tell you to do, do it. Do you understand? Don't make any scenes. Don't bite anybody, no matter what they may say about Luke. Just behave perfectly quietly and answer any question I may ask you—truthfully. Do you understand?"

"Very well. But do you think you will be able to get him off, Doctor?" asked Bob. "He's a good man, Doctor. He really is. There never was a better."

"We'll see, we'll see, Bob. It's a new thing I'm going to try. I'm not sure the judge will allow it. But . . . well, we'll see. It's time to go into the courtroom now. Don't forget what I told you. Remember: For heaven's sake, don't start biting anyone or you'll get us all put out and spoil everything."

· The Fifth Chapter ·
MENDOZA

INSIDE the courtroom everything was very solemn and wonderful. It was a high, big room. Raised above the floor, against the wall was the judge's desk, and here the judge was already sitting—an old, handsome man in a marvelous big wig of gray hair and a gown of black. Below him was another wide, long desk at which lawyers in white wigs sat. The whole thing reminded me of a mixture between a church and a school.

"Those twelve men at the side," whispered the Doctor, "—those in pews like a choir, they are what is called the jury. It is they who decide whether Luke is guilty—whether he did it or not."

"And look!" I said, "there's Luke himself in a sort of pulpit-thing with policemen each side of him. And there's another pulpit, the same kind, the other side of the room, see—only that one's empty."

"That one is called the witness-box," said the Doctor. "Now I'm going down to speak to one of those men in white wigs, and I want you to wait here and keep these two seats for us.

Bob will stay with you. Keep an eye on him—better hold on to his collar. I shan't be more than a minute or so."

With that, the Doctor disappeared into the crowd that filled the main part of the room.

Then I saw the judge take up a funny little wooden hammer and knock on his desk with it. This, it seemed, was to make people keep quiet, for immediately everyone stopped buzzing and talking and began to listen very respectfully. Then another man in a black gown stood up and began reading from a paper in his hand.

He mumbled away exactly as though he were saying his prayers and didn't want anyone to understand what language they were in. But I managed to catch a few words:

"*Biz . . . biz . . . biz . . . biz . . . biz . . .* otherwise known as Luke the Hermit, of *. . . biz . . . biz . . . biz . . . biz . . .* for killing his partner with *. . . biz . . . biz . . . biz . . .* otherwise known as Bluebeard Bill on the night of the *. . . biz . . . biz . . . biz . . .* in the *biz . . . biz . . . biz . . .* of Mexico. Therefore Her Majesty's *. . . biz . . . biz . . . biz . . .*"

At this moment I felt someone take hold of my arm from the back, and turning around I found the Doctor had returned with one of the men in white wigs.

"Stubbins, this is Mr. Percy Jenkyns," said the Doctor. "He is Luke's lawyer. It is his business to get Luke off—if he can."

Mr. Jenkyns seemed to be an extremely young man with a round smooth face like a boy. He shook hands with me and then immediately turned and went on talking with the Doctor.

"Oh, I think it is a perfectly precious idea," he was saying. "Of *course* the dog must be admitted as a witness; He was the only one who saw the thing take place. I'm awfully glad you

came. I wouldn't have missed this for anything. My hat!
Won't it make the old court sit up? This will stir things. A
bulldog witness for the defense! I do hope there are plenty of
reporters present. . . . Yes, there's one making a sketch of
the prisoner. I shall become known after this. . . . And
won't Conkey be pleased? My hat!"

He put his hand over his mouth to smother a laugh and his
eyes fairly sparkled with mischief.

"Who is Conkey?" I asked the Doctor.

"Sh! He is speaking of the judge up there, the Honorable
Eustace Beauchamp Conckley."

"Now," said Mr. Jenkyns, bringing out a notebook, "tell me
a little more about yourself, Doctor. You took your degree as
Doctor of Medicine at Durham, I think you said. And the
name of your last book was . . . ?"

I could not hear any more for they talked in whispers, and
I fell to looking around the court again.

Of course I could not understand everything that was going
on, though it was all very interesting. People kept getting up
in the place the Doctor called the witness-box, and the lawyers at the long table asked them questions about "the night
of the 29th." Then the people would get down again and
somebody else would get up and be questioned.

One of the lawyers (who, the Doctor told me afterward,
was called the prosecutor) seemed to be doing his best to get
the Hermit into trouble by asking questions that made it look
as though he had always been a very bad man. He was a
nasty lawyer, this prosecutor, with a long nose.

Most of the time I could hardly keep my eyes off poor
Luke, who sat there between his two policemen, staring at
the floor as though he weren't interested. The only time I saw
him take any notice at all was when a small dark man with

wicked little watery eyes got up into the witness-box. I heard Bob snarl under my chair as this person came into the court-room and Luke's eyes just blazed with anger and contempt.

This man said his name was Mendoza and that he was the one who had guided the Mexican police to the mine after Bluebeard Bill had been killed. And at every word he said I could hear Bob down below me muttering between his teeth, "It's a lie! It's a lie! I'll chew his face! It's a lie!"

And both the Doctor and I had hard work keeping the dog under the seat.

Then I noticed that our Mr. Jenkyns had disappeared from the Doctor's side. But presently I saw him stand up at the long table to speak to the judge.

"Your Honor," said he, "I wish to introduce a new witness for the defense, Doctor John Dolittle, the naturalist. Will you please step into the witness stand, Doctor?"

There was a buzz of excitement as the Doctor made his way across the crowded room, and I noticed the nasty lawyer with the long nose lean down and whisper something to a friend, smiling in an ugly way that made me want to pinch him.

Then Mr. Jenkyns asked the Doctor a whole lot of questions about himself and made him answer in a loud voice so the whole court could hear. He finished up by saying, "And you are prepared to swear, Doctor Dolittle, that you understand the language of dogs and can make them understand you. Is that so?"

"Yes," said the Doctor, "that is so."

"And what, might I ask," put in the judge in a very quiet, dignified voice, "has all this to do with the killing of er, er, Bluebeard Bill?"

"This, Your Honor," said Mr. Jenkyns, talking in a very

grand manner as though he were on a stage in a theater. "There is in this courtroom at the present moment a bulldog, who was the only living thing that saw the man killed. With the court's permission I propose to put that dog in the witness stand and have him questioned before you by the eminent scientist, Doctor John Dolittle."

· The Sixth Chapter ·
THE JUDGE'S DOG

T first there was a dead silence in the court. Then everybody began whispering or giggling at the same time till the whole room sounded like a great hive of bees. Many people seemed to be shocked; most of them were amused; and a few were angry.

Presently up sprang the nasty lawyer with the long nose.

"I protest, Your Honor," he cried, waving his arms wildly to the judge. "I object. The dignity of this court is in peril. I protest."

"I am the one to take care of the dignity of this court," said the judge.

Then Mr. Jenkyns got up again. (If it hadn't been such a serious matter, it was almost like a Punch-and-Judy show: Somebody was always popping down and somebody else popping up.)

"If there is any doubt on the score of our being able to do as we say, Your Honor will have no objection, I trust, to the Doctor's giving the court a demonstration of his powers—to show that he actually can understand the speech of animals?"

I thought I saw a twinkle of amusement come into the old

judge's eyes as he sat considering a moment before he answered.

"No," he said at last, "I don't think so." Then he turned to the Doctor.

"Are you quite sure you can do this?" he asked.

"Quite, Your Honor," said the Doctor, "—quite sure."

"Very well, then," said the judge. "If you can satisfy us that you really are able to understand canine testimony, the dog shall be admitted as a witness. I do not see, in that case, how I could object to his being heard. But I warn you that if you are trying to make a laughingstock of this court it will go hard with you."

"I protest, I protest!" yelled the long-nosed prosecutor. "This is a scandal, an outrage to the bar!"

"Sit down!" said the judge in a very stern voice.

"What animal does Your Honor wish me to talk with?" asked the Doctor.

"I would like you to talk to my own dog," said the judge. "He is outside in the cloakroom. I will have him brought in, and then we shall see what you can do."

Then someone went out and fetched the judge's dog, a lovely great Russian wolfhound with slender legs and a shaggy coat. He was a proud and beautiful creature.

"Now, Doctor," said the judge, "did you ever see this dog before? Remember, you are in the witness stand and under oath."

"No, Your Honor, I never saw him before."

"Very well, then, will you please ask him to tell you what I had for supper last night? He was with me and watched me while I ate."

Then the Doctor and the dog started talking to one another in signs and sounds, and they kept at it for quite a long time.

And the Doctor began to giggle and get so interested that he seemed to forget all about the court and the judge and everything else.

"What a time he takes!" I heard a fat woman in front of me whispering. "He's only pretending. Of course he can't do it! Who ever heard of talking to a dog? He must think we're children."

"Haven't you finished yet?" the judge asked the Doctor. "It shouldn't take that long just to ask what I had for supper."

"Oh, no, Your Honor," said the Doctor. "The dog told me that long ago. But then he went on to tell me what you did after supper."

"Never mind that," said the judge. "Tell me what answer he gave you to my question."

"He says you had a mutton chop, two baked potatoes, a pickled walnut, and a glass of ale."

The Honorable Eustace Beauchamp Conckley went white to the lips.

"Sounds like witchcraft," he muttered. "I never dreamed—"

"And after your supper," the Doctor went on, "he says you went to see a prizefight and then sat up playing cards for money till twelve o'clock and came home singing, 'We won't get—'"

"That will do," the judge interrupted, "I am satisfied you can do as you say. The prisoner's dog shall be admitted as a witness."

"I protest, I object!" screamed the prosecutor. "Your Honor, this is—"

"Sit down!" roared the judge. "I say the dog shall be heard. That ends the matter. Put the witness in the stand."

And then for the first time in the solemn history of England a dog was put in the witness stand of Her Majesty's Court.

"Sat scowling down upon the amazed and gaping jury"

And it was I, Tommy Stubbins (when the Doctor made a sign to me across the room), who proudly led Bob up the aisle, through the astonished crowd, past the frowning, spluttering, long-nosed prosecutor, and made him comfortable on a high chair in the witness-box; from where the old bulldog sat scowling down over the rail upon the amazed and gaping jury.

· The Seventh Chapter ·
THE END OF THE MYSTERY

THE trial went swiftly forward after that. Mr. Jenkyns told the Doctor to ask Bob what he saw on the night of the 29th, and when Bob had told all he knew and the Doctor had turned it into English for the judge and the jury, this was what he had to say:

"On the night of the 29th of November, 1824, I was with my master, Luke Fitzjohn (otherwise known as Luke the Hermit), and his two partners, Manuel Mendoza and William Boggs (otherwise known as Bluebeard Bill) in their gold mine in Mexico. For a long time these three men had been hunting for gold, and they had dug a deep hole in the ground. On the morning of the 29th gold was discovered, lots of it, at the bottom of this hole. And all three, my master and his two partners, were very happy about it because now they would be rich. But Manuel Mendoza asked Bluebeard Bill to go for a walk with him. These two men I had always suspected of being bad. So when I noticed that they left my master behind, I followed them secretly to see what they were up to. And in a deep cave in the mountains I heard them arrange together to kill Luke the Hermit so that they should get all the gold and he have none."

At this point the judge asked, "Where is the witness Mendoza? Constable, see that he does not leave the court."

But the wicked little man with the watery eyes had already sneaked out when no one was looking, and he was never seen in Puddleby again.

"Then," Bob's statement went on, "I went to my master and tried very hard to make him understand that his partners were dangerous men. But it was no use. He did not understand dog language. So I did the next best thing: I never let him out of my sight but stayed with him every moment of the day and night.

"Now the hole that they had made was so deep that to get down and up it you had to go in a big bucket tied on the end of a rope, and the three men used to haul one another up and let one another down the mine in this way. That was how the gold was brought up, too—in the bucket. Well, about seven o'clock in the evening my master was standing at the top of the mine, hauling up Bluebeard Bill who was in the bucket. Just as he had got Bill halfway up I saw Mendoza come out of the hut where we all lived. Mendoza thought that Bill was away buying groceries. But he wasn't, he was in the bucket. And when Mendoza saw Luke hauling and straining on the rope, he thought he was pulling up a bucketful of gold. So he drew a pistol from his pocket and came sneaking up behind Luke to shoot him.

"I barked and barked to warn my master of the danger he was in, but he was so busy hauling up Bill (who was a heavy, fat man) that he took no notice of me. I saw that if I didn't do something quick he would surely be shot. So I did a thing I've never done before: Suddenly and savagely I bit my master in

HUGH LOFTING

" 'He drew a pistol and came sneaking up' "

the leg from behind. Luke was so hurt and startled that he did just what I wanted him to do: He let go the rope with both hands at once and turned around. And then—*crash!*—down went Bill in his bucket to the bottom of the mine and he was killed.

"While my master was busy scolding me Mendoza put his pistol in his pocket, came up with a smile on his face, and looked down the mine.

" 'Why, good gracious!' said he to Luke. 'You've killed Blue-beard Bill. I must go and tell the police'—hoping, you see, to get the whole mine to himself when Luke should be put in prison. Then he jumped on his horse and galloped away.

"And soon my master grew afraid, for he saw that if Mendoza only told enough lies to the police, it *would* look as though he had killed Bill on purpose. So while Mendoza was gone he and I stole away together secretly and came to England. Here he shaved off his beard and became a hermit. And ever since, for fifteen years, we've remained in hiding. This is all I have to say. And I swear it is the truth, every word."

When the Doctor finished reading Bob's long speech the excitement among the twelve men of the jury was positively terrific. One, a very old man with white hair, began to weep in a loud voice at the thought of poor Luke hiding on the fen for fifteen years for something he couldn't help. And all the others set to whispering and nodding their heads to one another.

In the middle of all this up got that horrible prosecutor again, waving his arms more wildly than ever.

"Your Honor," he cried, "I must object to this evidence as biased. Of course the dog would not tell the truth against his own master. I object. I protest."

"Very well," said the judge, "you are at liberty to cross-examine. It is your duty as prosecutor to prove his evidence untrue. There is the dog: Question him, if you do not believe what he says."

I thought the long-nosed lawyer would have a fit. He looked first at the dog, then at the Doctor, then at the judge, then back at the dog scowling from the witness-box. He opened his mouth to say something, but no words came. He waved his arms some more. His face got redder and redder. At last, clutching his forehead, he sank weakly into his seat and had to be helped out of the courtroom by two friends. As he was half carried through the door he was still feebly murmuring, "I protest . . . I object . . . I protest!"

· The Eighth Chapter ·
THREE CHEERS

EXT the judge made a very long speech to
the jury, and when it was over all the twelve jurymen got up
and went out into the next room. And at that point the Doctor
came back, leading Bob, to the seat beside me.

"What have the jurymen gone out for?" I asked.

"They always do that at the end of a trial, to make up their
minds whether the prisoner did it or not."

"Couldn't you and Bob go in with them and help them
make up their minds the right way?" I asked.

"No, that's not allowed. They have to talk it over in secret.
Sometimes it takes . . . my gracious, look, they're coming
back already! They didn't spend long over it."

Everybody kept quite still while the twelve men came
tramping back into their places in the pews. Then one of
them, the leader—a little man—stood up and turned to the
judge. Everyone was holding his breath, especially the Doctor
and myself, to see what he was going to say. You could have
heard a pin drop while the whole courtroom, the whole of
Puddleby in fact, waited with craning necks and straining
ears to hear the weighty words.

"Your Honor," said the little man, "the jury returns a verdict of *Not Guilty*."

"What's that mean?" I asked, turning to the Doctor.

But I found Doctor John Dolittle, the famous naturalist, standing on top of a chair, dancing about on one leg like a schoolboy.

"It means he's free!" he cried. "Luke is free!"

"Then he'll be able to come on the voyage with us, won't he?"

But I could not hear his answer, for the whole courtroom seemed to be jumping up on chairs like the Doctor. The crowd had suddenly gone crazy. All the people were laughing and calling and waving to Luke to show him how glad they were that he was free. The noise was deafening.

Then it stopped. All was quiet again, and the people stood up respectfully while the judge left the court. For the trial of Luke the Hermit, that famous trial which to this day they are still talking of in Puddleby, was over.

In the hush while the judge was leaving, a sudden shriek rang out, and there, in the doorway stood a woman, her arms outstretched to the Hermit.

"Luke!" she cried, "I've found you at last!"

"It's his wife," the fat woman in front of me whispered. "She ain't seen 'im in fifteen years, poor dear! What a lovely reunion. I'm glad I came. I wouldn't have missed this for anything!"

As soon as the judge had gone the noise broke out again, and now the folks gathered around Luke and his wife and shook them by the hand and congratulated them and laughed over them and cried over them.

"Come along, Stubbins," said the Doctor, taking me by the arm, "let's get out of this while we can."

"But aren't you going to speak to Luke?" I said, "—to ask him if he'll come on the voyage?"

"It wouldn't be a bit of use," said the Doctor. "His wife's come for him. No man stands any chance of going on a voyage when his wife hasn't seen him in fifteen years. Come along. Let's get home to tea. We didn't have any lunch, remember. And we've earned something to eat. We'll have one of those mixed meals, lunch and tea combined—with watercress and ham. Nice change. Come along."

Just as we were going to step out at a side door I heard the crowd shouting, "The Doctor! The Doctor! Where's the Doctor? The Hermit would have hanged if it hadn't been for the Doctor. Speech! Speech! The Doctor!"

And a man came running up to us and said, "The people are calling for you, sir."

"I'm very sorry," said the Doctor, "but I'm in a hurry."

"The crowd won't be denied, sir," said the man. "They want you to make a speech in the marketplace."

"Beg them to excuse me," said the Doctor, "—with my compliments. I have an appointment at my house—a very important one that I may not break. Tell Luke to make a speech. Come along, Stubbins, this way."

"Oh, Lord!" he muttered as we got out into the open air and found another crowd waiting for him at the side door. "Let's go up that alleyway to the left. Quick! Run!"

We took to our heels, darted through a couple of side streets and just managed to get away from the crowd.

It was not till we had gained the Oxenthorpe Road that we dared to slow down to a walk and take our breath. And even when we reached the Doctor's gate and turned to look backward toward the town, the faint murmur of many voices still reached us on the evening wind.

"They're still clamoring for you," I said. "Listen!"

The murmur suddenly swelled up into a low distant roar, and although it was a mile and half away you could distinctly hear the words,

"Three cheers for Luke the Hermit: Hooray!—Three cheers for his dog: Hooray!—Three cheers for his wife: Hooray!—Three cheers for the Doctor: Hooray! Hooray! HOO-R-A-Y!"

· The Ninth Chapter ·
THE PURPLE BIRD OF PARADISE

OLYNESIA was waiting for us on the front porch.
She looked full of some important news.

"Doctor," said she, "the purple bird of paradise has arrived!"

"At last!" said the Doctor. "I had begun to fear some accident had befallen her. And how is Miranda?"

From the excited way in which the Doctor fumbled his key into the lock, I guessed that we were not going to get our tea right away, even now.

"Oh, she seemed all right when she arrived," said Polynesia, "—tired from her long journey, of course, but otherwise all right. But what *do* you think? That mischief-making sparrow, Cheapside, insulted her as soon as she came into the garden. When I arrived on the scene she was in tears and was all for turning around and going straight back to Brazil tonight. I had the hardest work persuading her to wait till you came. She's in the study. I shut Cheapside in one of your bookcases and told him I'd tell you exactly what had happened, the moment you got home."

The Doctor frowned, then walked silently and quickly to the study.

Here we found the candles lit, for the daylight was nearly gone. Dab-Dab was standing on the floor mounting guard over the glass-fronted bookcases in which Cheapside had been imprisoned. The noisy little sparrow was still fluttering angrily behind the glass when we came in.

In the center of the big table, perched on the inkstand, stood the most beautiful bird I have ever seen. She had a deep violet-colored breast, scarlet wings, and a long, long, sweeping tail of gold. She was unimaginably beautiful but looked dreadfully tired. Already she had her head under her wing, and she swayed gently from side to side on top of the ink-stand like a bird that has flown long and far.

"Sh!" said Dab-Dab. "Miranda is asleep. I've got this little imp Cheapside in here. Listen, Doctor, for heaven's sake send that sparrow away before he does any more mischief. He's nothing but a vulgar little nuisance. We've had a perfectly awful time trying to get Miranda to stay. Shall I serve your tea in here, or will you come into the kitchen when you're ready?"

"We'll come into the kitchen, Dab-Dab," said the Doctor. "Let Cheapside out before you go, please."

Dab-Dab opened the bookcase door and Cheapside strutted out trying hard not to look guilty.

"Cheapside," said the Doctor sternly, "what did you say to Miranda when she arrived?"

"I didn't say nothing, Doc, straight I didn't. That is, nothing much. I was picking up crumbs off the gravel path when she comes swanking into the garden, turning up her nose in all directions, as though she owned the earth—just because she's got a lot of colored plumage. A London sparrow's as good as her any day. I don't hold by these gawdy, bedizened foreigners, nohow. Why don't they stay in their own country?"

"But what did you say to her that got her so offended?"

"All I said was, 'You don't belong in an English garden; you ought to be in a milliner's window.' That's all."

"You ought to be ashamed of yourself, Cheapside. Don't you realize that this bird has come thousands of miles to see me—only to be insulted by your impertinent tongue as soon as she reaches my garden? What do you mean by it? If she had gone away again before I got back tonight, I would never have forgiven you. Leave the room."

Sheepishly, but still trying to look as though he didn't care, Cheapside hopped out into the passage and Dab-Dab closed the door.

The Doctor went up to the beautiful bird on the inkstand and gently stroked its back. Instantly, its head popped out from under its wing.

· The Tenth Chapter ·

LONG ARROW,
THE SON OF GOLDEN ARROW

WELL, Miranda," said the Doctor. "I'm terribly sorry this has happened. But you mustn't mind Cheapside; he doesn't know any better. He's a city bird, and all his life he has had to squabble for a living. You must make allowances. He doesn't know any better."

Miranda stretched her gorgeous wings wearily. Now that I saw her awake and moving, I noticed what a superior, well-bred manner she had. There were tears in her eyes and her beak was trembling.

"I wouldn't have minded so much," she said in a high silvery voice, "if I hadn't been so dreadfully worn out. . . . That and something else," she added beneath her breath.

"Did you have a hard time getting here?" asked the Doctor.

"The worst passage I ever made," said Miranda. "The weather—well, there. What's the use? I'm here anyway."

"Tell me," said the Doctor as though he had been impatiently waiting to say something for a long time, "what did Long Arrow say when you gave him my message?"

The purple bird of paradise hung her head.

"That's the worst part of it," she said. "I might almost as

well have not come at all. I wasn't able to deliver your message. I couldn't find him. *Long Arrow, the son of Golden Arrow, has disappeared!*"

"Disappeared!" cried the Doctor. "Why, what's become of him?"

"Nobody knows," Miranda answered. "He had often disappeared before, as I have told you—so that the Indians didn't know where he was. But it's a mighty hard thing to hide away from the birds. I had always been able to find some owl or martin who could tell me where he was, if I wanted to know. But not this time. That's why I'm nearly a fortnight late in coming to you: I kept hunting and hunting, asking everywhere. I went over the whole length and breadth of South America. But there wasn't a living thing could tell me where he was."

There was a sad silence in the room after she had finished; the Doctor was frowning in a peculiar sort of way and Polynesia scratched her head.

"Did you ask the black parrots?" asked Polynesia. "They usually know everything."

"Certainly I did," said Miranda. "And I was so upset at not being able to find out anything that I forgot all about observing the weather signs before I started my flight here. I didn't even bother to break my journey at the Azores, but cut right across, making for the Straits of Gibraltar—as though it were June or July. And of course I ran into a perfectly frightful storm in mid-Atlantic. I really thought I'd never come through it. Luckily I found a piece of a wrecked vessel floating in the sea after the storm had partly died down, and I roosted on it and took some sleep. If I hadn't been able to take that rest, I wouldn't be here to tell the tale."

"Poor Miranda! What a time you must have had!" said the

Doctor. "But tell me, were you able to find out whereabouts Long Arrow was last seen?"

"Yes. A young albatross told me he had seen him on Spider Monkey Island."

"Spider Monkey Island? That's somewhere off the coast of Brazil, isn't it?"

"Yes, that's it. Of course I flew there right away and asked every bird on the island—and it is a big island, a hundred miles long. It seems that Long Arrow was visiting some peculiar Indians that live there, and that when last seen he was going up into the mountains looking for rare medicine plants. I got that from a tame hawk, a pet, which the Chief of the Indians keeps for hunting partridges with. I nearly got caught and put in a cage for my pains, too. That's the worst of having beautiful feathers: It's as much as your life is worth to go near most humans. They say, 'oh, how pretty!' and shoot an arrow or a bullet into you. You and Long Arrow were the only two men that I would ever trust myself near—out of all the people in the world."

"But was he never known to have returned from the mountains?"

"No. That was the last that was seen or heard of him. I questioned the seabirds around the shores to find out if he had left the island in a canoe. But they could tell me nothing."

"Do you think that some accident has happened to him?" asked the Doctor in a fearful voice.

"I'm afraid it must have," said Miranda shaking her head.

"Well," said John Dolittle slowly, "if I could never meet Long Arrow face to face, it would be the greatest disappointment in my whole life. Not only that, but it would be a great loss to the knowledge of the human race. For, from what you

" 'What else can I think?' "

have told me of him, he knew more natural science than all the rest of us put together; and if he has gone without anyone to write it down for him so the world may be the better for it, it would be a terrible thing. But you don't really think that he is dead, do you?"

"What else can I think?" asked Miranda, bursting into tears, "when for six whole months he has not been seen by flesh, fish, or fowl."

· The Eleventh Chapter ·
BLIND TRAVEL

THIS news about Long Arrow made us all very sad. And I could see from the silent dreamy way the Doctor took his tea that he was dreadfully upset. Every once in a while he would stop eating altogether and sit staring at the spots on the kitchen tablecloth as though his thoughts were far away, till Dab-Dab, who was watching to see that he got a good meal, would cough or rattle the pots in the sink.

I did my best to cheer him up by reminding him of all he had done for Luke and his wife that afternoon. And when that didn't seem to work, I went on talking about our preparations for the voyage.

"But you see, Stubbins," said he as we rose from the table and Dab-Dab and Chee-Chee began to clear away, "I don't know where to go now. I feel sort of lost since Miranda brought me this news. On this voyage I had planned going to see Long Arrow. I had been looking forward to it for a whole year. I felt he might help me in learning the language of the shellfish—and perhaps in finding some way of getting to the bottom of the sea. But now? He's gone! And all his great knowledge has gone with him."

Then he seemed to fall a-dreaming again.

"Just to think of it!" he murmured. "Long Arrow and I, two students. Although I'd never met him, I felt as though I knew him quite well. For, in his way—without any schooling—he has all his life been trying to do the very things that I have tried to do in mine. And now he's gone! A whole world lay between us—and only a bird knew us both!"

We went back into the study, where Jip brought the Doctor his slippers and his pipe. And after the pipe was lit and the smoke began to fill the room the old man seemed to cheer up a little.

"But you will go on some voyage, Doctor, won't you?" I asked, "—even if you can't go to find Long Arrow."

He looked up sharply into my face, and I suppose he saw how anxious I was. Because he suddenly smiled his old, boy-ish smile and said, "Yes, Stubbins. Don't worry. We'll go. We mustn't stop working and learning, even if poor Long Arrow has disappeared. But where to go: That's the question. Where shall we go?"

There were so many places that I wanted to go that I couldn't make up my mind right away. And while I was still thinking, the Doctor sat up in his chair and said, "I tell you what we'll do, Stubbins: It's a game I used to play when I was young—before Sarah came to live with me. I used to call it Blind Travel. Whenever I wanted to go on a voyage and I couldn't make up my mind where to go, I would take the atlas and open it with my eyes shut. Next, I'd wave a pencil, still without looking, and stick it down on whatever page had fallen open. Then I'd open my eyes and look. It's a very excit-ing game, is Blind Travel. Because you have to swear before you begin that you will go to the place the pencil touches, come what may. Shall we play it?"

"Oh, let's!" I almost yelled. "How thrilling! I hope it's China . . . or Borneo . . . or Bagdad."

And in a moment I had scrambled up the bookcase, dragged the big atlas from the top shelf, and laid it on the table before the Doctor.

I knew every page in that atlas by heart. How many days and nights I had lingered over its old faded maps, following the blue rivers from the mountains to the sea, wondering what the little towns really looked like and how wide were the sprawling lakes!

As the Doctor began sharpening his pencil a thought came to me.

"What if the pencil falls upon the North Pole?" I asked. "Will we have to go there?"

"No. The rules of the game say you don't have to go any place you've been to before. You are allowed another try. I've been to the North Pole," he ended quietly, "so we shan't have to go there."

I could hardly speak with astonishment.

"You've been to the North Pole!" I managed to gasp out at last. "But I thought it was still undiscovered. The map shows all the places explorers have reached, *trying* to get there. Why isn't your name down if you discovered it?"

"I promised to keep it a secret. And you must promise me never to tell anyone. Yes, I discovered the North Pole in April, 1809. But shortly after I got there the polar bears came to me in a body and told me there was a great deal of coal there, buried beneath the snow. They knew, they said, that human beings would do anything and go anywhere to get coal. So would I please keep it a secret. Because once people began coming up there to start coal mines, their beautiful white

HUGH LOFTING

"It was a tense and fearful moment"

country would be spoiled—and there was nowhere else in the world cold enough for polar bears to be comfortable. So of course I had to promise them I would. Ah, well, it will be discovered again someday, by somebody else. But I want the polar bears to have their playground to themselves as long as possible. And I daresay it will be a good while yet, for it certainly is a fiendish place to get to. Well, now, are we ready? Good! Take the pencil and stand here close to the table. When the book falls open, wave the pencil around three times and jab it down. Ready? All right, shut your eyes."

It was a tense and fearful moment—but very thrilling. We both had our eyes shut tight. I heard the atlas fall open with a bang. I wondered what page it was: England or Asia. If it should be the map of Asia, so much would depend on where that pencil would land. I waved three times in a circle. I began to lower my hand. The pencil point touched the page.

"All right," I called out, "it's done."

· The Twelfth Chapter ·
DESTINY AND DESTINATION

WE both opened our eyes, then bumped our heads together with a crack, in our eagerness to lean over and see where we were to go.

The atlas lay open at a map called *Chart of the South Atlantic Ocean*. My pencil point was resting right in the center of a tiny island. The name of it was printed so small that the Doctor had to get out his strong spectacles to read it. I was trembling with excitement.

"Spider Monkey Island," he read out slowly. Then he whistled softly beneath his breath. "Of all the extraordinary things! You've hit upon the very island where Long Arrow was last seen on earth. I wonder . . . Well, well! How very singular!"

"We'll go there, Doctor, won't we?" I asked.

"Of course we will. The rules of the game say we've got to."

"I'm so glad it wasn't Oxenthorpe or Bristol," I said. "It'll be a grand voyage, this. Look at all the sea we've got to cross. Will it take us long?"

"Oh, no," said the Doctor, "—not very. With a good boat and a good wind we should make it easily in four weeks. But isn't it extraordinary? Of all the places in the world you picked out that one with your eyes shut. Spider Monkey Island after all!—Well, there's one good thing about it: I shall be able to get some jabizri beetles."

"What are jabizri beetles?"

"They are a very rare kind of beetles with peculiar habits. I want to study them. There are only three countries in the world where they are to be found. Spider Monkey Island is one of them. But even there they are very scarce."

"What is this little question mark after the name of the island for?" I asked, pointing to the map.

"That means that the island's position in the ocean is not known very exactly—that it is somewhere *about* there. Ships have probably seen it in that neighborhood, that is all, most likely. It is quite possible we shall be the first to land there. But I daresay we shall have some difficulty in finding it first."

How like a dream it all sounded! The two of us sitting there at the big study table, the candles lit, the smoke curling toward the dim ceiling from the Doctor's pipe—the two of us sitting there, talking about finding an island in the ocean and being the first Europeans to land upon it!

"I'll bet it will be a great voyage," I said. "It looks a lovely island on the map. Will there be natives there?"

"A peculiar tribe of Indians lives on it, Miranda tells me."

At this point the poor bird of paradise stirred and woke up. In our excitement we had forgotten to speak low.

"We are going to Spider Monkey Island, Miranda," said the Doctor. "You know where it is, do you not?"

"I know where it was the last time I saw it," said the bird. "But whether it will be there still, I can't say."

"What do you mean?" asked the Doctor. "It is always in the same place, surely?"

"Not by any means," said Miranda. "Why, didn't you know? Spider Monkey Island is a *floating* island. It moves around all over the place—usually somewhere near southern South America. But of course I could surely find it for you, if you want to go there."

At this fresh piece of news I could contain myself no longer. I was bursting to tell someone. I ran dancing and singing from the room to find Chee-Chee.

At the door I tripped over Dab-Dab, who was just coming in with her wings full of plates, and fell headlong on my nose.

"Has the boy gone crazy?" cried the duck. "Where do you think you're going, ninny?"

"To Spider Monkey Island!" I shouted, picking myself up and doing cartwheels down the hall. "Spider Monkey Island! Hooray! . . . And it's a *floating* island!"

"You're going to Bedlam, I should say," snorted the housekeeper. "Look what you've done to my best china!"

But I was far too happy to listen to her scolding, and I ran on, singing, into the kitchen to find Chee-Chee.

PART III

· The First Chapter ·
THE THIRD MAN

THAT same week we began our preparations for the voyage.

Joe, the mussel man, had *The Curlew* moved down the river and tied it up along the river wall, so it would be more handy for loading. And for three whole days we carried provisions down to our beautiful new boat and stowed them away.

I was surprised to find how roomy and big she was inside. There were three little cabins, a saloon (or dining room), and underneath all this, a big place called the hold, where the food and extra sails and other things were kept.

I think Joe must have told everybody in the town about our coming voyage because there was always a regular crowd watching us when we brought the things down to put aboard. And of course, sooner or later, old Matthew Mugg was bound to turn up.

"My goodness, Tommy," said he, as he watched me carrying on some sacks of flour, "but that's a pretty boat! Where might the Doctor be going to this voyage?"

"We're going to Spider Monkey Island," I said proudly.

"And be you the only one the Doctor's taking along?"

"Well, he has spoken of wanting to take another man," I said, "but so far he hasn't made up his mind."

Matthew grunted, then squinted up at the graceful masts of *The Curlew*.

"You know, Tommy," said he, "if it wasn't for my rheumatism I've half a mind to come with the Doctor myself. There's something about a boat standing ready to sail that always did make me feel venturesome and travelish-like. What's that stuff in the cans you're taking on?"

"This is treacle," I said, "—twenty pounds of treacle."

"My goodness," he sighed, turning away sadly. "That makes me feel more like going with you than ever. But my rheumatism is that bad I can't hardly—"

I didn't hear any more, for Matthew had moved off, still mumbling, into the crowd that stood about the wharf. The clock in Puddleby Church struck noon and I turned back, feeling very busy and important, to the task of loading.

But it wasn't very long before someone else came along and interrupted my work. This was a huge, big burly man with a red beard and tattoo marks all over his arms. He wiped his mouth with the back of his hand, spat twice onto the river wall and said, "Boy, where's the skipper?"

"The *skipper*! . . . Who do you mean?" I asked.

"The captain. . . . Where's the captain of this craft?" he said, pointing to *The Curlew*.

"Oh, you mean the Doctor," said I. "Well, he isn't here at present."

At that moment the Doctor arrived with his arms full of notebooks and butterfly nets and glass cases and other natural history things. The big man went up to him, respectfully touching his cap.

" 'Boy, where's the skipper?' "

"Good morning, Captain," said he. "I heard you was in need of hands for a voyage. My name's Ben Butcher, able seaman."

"I am very glad to know you," said the Doctor. "But I'm afraid I shan't be able to take on any more crew."

"Why, but Captain," said the able seaman, "you surely ain't going to face deep-sea weather with nothing more than this bit of a lad to help you—and with a cutter that big!"

The Doctor assured him that he was, but the man didn't go away. He hung around and argued. He told us he had known of many ships being sunk through "undermanning." He got out what he called his *stiffikit*—a paper which said what a good sailor he was—and implored us, if we valued our lives, to take him.

But the Doctor was quite firm—polite but determined—and finally the man walked sorrowfully away, telling us he never expected to see us alive again.

Callers of one sort and another kept us quite busy that morning. The Doctor had no sooner gone below to stow away his notebooks than another visitor appeared upon the gangplank. This was a black man, very fashionably dressed.

"Pardon me," said he, bowing elegantly, "but is this the ship of the physician Dolittle?"

"Yes," I said, "did you wish to see him?"

"I did—if it will not be discommodious," he answered.

"Who shall I say it is?"

"I am Bumpo Kahbooboo, Crown Prince of Jolliginki."

I ran downstairs at once and told the Doctor.

"How fortunate!" cried John Dolittle. "My old friend Bumpo! Well, well! He's studying at Oxford, you know. How good of him to come all this way to call on me!" And he tumbled up the ladder to greet his visitor.

The strange man seemed to be overcome with joy when the Doctor appeared and shook him warmly by the hand.

"News reached me," he said, "that you were about to sail upon a voyage. I hastened to see you before your departure. I am sublimely ecstasied that I did not miss you."

"You very nearly did miss us," said the Doctor. "As it happened, we were delayed somewhat in getting the necessary number of men to sail our boat. If it hadn't been for that, we would have been gone three days ago."

"How many men does your ship's company yet require?" asked Bumpo.

"Only one," said the Doctor, "—but it is so hard to find the right one."

"Methinks I detect something of the finger of Destination in this," said Bumpo. "How would I do?"

"Splendidly," said the Doctor. "But what about your studies? You can't very well just go off and leave your university career to take care of itself, you know."

"I need a holiday," said Bumpo. "Even had I not gone with you, I intended at the end of this term to take a three-months' abiscission. But besides, I shall not be neglecting my edification if I accompany you. Before I left Jolliginki my august father, the King, told me to be sure and travel plenty. You are a man of great studiosity. To see the world in your company is an opportunity not to be sneezed upon. No, no, indeed."

"How did you like the life at Oxford?" asked the Doctor.

"Oh, passably, passably," said Bumpo. "I liked it all except the algebra and the shoes. The algebra hurt my head and the shoes hurt my feet. I threw the shoes over a wall as soon as I got out of the college quadrilateral this morning, and the algebra I am happily forgetting very fast. I liked Cicero—yes, I think Cicero's fine—so simultaneous. By the way, they tell me his son is rowing for our college next year—charming fellow."

The Doctor looked down at the man's huge bare feet thoughtfully a moment.

"Well," he said slowly, "there is something in what you say, Bumpo, about getting education from the world as well as from the college. And if you are really sure that you want to come, we shall be delighted to have you. Because, to tell you the truth, I think you are exactly the man we need."

· The Second Chapter ·
GOOD-BYE!

TWO days after that we had all in readiness for our departure.

On this voyage Jip begged so hard to be taken that the Doctor finally gave in and said he could come. Polynesia and Chee-Chee were the only other animals to go with us. Dab-Dab was left in charge of the house and the animal family we were to leave behind.

Of course, as is always the way, at the last moment we kept remembering things we had forgotten, and when we finally closed the house up and went down the steps to the street, we were all burdened with armfuls of odd packages.

Halfway to the river, the Doctor suddenly remembered that he had left the stockpot boiling on the kitchen fire. However, we saw a blackbird flying by who nested in our garden, and the Doctor asked her to go back for us and tell Dab-Dab about it.

Down at the river wall we found a great crowd waiting to see us off.

Standing right near the gangplank were my mother and father. I hoped that they would not make a scene or burst into tears, or anything like that. But as a matter of fact they behaved quite well—for parents. My mother said something about being sure not to get my feet wet; and my father just smiled a crooked sort of smile, patted me on the back, and wished me luck.

We were a little surprised not to see Matthew Mugg among the crowd. We had felt sure that he would be there, and the Doctor had intended to give him some extra instructions about the food for the animals we had left at the house.

At last, after much pulling and tugging, we got the anchor up and undid a lot of mooring ropes. Then *The Curlew* began to move gently down the river with the out-running tide, while the people on the wall cheered and waved their handkerchiefs.

We bumped into one or two other boats getting out into the stream, and at one sharp bend in the river we got stuck on a mudbank for a few minutes. But though the people on the shore seemed to get very excited at these things, the Doctor did not appear to be disturbed by them in the least.

"These little accidents will happen in the most carefully regulated voyages," he said as he leaned over the side and fished for his boots, which had gotten stuck in the mud while we were pushing off. "Sailing is much easier when you get out into the open sea. There aren't so many silly things to bump into."

For me indeed it was a great and wonderful feeling, that getting out into the open sea, when at length we passed the little lighthouse at the mouth of the river and found ourselves free of the land. It was all so new and different: just the sky above you and sea below. This ship, which was to be our house and our street, our home and our garden, for so many days to come, seemed so tiny in all this wide water—so tiny and yet so snug, sufficient, safe.

I looked around me and took in a deep breath. The Doctor was at the wheel steering the boat which was now leaping and plunging gently through the waves. (I had expected to feel seasick at first but was delighted to find that I didn't.) Bumpo had been told to go downstairs and prepare dinner for us. Chee-Chee was coiling up ropes in the stern and laying them in neat piles. My work was fastening down the things on the deck so that nothing could roll about if the weather should grow rough when we got farther from the land. Jip was up in the peak of the boat with ears cocked and nose stuck out—like a statue, so still—his keen old eyes keeping a sharp lookout for floating wrecks, sandbars, and other dangers. Each one of us had some special job to do, part of the proper running of a ship. Even old Polynesia was taking the sea's temperature with the Doctor's bath thermometer tied on the end of a string, to make sure there were no icebergs near us. As I listened to her swearing softly to herself because she couldn't read the pesky figures in the fading light, I realized that the voyage had begun in earnest and that very soon it would be night—my first night at sea!

· The Third Chapter ·
OUR TROUBLES BEGIN

JUST before suppertime Bumpo appeared from downstairs and went to the Doctor at the wheel.

"A stowaway in the hold, sir," said he in a very businesslike seafaring voice. "I just discovered him, behind the flour bags."

"Dear me!" said the Doctor. "What a nuisance! Stubbins, go down with Bumpo and bring the man up. I can't leave the wheel just now."

So Bumpo and I went down into the hold; and there, behind the flour bags, plastered in flour from head to foot, we found a man. After we had swept most of the flour off him with a broom, we discovered that it was Matthew Mugg. We hauled him upstairs sneezing and took him before the Doctor.

"Why, Matthew!" said John Dolittle. "What on earth are you doing here?"

"The temptation was too much for me, Doctor," said the cat's-meat man. "You know I've often asked you to take me on voyages with you and you never would. Well, this time, knowing that you needed an extra man, I thought if I stayed hid till the ship was well at sea you would find I came in handy-like and keep me. But I had to lie so doubled up for hours behind them flour bags that my rheumatism came on something awful. I just had to change my position, and of course just as I stretched out my legs, along comes this here African cook of yours and sees my feet sticking out. . . . Don't this ship roll something awful! How long has this storm been going on? I reckon this damp sea air wouldn't be very good for my rheumatics."

"No, Matthew, it really isn't. You ought not to have come. You are not in any way suited to this kind of a life. I'm sure you wouldn't enjoy a long voyage a bit. We'll stop in at Penzance and put you ashore. Bumpo, please go downstairs to my bunk, and, listen, in the pocket of my dressing gown you'll find some maps. Bring me the small one—with blue pencil marks at the top. I know Penzance is over here on our left somewhere. But I must find out what lighthouses there are before I change the ship's course and sail inshore."

"Very good, sir," said Bumpo, turning around smartly and making for the stairway.

"Now, Matthew," said the Doctor, "you can take the coach from Penzance to Bristol. And from there it is not very far to Puddleby, as you know. Don't forget to take the usual provisions to the house every Thursday, and be particularly careful to remember the extra supply of herring for the baby minks."

While we were waiting for the maps Chee-Chee and I set about lighting the lamps: a green one on the right side of the ship, a red one on the left, and a white one on the mast.

At last we heard someone trundling on the stairs again and the Doctor said, "Ah, here's Bumpo with the maps at last!"

But to our great astonishment it was not Bumpo alone that appeared but *three* people.

"Good Lord, deliver us! Who are these?" cried John Dolittle.

"Two more stowaways, sir," said Bumpo, stepping forward briskly. "I found them in your cabin hiding under the bunk. One woman and one man, sir. Here are the maps."

"This is too much," said the Doctor feebly. "Who are they? I can't see their faces in this dim light. Strike a match, Bumpo."

You could never guess who it was. It was Luke and his wife. Mrs. Luke appeared to be very miserable and seasick.

They explained to the Doctor that after they had settled down to live together in the little shack out on the fens, so many people came to visit them (having heard about the great trial) that life became impossible; and they had decided to escape from Puddleby in this manner—for they had no money to leave any other way—and try to find some new place to live where they and their story wouldn't be so well known. But as soon as the ship had begun to roll Mrs. Luke had gotten most dreadfully unwell.

Poor Luke apologized many times for being such a nuisance and said that the whole thing had been his wife's idea.

The Doctor, after he had sent below for his medicine bag and had given Mrs. Luke some *sal volatile* and smelling salts, said he thought the best thing to do would be for him to lend them some money and put them ashore at Penzance with Matthew. He also wrote a letter for Luke to take with him to a friend the Doctor had in the town of Penzance who, it was hoped, would be able to find Luke work to do there.

As the Doctor opened his purse and took out some gold coins I heard Polynesia, who was sitting on my shoulder watching the whole affair, mutter beneath her breath, "There he goes—lending his last blessed penny—three pounds ten— all the money we had for the whole trip! Now we haven't the price of a postage stamp aboard if we should lose an anchor or have to buy a pint of tar. Well, let's pray we don't run out of food. Why doesn't he give them the ship and walk home?"

Presently with the help of the map the course of the boat was changed and, to Mrs. Luke's great relief, we made for Penzance and dry land.

I was tremendously interested to see how a ship could be steered into a port at night with nothing but lighthouses and a compass to guide you. It seemed to me that the Doctor missed all the rocks and sandbars very cleverly.

We got into that funny little Cornish harbor about eleven o'clock that night. The Doctor took his stowaways on shore in our small rowboat, which we kept on the deck of *The Curlew*, and found them rooms at the hotel there. When he got back he told us that Mrs. Luke had gone straight to bed and was feeling much better.

It was now after midnight, so we decided to stay in the harbor and wait till morning before setting out again.

I was glad to get to bed, although I felt that staying up so tremendously late was great fun. As I climbed into the bunk over the Doctor's and pulled the blankets snugly around me, I found I could look out of the porthole at my elbow, and, without raising my head from the pillow, could see the lights of Penzance swinging gently up and down with the motion of the ship at anchor. It was like being rocked to sleep with a little show going on to amuse you. I was just deciding that I liked the life of the sea very much when I fell fast asleep.

· The Fourth Chapter ·
OUR TROUBLES CONTINUE

THE next morning when we were eating a very excellent breakfast of kidneys and bacon, prepared by our good cook Bumpo, the Doctor said to me, "I was just wondering, Stubbins, whether I should stop at the Capa Blanca Islands or run right across for the coast of Brazil. Miranda said we could expect a spell of excellent weather now—for four and a half weeks at least."

"Well," I said, spooning out the sugar at the bottom of my cocoa cup, "I should think it would be best to make straight across while we are sure of good weather. And, besides, the purple bird of paradise is going to keep a lookout for us, isn't she? She'll be wondering what's happened to us if we don't get there in about a month."

"True, quite true, Stubbins. On the other hand, the Capa Blancas make a very convenient stopping place on our way across. If we should need supplies or repairs, it would be very handy to put in there."

"How long will it take us from here to the Capa Blancas?" I asked.

"About six days," said the Doctor. "—Well, we can decide

later. For the next two days, at any rate, our direction would be the same practically in either case. If you have finished breakfast let's go and get under way."

Upstairs I found our vessel surrounded by white and gray seagulls who flashed and circled about in the sunny morning air, looking for food scraps thrown out by the ships into the harbor.

By about half past seven we had the anchor up and the sails set to a nice steady breeze, and this time we got out into the open sea without bumping into a single thing. We met the Penzance fishing fleet coming in from the night's fishing, and very trim and neat they looked, in a line like soldiers, with their red-brown sails all leaning over the same way and the white water dancing before their bows.

For the next three or four days everything went smoothly. We divided the twenty-four hours of the day into three spells, and we took it in turns to sleep our eight hours and be awake sixteen. So the ship was well looked after, with two of us always on duty.

Besides that, Polynesia, who was an older sailor than any of us, and really knew a lot about running ships, seemed to be always awake—except when she took her couple of winks in the sun, standing on one leg beside the wheel. You may be sure that no one ever got a chance to stay abed more than his eight hours while Polynesia was around. She used to watch the ship's clock, and if you overslept a half minute, she would come down to the cabin and peck you gently on the nose till you got up.

I very soon grew to be quite fond of our funny friend Bumpo, with his grand way of speaking and his enormous feet which someone was always stepping on or falling over. Although he was much older than I was and had been to college, he never tried to lord it over me. He seemed to be forever smiling and kept all of us in good humor. It wasn't long before I began to see the Doctor's good sense in bringing him—in spite of the fact that he knew nothing whatever about sailing or travel.

On the morning of the fifth day out, just as I was taking the wheel over from the Doctor, Bumpo appeared and said, "The salt beef is nearly all gone, sir."

"The salt beef!" cried the Doctor. "Why, we brought a hundred and twenty pounds with us. We couldn't have eaten that in five days. What can have become of it?"

"I don't know, sir, I'm sure. Every time I go down to the stores I find another hunk missing. If it is rats that are eating it, then they are certainly colossal rodents."

Polynesia, who was walking up and down a stayrope taking her morning exercise, put in, "We must search the hold. If this is allowed to go on, we will all be starving before a week is out. Come downstairs with me, Tommy, and we will look into this matter."

So we went downstairs into the storeroom and Polynesia told us to keep quite still and listen. This we did. And presently we heard from a dark corner of the hold the distinct sound of someone snoring.

"Ah, I thought so," said Polynesia. "It's a man—and a big one. Climb in there, both of you, and haul him out. It sounds as though he were behind that barrel. Gosh! We seem to have brought half of Puddleby with us. Haul him out."

So Bumpo and I lit a lantern and climbed over the stores. And there behind the barrel, sure enough, we found an enormous bearded man fast asleep with a well-fed look on his face. We woke him up.

"Washamarrer?" he said sleepily.

It was Ben Butcher, the able seaman.

Polynesia spluttered like an angry firecracker.

"This is the last straw," said she. "The one man in the world we least wanted. Shiver my timbers, what cheek!"

"Would it not be advisable," suggested Bumpo, "while the varlet is still sleepy, to strike him on the head with some heavy object and push him through a porthole into the sea?"

"No. We'd get into trouble," said Polynesia. "Besides, there never was a porthole big enough to push that man through. Bring him upstairs to the Doctor."

So we led the man to the wheel, where he respectfully touched his cap to the Doctor.

"Another stowaway, sir," said Bumpo smartly.

I thought the poor Doctor would have a fit.

"Good morning, Captain," said the man. "Ben Butcher, able seaman, at your service. I knew you'd need me, so I took the liberty of stowing away—much against my conscience. But I just couldn't bear to see you poor landsmen set out on this voyage without a single real seaman to help you. You'd never have gotten home alive if I hadn't come. Why look at your mainsail, sir—all loose at the throat. First gust of wind come along, and away goes your canvas overboard. Well, it's all right now I'm here. We'll soon get things in shipshape."

"No, it isn't all right," said the Doctor, "it's all wrong. And I'm not at all glad to see you. I told you in Puddleby I didn't want you. You had no right to come."

"But, Captain," said the able seaman, "you can't sail this ship without me. You don't understand navigation. Why, look at the compass now: You've let her swing a point and a half off her course. It's madness for you to try to do this trip alone —if you'll pardon my saying so, sir. Why . . . why, you'll lose the ship!"

"Look here," said the Doctor, a sudden stern look coming into his eyes, "losing a ship is nothing to me. I've lost ships before and it doesn't bother me in the least. When I set out to go to a place, I get there. Do you understand? I may know nothing whatever about sailing and navigation, but I get there just the same. Now you may be the best seaman in the world, but on *this* ship you're just a plain ordinary nuisance —very plain and very ordinary. And I am now going to call at the nearest port and put you ashore."

"Yes, and think yourself lucky," Polynesia put in, "that you are not locked up for stowing away and eating all our salt beef."

"I don't know what the mischief we're going to do now," I heard her whisper to Bumpo. "We've no money to buy any more, and that salt beef was the most important part of the stores."

"Would it not be good political economy," Bumpo whispered back, "if we salted the able seaman and ate him instead? I should judge that he would weigh more than a hundred and twenty pounds."

"Don't be silly," snapped Polynesia. "Those things are not done anymore. —Still," she murmured after a moment's thought, "it's an awfully bright idea. I don't suppose anybody saw him come onto the ship. . . . Oh, but heavens! we haven't got enough salt. Besides, he'd be sure to taste of tobacco."

· The Fifth Chapter ·
POLYNESIA HAS A PLAN

THEN the Doctor told me to take the wheel while he made a little calculation with his map and worked out what new course we should take.

"I shall have to run for the Capa Blancas after all," he told me when the seaman's back was turned. "Dreadful nuisance! But I'd sooner swim back to Puddleby than have to listen to that fellow's talk all the way to Brazil."

Indeed he was a terrible person, this Ben Butcher. You'd think that anyone after being told he wasn't wanted would have had the decency to keep quiet. But not Ben Butcher. He kept going around the deck pointing out all the things we had wrong. According to him, there wasn't a thing right on the whole ship. The anchor was hitched up wrong; the hatches weren't fastened down properly; the sails were put on back to front; all our knots were the wrong kind of knots.

At last the Doctor told him to stop talking and go downstairs. He refused—said he wasn't going to be sunk by landlubbers while he was still able to stay on deck.

This made us feel a little uneasy. He was such an enormous

man there was no knowing what he might do if he got really obstreperous.

Bumpo and I were talking about this downstairs in the dining saloon when Polynesia, Jip, and Chee-Chee came and joined us. And, as usual, Polynesia had a plan.

"Listen," she said, "I am certain this Ben Butcher is a smuggler and a bad man. I am a very good judge of seamen, remember, and I don't like the cut of this man's jib. I—"

"Do you really think," I interrupted, "that it *is* safe for the Doctor to cross the Atlantic without any regular seamen on his ship?"

You see it had upset me quite a good deal to find that all the things we had been doing were wrong; and I was beginning to wonder what might happen if we ran into a storm—particularly as Miranda had said the weather would be good only for a certain time, and we seemed to be having so many delays. But Polynesia merely tossed her head scornfully.

"Oh, bless you, my boy," said she, "you're always safe with John Dolittle. Remember that. Don't take any notice of that stupid old salt. Of course it is perfectly true the Doctor does do everything wrong. But with him it doesn't matter. Mark my words, if you travel with John Dolittle you always get there, as you heard him say. I've been with him lots of times and I know. Sometimes the ship is upside down when you get there, and sometimes it's right way up. But you get there just the same. And then of course there's another thing about the Doctor," she added thoughtfully, "he always has extraordinary good luck. He may have his troubles, but with him things seem to have a habit of turning out all right in the end. I remember once when we were going through the Straits of Magellan the wind was so strong—"

"But what are we going to do about Ben Butcher?" Jip put in. "You had some plan, Polynesia, hadn't you?"

"Yes. What I'm afraid of is that he may hit the Doctor on the head when he's not looking and make himself captain of *The Curlew*. Bad sailors do that sometimes. Then they run the ship their own way and take it where they want. That's what you call a mutiny."

"Yes," said Jip, "and we ought to do something pretty quick. We can't reach the Capa Blancas before the day after tomorrow, at best. I don't like to leave the Doctor alone with him for a minute. He smells like a very bad man to me."

"Well, I've got it all worked out," said Polynesia. "Listen, is there a key in that door?"

We looked outside the dining room and found that there was.

"All right," said Polynesia. "Now Bumpo lays the table for lunch and we all go and hide. Then at twelve o'clock Bumpo rings the dinner bell down here. As soon as Ben hears it he'll come down expecting more salt beef. Bumpo must hide behind the door outside. The moment that Ben is seated at the dining table Bumpo slams the door and locks it. Then we've got him. See?"

"How stratagenious!" Bumpo chuckled. "As Cicero said, *parrots cum parishioners facilime congregation*. I'll lay the table at once."

"Yes and take that Worcestershire sauce off the dresser with you when you go out," said Polynesia. "Don't leave any loose eatables around. That fellow has had enough to last any man for three days. Besides, he won't be so inclined to start a fight when we put him ashore at the Capa Blancas if we thin him down a bit before we let him out."

So we all went and hid ourselves in the passage where we

could watch what happened. And presently Bumpo came to the foot of the stairs and rang the dinner bell like mad. Then he hopped behind the dining room door and we all kept still and listened.

Almost immediately, *thump, thump, thump*, down the stairs tramped Ben Butcher, the able seaman. He walked into the dining saloon, sat himself down at the head of the table in the Doctor's place, tucked a napkin under his fat chin, and heaved a sigh of expectation.

Then, *bang*! Bumpo slammed the door and locked it.

"That settles *him* for a while," said Polynesia coming out from her hiding place. "Now let him teach navigation to the sideboard. Gosh, the cheek of the man! I've forgotten more about the sea than that lumbering lout will ever know. Let's go upstairs and tell the Doctor. Bumpo, you will have to serve the meals in the cabin for the next couple of days."

And bursting into a rollicking Norwegian sea song, she climbed up to my shoulder and we went on deck.

· The Sixth Chapter ·

THE BED MAKER
OF MONTEVERDE

WE remained three days in the Capa Blanca Islands.

There were two reasons why we stayed there so long when we were really in such a hurry to get away. One was the shortage in our provisions caused by the able seaman's enormous appetite. When we came to go over the stores and make a list, we found that he had eaten a whole lot of other things besides the beef. And having no money, we were sorely puzzled how to buy more. The Doctor went through his trunk to see if there was anything he could sell. But the only thing he could find was an old watch with the hands broken and the back dented in, and we decided this would not bring in enough money to buy much more than a pound of tea. Bumpo suggested that he sing comic songs in the streets which he had learned in Jolliginki. But the Doctor said he did not think that the islanders would pay for music when they could make their own.

The other thing that kept us was the bullfight. In these islands, which belonged to Spain, they had bullfights every Sunday. It was on a Friday that we arrived there, and after we had got rid of the able seaman we took a walk through the town.

It was a very funny little town, quite different from any that I had ever seen. The streets were all twisty and winding and so narrow that a wagon could only just pass along them. The houses overhung at the top and came so close together that people in the attics could lean out of the windows and shake hands with their neighbors on the opposite side of the street. The Doctor told us the town was very, very old. It was called Monteverde.

As we had no money of course we did not go to a hotel or anything like that. But on the second evening when we were passing by a bed maker's shop we noticed several beds, which the man had made, standing on the pavement outside. The Doctor started chatting in Spanish to the bed maker, who was sitting at his door whistling to a parrot in a cage. The Doctor and the bed maker got very friendly talking about birds and things. And as it grew near to suppertime the man asked us to stop and sup with him.

This of course we were very glad to do. And after the meal was over (very nice dishes they were, mostly cooked in olive oil—I particularly liked the fried bananas) we sat outside on the pavement again and went on talking far into the night.

At last when we got up to go back to our ship, this very nice shopkeeper wouldn't hear of our going away on any account. He said the streets down by the harbor were very badly lighted and there was no moon. We would surely get lost. He invited us to spend the night with him and go back to our ship in the morning.

Well, we finally agreed; and as our good friend had no spare bedrooms, the three of us, the Doctor, Bumpo and I, slept on the beds set out for sale on the pavement before the

"The Doctor started chatting in Spanish
to the bed maker"

shop. The night was so hot we needed no coverings. It was great fun to fall asleep out-of-doors like this, watching the people walking to and fro and the gay life of the streets. It seemed to me that Spanish people never went to bed at all. Late as it was, all the little restaurants and cafés around us were wide open, with customers drinking coffee and chatting merrily at the small tables outside. The sound of a guitar strumming softly in the distance mingled with the clatter of chinaware and the babble of voices.

Somehow it made me think of my mother and father far away in Puddleby, with their regular habits, the evening practice on the flute and the rest—doing the same thing every day. I felt sort of sorry for them, in a way, because they missed the fun of this traveling life, where we were doing something new all the time—even sleeping differently. But I suppose if they had been invited to go to bed on a pavement in front of a shop, they wouldn't have cared for the idea at all. It is funny how some people are.

· The Seventh Chapter ·
THE DOCTOR'S WAGER

N EXT morning we were awakened by a great racket. There was a procession coming down the street, a number of men in very gay clothes followed by a large crowd of admiring ladies and cheering children. I asked the Doctor who they were.

"They are the bullfighters," he said. "There is to be a bullfight tomorrow."

"What is a bullfight?" I asked.

To my great surprise the Doctor got red in the face with anger. It reminded me of the time when he had spoken of the lions and tigers in his private zoo.

"A bullfight is a stupid, cruel, disgusting business," said he. "These Spanish people are most lovable and hospitable folk. How they can enjoy these wretched bullfights is a thing I could never understand."

Then the Doctor went on to explain to me how a bull was first made very angry by teasing and then allowed to run into a circus where men came out with red cloaks, waved them at him, and ran away. Next the bull was allowed to tire himself out by tossing and killing a lot of poor, old, broken-down horses who couldn't defend themselves. Then, when the bull was thoroughly out of breath and wearied by this, a man came out with a sword and killed the bull.

"Every Sunday," said the Doctor, "in almost every big town in Spain there are six bulls killed like that and as many horses."

"But aren't the men ever killed by the bull?" I asked.

"Unfortunately very seldom," said he. "A bull is not nearly as dangerous as he looks, even when he's angry, if only you are quick on your feet and don't lose your head. These bullfighters are very clever and nimble. And the people, especially the Spanish ladies, think no end of them. A famous bullfighter (or matador, as they call them) is a more important man in Spain than a king— Here comes another crowd of them round the corner, look. See the girls throwing kisses to them. Ridiculous business!"

At that moment our friend the bed maker came out to see the procession go past. And while he was wishing us good morning and inquiring how we had slept, a friend of his walked up and joined us. The bed maker introduced this friend to us as Don Enrique Cardenas.

Don Enrique, when he heard where we were from, spoke to us in English. He appeared to be a well-educated, gentlemanly sort of person.

"And you go to see the bullfight tomorrow, yes?" he asked the Doctor pleasantly.

"Certainly not," said John Dolittle firmly. "I don't like bullfights—cruel, cowardly shows."

Don Enrique nearly exploded. I never saw a man get so excited. He told the Doctor that he didn't know what he was talking about. He said bullfighting was a noble sport and that the matadors were the bravest men in the world.

"Oh, rubbish!" said the Doctor. "You never give the poor bull a chance. It is only when he is all tired and dazed that your precious matadors dare to try and kill him."

I thought the Spaniard was going to strike the Doctor, he got so angry. While he was still spluttering to find words, the bed maker came between them and took the Doctor aside. He explained to John Dolittle in a whisper that this Don Enrique Cardenas was a very important person, that he it was who supplied the bulls—a special, strong black kind—from his own farm for all the bullfights in the Capa Blancas. He was a very rich man, the bed maker said, a most important personage. He mustn't be allowed to take offense on any account.

I watched the Doctor's face as the bed maker finished, and I saw a flash of boyish mischief come into his eyes as though an idea had struck him. He turned to the angry Spaniard.

"Don Enrique," he said, "you tell me your bullfighters are very brave men and skillful. It seems I have offended you by saying that bullfighting is a poor sport. What is the name of the best matador you have for tomorrow's show?"

"Pepito de Malaga," said Don Enrique, "one of the greatest names, one of the bravest men, in all Spain."

"Very well," said the Doctor, "I have a proposal to make to you. I have never fought a bull in my life. Now supposing I were to go into the ring tomorrow with Pepito de Malaga and any other matadors you choose, and if I can do more tricks with a bull than they can, would you promise to do something for me?"

Don Enrique threw back his head and laughed.

"Man," he said, "you must be mad! You would be killed at

once. One has to be trained for years to become a proper bullfighter."

"Supposing I were willing to take the risk of that . . . you are not afraid, I take it, to accept my offer?"

The Spaniard frowned.

"Afraid!" he cried. "Sir, if you can beat Pepito de Malaga in the bullring I'll promise you anything it is possible for me to grant."

"Very good," said the Doctor, "now I understand that you are quite a powerful man in these islands. If you wished to stop all bullfighting here after tomorrow, you could do it, couldn't you?"

"Yes," said Don Enrique proudly, "I could."

"Well, that is what I ask of you—if I win my wager," said John Dolittle. "If I can do more with angry bulls than can Pepito de Malaga, you are to promise me that there shall never be another bullfight in the Capa Blancas so long as you are alive to stop it. Is it a bargain?"

The Spaniard held out his hand.

"It is a bargain," he said. "I promise. But I must warn you that you are merely throwing your life away, for you will certainly be killed. However, that is no more than you deserve for saying that bullfighting is an unworthy sport. I will meet you here tomorrow morning if you should wish to arrange any particulars. Good day, sir."

As the Spaniard turned and walked into the shop with the bed maker, Polynesia, who had been listening as usual, flew up on to my shoulder and whispered in my ear, "I have a plan. Get hold of Bumpo and come some place where the Doctor can't hear us. I want to talk to you."

I nudged Bumpo's elbow and we crossed the street and

pretended to look into a jeweler's window, while the Doctor sat down upon his bed to lace up his boots, the only part of his clothing he had taken off for the night.

"Listen," said Polynesia, "I've been breaking my head trying to think up some way we can get money to buy those stores with, and at last I've got it."

"The money?" said Bumpo.

"No, the idea—to make the money with. Listen, the Doctor is simply bound to win this game tomorrow, sure as you're alive. Now all we have to do is to make a side bet with these Spaniards and the trick's done."

"What's a side bet?" I asked.

"Oh, I know what that is," said Bumpo proudly. "We used to have lots of them at Oxford when boat-racing was on. I go to Don Enrique and say, 'I bet you a hundred pounds the Doctor wins.' Then if he does win, Don Enrique pays me a hundred pounds; and if he doesn't, I have to pay Don Enrique."

"That's the idea," said Polynesia. "Only don't say a hundred pounds—say two thousand five hundred pesetas. Now, come and find old Don Ricky-ticky and try to look rich."

So we crossed the street again and slipped into the bed maker's shop while the Doctor was still busy with his boots.

"Don Enrique," said Bumpo, "allow me to introduce myself. I am the Crown Prince of Jolliginki. Would you care to have a small bet with me on tomorrow's bullfight?"

Don Enrique bowed.

"Why certainly," he said, "I shall be delighted. But I must warn you that you are bound to lose. How much?"

"Oh a mere truffle," said Bumpo, "—just for the fun of the thing, you know. What do you say to three thousand pesetas?"

"I agree," said the Spaniard, bowing once more. "I will meet you after the bullfight tomorrow."

"So that's all right," said Polynesia as we came out to join the Doctor. "I feel as though quite a load had been taken off my mind."

· The Eighth Chapter ·
THE GREAT BULLFIGHT

THE next day was a great day in Monteverde. All the streets were hung with flags, and everywhere gaily dressed crowds were to be seen flocking toward the bullring, as the big circus was called where the fights took place.

The news of the Doctor's challenge had gone around the town and, it seemed, had caused much amusement to the islanders. The very idea of a mere foreigner daring to match himself against the great Pepito de Malaga! . . . Serve him right if he got killed!

The Doctor had borrowed a bullfighter's suit from Don Enrique; and very gay and wonderful he looked in it, though Bumpo and I had hard work getting the waistcoat to close in front and, even then, the buttons kept bursting off it in all directions.

When we set out from the harbor to walk to the bullring, crowds of small boys ran after us making fun of the Doctor's fatness, calling out, *"Juan Hagapoco, el grueso matador!"* which is the Spanish for "John Dolittle, the fat bullfighter."

As soon as we arrived the Doctor said he would like to take a look at the bulls before the fight began, and we were at once

157

led to the bull pen where, behind a high railing, six enormous black bulls were tramping around wildly.

In a few hurried words and signs the Doctor told the bulls what he was going to do and gave them careful instructions for their part of the show. The poor creatures were tremendously glad when they heard that there was a chance of bull-fighting being stopped, and they promised to do exactly as they were told.

Of course the man who took us in there didn't understand what we were doing. He merely thought the fat Englishman was crazy when he saw the Doctor making signs and talking in ox tongue.

From there the Doctor went to the matadors' dressing rooms while Bumpo and I with Polynesia made our way into the bullring and took our seats in the great open-air theater.

It was a very gay sight. Thousands of ladies and gentlemen were there, all dressed in their smartest clothes, and everybody seemed very happy and cheerful.

Right at the beginning Don Enrique got up and explained to the people that the first item on the program was to be a match between the English Doctor and Pepito de Malaga. He told them what he had promised if the Doctor should win. But the people did not seem to think there was much chance of that. A roar of laughter went up at the very mention of such a thing.

When Pepito came into the ring everybody cheered, the ladies blew kisses, and the men clapped and waved their hats.

Presently a large door on the other side of the ring was rolled back and in galloped one of the bulls; then the door was closed again. At once the matador became very much on the alert. He waved his red cloak and the bull rushed at him. Pepito stepped nimbly aside and the people cheered again.

This game was repeated several times. But I noticed that whenever Pepito got into a tight place and seemed to be in real danger from the bull, an assistant of his, who always hung around somewhere near, drew the bull's attention upon himself by waving another red cloak. Then the bull would chase the assistant and Pepito was left in safety. Most often, as soon as he had drawn the bull off, this assistant ran for the high fence and vaulted out of the ring to save himself. They evidently had it all arranged, these matadors, and it didn't seem to me that they were in any very great danger from the poor clumsy bull so long as they didn't slip and fall.

After about ten minutes of this kind of thing the small door into the matadors' dressing room opened and the Doctor strolled into the ring. As soon as his fat figure, dressed in sky-blue velvet, appeared, the crowd rocked in their seats with laughter.

Juan Hagapoco, as they had called him, walked out into the center of the ring and bowed ceremoniously to the ladies in the boxes. Then he bowed to the bull. Then he bowed to Pepito. While he was bowing to Pepito's assistant the bull started to rush at him from behind.

"Look out! Look out! The bull! You will be killed!" yelled the crowd.

But the Doctor calmly finished his bow. Then turning round he folded his arms, fixed the onrushing bull with his eye and frowned a terrible frown.

Presently a curious thing happened: The bull's speed got slower and slower. It almost looked as though he were afraid of that frown. Soon he stopped altogether. The Doctor shook his finger at him. He began to tremble. At last, tucking his tail between his legs, the bull turned around and ran away.

The crowd gasped. The Doctor ran after him. Around and

around the ring they went, both of them puffing and blowing like grampuses. Excited whispers began to break out among the people. This was something new in bullfighting, to have the bull running away from the man instead of the man away from the bull. At last in the tenth lap, with a final burst of speed, Juan Hagapoco, the English matador, caught the poor bull by the tail.

Then leading the now timid creature into the middle of the ring, the Doctor made him do all manner of tricks: standing on the hind legs, standing on the front legs, dancing, hopping, rolling over. He finished up by making the bull kneel down; then he got onto his back and did handsprings and other acrobatics on the beast's horns.

Pepito and his assistant had their noses sadly out of joint. The crowd had forgotten them entirely. They were standing together by the fence not far from where I sat, muttering to one another and slowly growing green with jealousy.

Finally the Doctor turned toward Don Enrique's seat and bowing said in a loud voice, "This bull is no good anymore. He's terrified and out of breath. Take him away, please."

"Does the caballero wish for a fresh bull?" asked Don Enrique.

"No," said the Doctor, "I want five fresh bulls. And I would like them all in the ring at once, please."

At this, a cry of horror burst from the people. They had been used to seeing matadors escaping from one bull at a time. But *five*! . . . That must mean certain death.

Pepito sprang forward and called to Don Enrique not to allow it, saying it was against all the rules of bullfighting. ("Ha!" Polynesia chuckled into my ear. "It's like the Doctor's navigation: He breaks all the rules, but he gets there. If they'll only let him, he'll give them the best show for their money

"Did acrobatics on the beast's horns"

they ever saw.") A great argument began. Half the people seemed to be on Pepito's side and half on the Doctor's side. At last the Doctor turned to Pepito and made another very grand bow which burst the last button off his waistcoat.

"Well, of course if the caballero is afraid—" he began with a bland smile.

"Afraid!" screamed Pepito. "I am afraid of nothing on earth. I am the greatest matador in Spain. With this right hand I have killed nine hundred and fifty-seven bulls."

"All right then," said the Doctor, "let us see if you can kill five more. Let the bulls in!" he shouted. "Pepito de Malaga is not afraid."

A dreadful silence hung over the great theater as the heavy door into the bull pen was rolled back. Then with a roar the five big bulls bounded into the ring.

"Look fierce," I heard the Doctor call to them in cattle language. "Don't scatter. Keep close. Get ready for a rush. Take Pepito, the one in purple, first. But for heaven's sake don't kill him. Just chase him out of the ring. Now then, all together, go for him!"

The bulls put down their heads and all in line, like a squadron of cavalry, charged across the ring straight for poor Pepito.

For one moment the Spaniard tried his hardest to look brave. But the sight of the five pairs of horns coming at him at full gallop was too much. He turned white to the lips, ran for the fence, vaulted it, and disappeared.

"Now the other one," the Doctor hissed. And in two seconds the gallant assistant was nowhere to be seen. Juan Hagapoco, the fat matador, was left alone in the ring with five rampaging bulls.

The rest of the show was really well worth seeing. First, all five bulls went raging around the ring, butting at the fence with their horns, pawing up the sand, hunting for something to kill. Then each one in turn would pretend to catch sight of the Doctor for the first time and, giving a bellow of rage, would lower his wicked-looking horns and shoot like an arrow across the ring as though he meant to toss him to the sky.

It was really frightfully exciting. And even I, who knew it was all arranged beforehand, held my breath in terror for the Doctor's life when I saw how near they came to sticking him. But just at the last moment, when the horns' points were two inches from the sky-blue waistcoat, the Doctor would spring nimbly to one side and the great brutes would go thundering harmlessly by, missing him by no more than a hair.

Then all five of them went for him together, completely surrounding him, slashing at him with their horns and bellowing with fury. How he escaped alive I don't know. For several minutes his round figure could hardly be seen at all in that scrimmage of tossing heads, stamping hoofs, and waving tails. It was, as Polynesia had prophesied, the greatest bullfight ever seen.

One woman in the crowd got quite hysterical and screamed up to Don Enrique, "Stop the fight! Stop the fight! He is too brave a man to be killed. This is the most wonderful matador in the world. Let him live! Stop the fight!"

But presently the Doctor was seen to break loose from the mob of animals that surrounded him. Then catching each of them by the horns, one after another, he would give their heads a sudden twist and throw them down flat on the sand. The great fellows acted their parts extremely well. I have never seen trained animals in a circus do better. They lay there panting on the ground where the Doctor threw them as if they were exhausted and completely beaten.

Then with a final bow to the ladies John Dolittle took a cigar from his pocket, lit it, and strolled out of the ring.

· The Ninth Chapter ·
WE DEPART IN A HURRY

AS soon as the door closed behind the Doctor the most tremendous noise I have ever heard broke loose. Some of the men appeared to be angry (friends of Pepito's, I suppose), but the ladies called and called to have the Doctor come back into the ring.

When at length he did so, the women seemed to go entirely mad over him. They blew kisses to him. They called him a darling. Then they started taking off their flowers, their rings, their necklaces, and their brooches and threw them down at his feet. You never saw anything like it—a perfect shower of jewelry and roses.

But the Doctor just smiled up at them, bowed once more, and backed out.

"Now, Bumpo," said Polynesia, "this is where you go down and gather up all those trinkets and we'll sell 'em. That's what the big matadors do: leave the jewelry on the ground and their assistants collect it for them. We might as well lay in a good supply of money while we've got the chance—you never know when you may need it when you're traveling with the Doctor. Never mind the roses—you can leave them—but don't leave any rings. And when you've finished go and get your three thousand pesetas out of Don Ricky-ticky. Tommy and I will meet you outside and we'll pawn the gewgaws at that shop opposite the bed maker's. Run along—and not a word to the Doctor, remember."

Outside the bullring we found the crowd still in a great state of excitement. Violent arguments were going on everywhere. Bumpo joined us with his pockets bulging in all directions, and we made our way slowly through the dense crowd to that side of the building where the matadors' dressing room was. The Doctor was waiting at the door for us.

"Good work, Doctor!" said Polynesia, flying on to his shoulder. "Great work! But listen, I smell danger. I think you had better get back to the ship now as quickly and as quietly as you can. Put your overcoat on over that giddy suit. I don't like the looks of this crowd. More than half of them are furious because you've won. Don Ricky-ticky must now stop the bullfighting—and you know how they love it. What I'm afraid of is that some of these matadors who are just mad with jealousy may start some dirty work. I think this would be a good time for us to get away."

"I daresay you're right, Polynesia," said the Doctor, "—you usually are. The crowd does seem to be a bit restless. I'll slip down to the ship alone so I shan't be so noticeable, and I'll wait for you there. You come by some different way. But don't be long about it. Hurry!"

As soon as the Doctor had departed Bumpo sought out Don Enrique and said, "Honorable Sir, you owe me three thousand pesetas."

Without a word, but looking cross-eyed with annoyance, Don Enrique paid his bet.

We next set out to buy the provisions, and on the way we hired a cab and took it along with us.

Not very far away we found a big grocer's shop which seemed to sell everything to eat. We went in and bought up the finest lot of food you ever saw in your life.

As a matter of fact, Polynesia had been right about the danger we were in. The news of our victory must have spread like lightning through the whole town. For as we came out of the shop and loaded the cab up with our stores, we saw various little knots of angry men hunting around the streets, waving sticks and shouting, "The Englishmen! Where are those accursed Englishmen who stopped the bullfight? Hang them from a lamppost! Throw them in the sea! The Englishmen! . . . We want the Englishmen!"

After that we didn't waste any time, you may be sure. Bumpo grabbed the Spanish cabdriver and explained to him in signs that if he didn't drive down to the harbor as fast as he knew how and keep his mouth shut the whole way, he would choke the life out of him. Then we jumped into the cab on top of the food, slammed the door, pulled down the blinds, and away we went.

"We won't get a chance to pawn the jewelry now," said Polynesia, as we bumped over the cobbly streets. "But never mind—it may come in handy later on. And, anyway, we've got two thousand five hundred pesetas left out of the bet. Don't give the cabby more than two pesetas fifty, Bumpo. That's the right fare, I know."

Well, we reached the harbor all right and we were mighty glad to find that the Doctor had sent Chee-Chee back with the rowboat to wait for us at the landing wall.

Unfortunately, while we were in the middle of loading the supplies from the cab into the boat, the angry mob arrived upon the wharf and made a rush for us. Bumpo snatched up a big beam of wood that lay near and swung it around and around his head, letting out dreadful African battle yells the while. This kept the crowd off while Chee-Chee and I hustled the last of the stores into the boat and clambered in ourselves. Bumpo threw his beam of wood into the thick of the Spaniards and leapt in after us. Then we pushed off and rowed like mad for *The Curlew*.

The mob upon the wall howled with rage, shook their fists, and hurled stones and all manner of things after us. Poor old Bumpo got hit on the head with a bottle. But as he had a very strong head it only raised a small bump, while the bottle smashed into a thousand pieces.

When we reached the ship's side the Doctor had the anchor drawn up and the sails set and everything in readiness to get away. Looking back we saw boats coming out from the harbor wall after us, filled with angry, shouting men. So we didn't bother to unload our rowboat but just tied it on to the ship's stern with a rope and jumped aboard.

It took only a moment more to swing *The Curlew* around into the wind, and soon we were speeding out of the harbor on our way to Brazil.

"Ha!" sighed Polynesia, as we all flopped down on the deck to take a rest and get our breath. "That wasn't a bad adventure—quite reminds me of my old seafaring days when I sailed with the smugglers. Golly, that was the life! Never mind your head, Bumpo. It will be all right when the Doctor puts a little arnica on it. Think what we got out of the scrap: a boatload of ship's stores, pockets full of jewelry, and thousands of pesetas. Not bad, you know—not bad."

PART IV

· The First Chapter ·
SHELLFISH LANGUAGES AGAIN

IRANDA, the purple bird of paradise, had prophesied rightly when she had foretold a good spell of weather. For three weeks the good ship *Curlew* plowed her way through smiling seas before a steady powerful wind.

We did not pass many ships. When we did see one, the Doctor would get out his telescope and we would all take a look at it. Sometimes he would signal to it, asking for news by hauling up little colored flags upon the mast; and the ship would signal back to us in the same way. The meaning of all the signals was printed in a book that the Doctor kept in the cabin. He told me it was the language of the sea and that all ships could understand it, whether they be English, Dutch, or French.

Our greatest happening during those first weeks was passing an iceberg. When the sun shone on it, it burst into a hundred colors, sparkling like a jeweled palace in a fairy story. Through the telescope we saw a mother polar bear with a cub sitting on it, watching us. The Doctor recognized her as one of the bears who had spoken to him when he was discovering the North Pole. So he sailed the ship up close and offered to

171

" 'He talks English!' "

take her and her baby onto *The Curlew* if she wished it. But she only shook her head, thanking him. She said it would be far too hot for the cub on the deck of our ship, with no ice to keep his feet cool. It had been indeed a very hot day, but the nearness of that great mountain of ice made us all turn up our coat collars and shiver with the cold.

One afternoon we saw, floating around us, great quantities of stuff that looked like dead grass. The Doctor told me this was gulfweed. A little further on it became so thick that it covered all the water as far as the eye could reach. It made *The Curlew* look as though she were moving across a meadow instead of sailing the Atlantic.

Crawling about upon this weed, many crabs were to be seen. And the sight of them reminded the Doctor of his dream of learning the language of the shellfish. He fished several of these crabs up with a net and put them in his listening-tank to see if he could understand them. Among the crabs he also caught a strange-looking, chubby little fish which he told me was called a silver fidgit.

After he had listened to the crabs for a while with no success, he put the fidgit into the tank and began to listen to that. I had to leave him at this moment to go and attend to some duties on the deck. But presently I heard him below shouting for me to come down again.

"Stubbins," he cried as soon as he saw me, "a most extraordinary thing . . . quite unbelievable . . . I'm not sure whether I'm dreaming . . . can't believe my own senses. I—I —I—"

"Why, Doctor," I said, "what is it? What's the matter?"

"The fidgit," he whispered, pointing with a trembling finger to the listening-tank in which the little round fish was still swimming quietly, "he talks English! And . . . and . . . and *he whistles tunes*—English tunes!"

"Talks English!" I cried. "Whistles! Why, it's impossible."

"It's a fact," said the Doctor. "It's only a few words, scattered, with no particular sense to them—all mixed up with his own language, which I can't make out yet. But they're English words, unless there's something very wrong with my hearing. And the tune he whistles, it's as plain as anything—always the same tune. Now, you listen and tell me what you make of it. Tell me everything you hear. Don't miss a word."

I went to the glass tank upon the table while the Doctor grabbed a notebook and a pencil. Undoing my collar I stood upon the empty packing case he had been using for a stand and put my right ear down under the water.

For some moments I detected nothing at all—except, with my dry ear, the heavy breathing of the Doctor as he waited, all stiff and anxious, for me to say something. At last from within the water, sounding like a child singing miles and miles away, I heard an unbelievably thin, small voice.

"Ah!" I said.

"What is it?" asked the Doctor in a hoarse, trembly whisper. "What does he say?"

"I can't quite make it out," I said. "It's mostly in some strange fish language. Oh, but wait a minute! Yes, now I get it: 'No smoking'. . . . 'My, here's a queer one!' 'Popcorn and picture postcards here'. . . . 'This way out'. . . . 'Don't spit' —what funny things to say, Doctor! Oh, but wait! Now he's whistling the tune."

"What tune is it?" gasped the Doctor.

"John Peel."

"Aha!" cried the Doctor. "That's what I made it out to be!" And he wrote furiously in his notebook.

I went on listening.

"This is most extraordinary!" the Doctor kept muttering to himself as his pencil went wiggling over the page. "Most extraordinary, but frightfully thrilling! I wonder where he—"

"Here's some more," I cried, "—some more English: *The big tank needs cleaning*'. . . . That's all. Now he's talking fish talk again."

"The big tank!" the Doctor murmured frowning in a puzzled kind of way. "I wonder where on earth he learned—"

Then he bounded up out of his chair.

"I have it!" he yelled. "This fish has escaped from an aquarium! Why, of course! Look at the kind of things he has learned: 'Picture postcards'—they always sell them in aquariums; 'Don't spit'; 'No smoking'; 'This way out'—the things the attendants say. And then, 'My, here's a queer one!' That's the kind of thing that people exclaim when they look into the tanks. It all fits. There's no doubt about it, Stubbins: We have here a fish who has escaped from captivity. And it's quite possible—not certain, by any means, but quite possible—that I may now, through him, be able to establish communication with the shellfish. This is a great piece of luck."

· The Second Chapter ·
THE FIDGIT'S STORY

WELL, now that he was started once more upon his old hobby of the shellfish languages, there was no stopping the Doctor. He worked right through the night.

A little after midnight I fell asleep in a chair; about two in the morning Bumpo fell asleep at the wheel; and for five hours *The Curlew* was allowed to drift where she liked. But still John Dolittle worked on, trying his hardest to understand the fidgit's language, struggling to make the fidgit understand him.

When I woke up it was broad daylight again. The Doctor was still standing at the listening-tank, looking as tired as an owl and dreadfully wet. But on his face there was a proud and happy smile.

"Stubbins," he said as soon as he saw me stir, "I've done it. I've got the key to the fidgit's language. It's a frightfully difficult language—quite different from anything I ever heard. The only thing it reminds me of—slightly—is ancient Hebrew. It isn't shellfish, but it's a big step toward it. Now, the next thing, I want you to take a pencil and a fresh notebook and write down everything I say. The fidgit has promised to tell me the story of his life. I will translate it into English and you put it down in the book. Are you ready?"

Once more the Doctor lowered his ear beneath the level of the water; and as he began to speak, I started to write. And this is the story that the fidgit told us.

Thirteen Months in an Aquarium

"I was born in the Pacific Ocean, close to the coast of Chile. I was one of a family of two thousand five hundred and ten. Soon after our mother and father left us, we youngsters got scattered. The family was broken up by a herd of whales who chased us. I and my sister Clippa (she was my favorite sister) had a very narrow escape for our lives. As a rule, whales are not very hard to get away from if you are good at dodging—if you've only got a quick swerve. But this one that came after Clippa and myself was a very mean whale. Every time he lost us under a stone or something, he'd come back and hunt and hunt till he routed us out into the open again. I never saw such a nasty, persevering brute.

"Well, we shook him at last—though not before he had worried us for hundreds of miles northward, up the west coast of South America. But luck was against us that day. While we were resting and trying to get our breath, another family of fidgits came rushing by, shouting, 'Come on! Swim for your lives! The dogfish are coming!'

"Now dogfish are particularly fond of fidgits. We are, you might say, their favorite food—and for that reason we always keep away from deep, muddy waters. What's more, dogfish are not easy to escape from; they are terribly fast and clever hunters. So up we had to jump and on again.

"After we had gone a few more hundred miles we looked

back and saw that the dogfish were gaining on us. So we turned into a harbor. It happened to be one on the west coast of the United States. Here we guessed, and hoped, the dogfish would not be likely to follow us. As it happened, they didn't even see us turn in, but dashed on northward and we never saw them again. I hope they froze to death in the Arctic seas.

"But, as I said, luck was against us that day. While I and my sister were cruising gently around the ships anchored in the harbor looking for orange peels, a great delicacy with us— *swoop! bang!*—we were caught in a net.

"We struggled for all we were worth, but it was no use. The net was small-meshed and strongly made. Kicking and flipping we were hauled up the side of the ship and dumped down on the deck, high and dry in a blazing noonday sun.

"Here a couple of old men in whiskers and spectacles leaned over us, making strange sounds. Some codling had gotten caught in the net the same time as we were. These the old men threw back into the sea, but us they seemed to think very precious. They put us carefully into a large jar and after they had taken us on shore they went to a big house and changed us from the jar into glass boxes full of water. This house was on the edge of the harbor, and a small stream of seawater was made to flow through the glass tank so we could breathe properly. Of course we had never lived inside glass walls before, and at first we kept on trying to swim through them and got our noses awfully sore bumping the glass at full speed.

"Then followed weeks and weeks of weary idleness. They treated us well, so far as they knew how. The old fellows in spectacles came and looked at us proudly twice a day and saw that we had the proper food to eat, the right amount of light, and that the water was not too hot or too cold. But, oh, the dullness of that life! It seemed we were a kind of a show. At a certain hour every morning the big doors of the house were thrown open and everybody in the city who had nothing special to do came in and looked at us. There were other tanks filled with different kinds of fishes all around the walls of the big room. And the crowds would go from tank to tank, looking in at us through the glass—with their mouths open, like half-witted flounders. We got so sick of it that we used to open our mouths back at them, and this they seemed to think highly comical.

"One day my sister said to me, 'Think you, Brother, that these strange creatures who have captured us can talk?'

" 'Surely,' said I. 'Have you not noticed that some talk with the lips only, some with the whole face, and yet others discourse with the hands? When they come quite close to the glass you can hear them. Listen!'

"At that moment a female, larger than the rest, pressed her nose up against the glass, pointed at me and said to her young behind her, 'Oh, look, here's a queer one!'

"And then we noticed that they nearly always said this when they looked in. And for a long time we thought that such was the whole extent of the language, this being a people of but few ideas. To help pass away the weary hours we learned it by heart, 'Oh, look, here's a queer one!' But we never got to know what it meant. Other phrases, however, we did get the meaning of, and we even learned to read a little in man talk. Many big signs there were, set up upon the walls; and when we saw that the keepers stopped the people from spitting and smoking, pointed to these signs angrily and read them out loud, we knew then that these writings signified *No Smoking* and *Don't Spit*.

"Then in the evenings, after the crowd had gone, the same

aged male with one leg of wood, swept up the peanut shells with a broom every night. And while he was so doing he always whistled the same tune to himself. This melody we rather liked, and we learned that too by heart—thinking it was part of the language.

"Thus a whole year went by in this dismal place. Some days new fishes were brought in to the other tanks, and other days old fishes were taken out. At first we had hoped we would only be kept here for a while, and that after we had been looked at sufficiently we would be returned to freedom and the sea. But as month after month went by, and we were left undisturbed, our hearts grew heavy within our prison walls of glass and we spoke to one another less and less.

"One day, when the crowd was thickest in the big room, a woman with a red face fainted from the heat. I watched through the glass and saw that the rest of the people got highly excited—though to me it did not seem to be a matter of very great importance. They threw cold water on her and carried her out into the open air.

"This made me think mightily, and presently a great idea burst upon me.

"'Sister,' I said, turning to poor Clippa who was sulking at the bottom of our prison trying to hide behind a stone from the stupid gaze of the children who thronged about our tank, 'supposing that we pretended we were sick: do you think they would take us also from this stuffy house?'

"'Brother,' said she wearily, 'that they might do. But most likely they would throw us on a rubbish heap, where we would die in the hot sun.'

"'But,' said I, 'why should they go abroad to seek a rubbish heap when the harbor is so close? While we were being brought here I saw men throwing their rubbish into the water. If they would only throw us also there, we could quickly reach the sea.'

" 'The sea!' murmured poor Clippa with a faraway look in her eyes (she had fine eyes, had my sister Clippa). 'How like a dream it sounds—the sea! Oh, Brother, will we ever swim in it again, think you? Every night as I lie awake on the floor of this evil-smelling dungeon I hear its hearty voice ringing in my ears. How I have longed for it! Just to feel it once again, the nice, big, wholesome homeliness of it all! To jump, just to jump from the crest of an Atlantic wave, laughing in the trade wind's spindrift, down into the blue-green swirling trough! To chase the shrimps on a summer evening, when the sky is red and the light's all pink within the foam! To lie on the top, in the doldrums' noonday calm, and warm your tummy in the tropic sun! To wander hand in hand once more through the giant seaweed forests of the Indian Ocean, seeking the delicious eggs of the pop-pop! To play hide-and-seek among the castles of the coral towns with their pearl and jasper windows spangling the floor of the Spanish Main! To picnic in the anemone meadows, dim blue and lilac-gray, that lie in the lowlands beyond the South Sea Garden! To throw somersaults on the springy sponge beds of the Mexican Gulf! To poke about among the dead ships and see what wonders and adventures lie inside! And then, on winter nights when the northeaster whips the water into froth, to swoop down and down to get away from the cold, down to where the water's warm and dark, down and still down, till we spy the twinkle of the fire eels far below where our friends and cousins sit chatting around the council grotto— chatting, Brother, over the news and gossip of *the sea*! . . . Oh—'

"And then she broke down completely, sniffling.

" 'Stop it!' I said. 'You make me homesick. Look here, let's pretend we're sick—or better still—let's pretend we're dead and see what happens. If they throw us on a rubbish heap and we fry in the sun, we'll not be much worse off than we are here in this smelly prison. What do you say? Will you risk it?'

" 'I will,' she said, '—and gladly.'

"So next morning two fidgits were found by the keeper floating on the top of the water in their tank, stiff and dead. We gave a mighty good imitation of dead fish—although I say it myself. The keeper ran and got the old gentlemen with spectacles and whiskers. They threw up their hands in horror when they saw us. Lifting us carefully out of the water they laid us on wet cloths. That was the hardest part of all. If you're a fish and get taken out of the water you have to keep opening and shutting your mouth to breathe at all—and even that you can't keep up for long. And all this time we had to stay stiff as sticks and breathe silently through half-closed lips.

"Well, the old fellows poked us and felt us and pinched us till I thought they'd never be done. Then, when their backs were turned a moment, a wretched cat got up on the table and nearly ate us. Luckily the old men turned around in time and shooed her away. You may be sure though that we took a couple of good gulps of air while they weren't looking, and that was the only thing that saved us from choking. I wanted to whisper to Clippa to be brave and stick it out. But I couldn't even do that; because, as you know, most kinds of fish talk cannot be heard—not even a shout—unless you're under water.

"Then, just as we were about to give it up and let on that we were alive, one of the old men shook his head sadly, lifted us up, and carried us out of the building.

" 'Now for it!' I thought to myself. 'We'll soon know our fate: liberty or the garbage can.'

"Outside, to our unspeakable horror, he made straight for a large ash barrel, which stood against the wall on the other side of a yard. Most happily for us, however, while he was crossing this yard a very dirty man with a wagon and horses drove up and took the ash barrel away. I suppose it was his property.

"Then the old man looked around for some other place to throw us. He seemed about to cast us upon the ground. But he evidently thought that this would make the yard untidy and he desisted. The suspense was terrible. He moved outside the yard gate and my heart sank once more as I saw that he now intended to throw us in the gutter of the street. But (fortune was indeed with us that day), a large man in blue clothes and silver buttons stopped him in the nick of time. Evidently, from the way the large man lectured and waved a short, thick stick, it was against the rules of the town to throw dead fish in the streets.

"At last, to our unutterable joy, the old man turned and moved off with us toward the harbor. He walked so slowly, muttering to himself all the way and watching the man in blue out of the corner of his eye, that I wanted to bite his finger to make him hurry up. Both Clippa and I were actually at our last gasp.

"Finally he reached the sea wall and giving us one last sad look he dropped us into the waters of the harbor.

"Never had we realized anything like the thrill of that moment, as we felt the salt wetness close over our heads. With one flick of our tails we came to life again. The old man was so surprised that he fell right into the water, almost on top of us. From this he was rescued by a sailor with a boat hook; and the last we saw of him, the man in blue was dragging him away by the coat collar, lecturing him again. Apparently it was also against the rules of the town to throw dead fish into the harbor.

"But we? What time or thought had we for his troubles? *We were free!* In lightning leaps, in curving spurts, in crazy zigzags—whooping, shrieking with delight, we sped for home and the open sea!

"That is all of my story and I will now, as I promised last night, try to answer any questions you may ask about the sea, on condition that I am set at liberty as soon as you have done."

The Doctor: Is there any part of the sea deeper than that known as the Nero Deep—I mean the one near the Island of Guam?
The Fidgit: Why, certainly. There's one much deeper than that near the mouth of the Amazon River. But it's small and hard to find. We call it the Deep Hole. And there's another in the Antarctic Sea.
The Doctor: Can you talk any shellfish language yourself?
The Fidgit: No, not a word. We regular fishes don't have anything to do with the shellfish. We consider them a low class.
The Doctor: But when you're near them, can you hear the sound they make talking—I mean without necessarily understanding what they say?
The Fidgit: Only with the very largest ones. Shellfish have such weak, small voices it is almost impossible for any but their own kind to hear them. But with the bigger ones it is

different. They make a sad, booming noise, rather like an iron pipe being knocked with a stone—only not nearly so loud of course.

The Doctor: I am most anxious to get down to the bottom of the sea—to study many things. But we land animals, as you no doubt know, are unable to breathe under water. Have you any ideas that might help me?

The Fidgit: I think that for both your difficulties the best thing for you to do would be to try and get hold of the great glass sea snail.

The Doctor: Er—who, or what, is the great glass sea snail?

The Fidgit: He is an enormous saltwater snail, one of the winkle family, but as large as a big house. He talks quite loudly—when he speaks, but this is not often. He can go to any part of the ocean, at all depths because he doesn't have to be afraid of any creature in the sea. His shell is made of transparent mother-of-pearl so that you can see through it, but it's thick and strong. When he is out of his shell and he carries it empty on his back, there is room in it for a wagon and a pair of horses. He has been seen carrying his food in it when traveling.

The Doctor: I feel that that is just the creature I have been looking for. He could take me and my assistant inside his shell and we could explore the deepest depths in safety. Do you think you could get him for me?

The Fidgit: Alas, no. I would willingly if I could, but he is hardly ever seen by ordinary fish. He lives at the bottom of the Deep Hole, and seldom comes out. And into the Deep Hole, the lower waters of which are muddy, fishes such as we are afraid to go.

The Doctor: Dear me! That's a terrible disappointment. Are there many of this kind of snail in the sea?

The Fidgit: Oh, no. He is the only one in existence, since his second wife died long, long ago. He is the last of the giant shellfish. He belongs to past ages when the whales were land animals and all that. They say he is over seventy thousand years old.

The Doctor: Good gracious, what wonderful things he could tell me! I do wish I could meet him.

The Fidgit: Were there any more questions you wished to ask me? This water in your tank is getting quite warm and sickly. I'd like to be put back into the sea as soon as you can spare me.

The Doctor: Just one more thing: When Christopher Columbus crossed the Atlantic in 1492, he threw overboard two copies of his diary sealed up in barrels. One of them was never found. It must have sunk. I would like to get it for my library. Do you happen to know where it is?

The Fidgit: Yes, I do. That too is in the Deep Hole. When the barrel sank the currents drifted it northward down what we call the Orinoco Slope, till it finally disappeared into the Deep Hole. If it was any other part of the sea I'd try and get it for you, but not there.

The Doctor: Well, that is all, I think. I hate to put you back into the sea because I know that as soon as I do, I'll think of a hundred other questions I wanted to ask you. But I must keep my promise. Would you care for anything before you go?—it seems a cold day—some cracker crumbs or something?

The Fidgit: No, I won't stop. All I want just at present is fresh seawater.

The Doctor: I cannot thank you enough for all the information you have given me. You have been very helpful and patient.

The Fidgit: Pray, do not mention it. It has been a real pleasure to be of assistance to the great John Dolittle. You are, as of course you know, already quite famous among the better class of fishes. Good-bye and good luck to you, to your ship and to all your plans!

The Doctor carried the listening-tank to a porthole, opened it and emptied the tank into the sea.

"Good-bye!" he murmured as a faint splash reached us from without.

I dropped my pencil on the table and leaned back with a sigh. My fingers were so stiff with writer's cramp that I felt as though I should never be able to open my hand again. But I, at least, had had a night's sleep. As for the poor Doctor, he was so weary that he had hardly put the tank back upon the table and dropped into a chair, when his eyes closed and he began to snore.

In the passage outside Polynesia scratched angrily at the door. I rose and let her in.

"A nice state of affairs!" she stormed. "What sort of a ship is this? There's Bumpo upstairs asleep under the wheel; the Doctor asleep down here; and you making pothooks in a copybook with a pencil! Expect the ship to steer herself to Brazil? We're just drifting around the sea like an empty bottle —and a week behind time as it is. What's happened to you all?"

She was so angry that her voice rose to a scream. But it would have taken more than that to wake the Doctor.

I put the notebook carefully in a drawer and went on deck to take the wheel.

· The Third Chapter ·
BAD WEATHER

AS soon as I had *The Curlew* swung around upon her course again I noticed something peculiar: We were not going as fast as we had been. Our favorable wind had almost entirely disappeared.

This, at first, we did not worry about, thinking that at any moment it might spring up again. But the whole day went by, then two days, then a week, ten days—and the wind grew no stronger. *The Curlew* just dawdled along at the speed of a toddling babe.

I now saw that the Doctor was becoming uneasy. He kept getting out his sextant (an instrument that tells you what part of the ocean you are in) and making calculations. He was forever looking at his maps and measuring distances on them. The far edge of the sea, all around us, he examined with his telescope a hundred times a day.

"But, Doctor," I said when I found him one afternoon mumbling to himself about the misty appearance of the sky, "it wouldn't matter so much, would it, if we did take a little longer over the trip? We've got plenty to eat on board now, and the purple bird of paradise will know that we have been delayed by something that we couldn't help."

"Yes, I suppose so," he said thoughtfully. "But I hate to keep her waiting. At this season of the year she generally goes to the Peruvian mountains for her health. And, besides, the good weather she prophesied is likely to end any day now and delay us still further. If we could only keep moving at even a fair speed, I wouldn't mind. It's this hanging around, almost dead still, that gets me restless. Ah, here comes a wind. Not very strong—but maybe it'll grow."

A gentle breeze from the northeast came singing through the ropes, and we smiled up hopefully at *The Curlew's* leaning masts.

"We've got only another hundred and fifty miles to make, to sight the coast of Brazil," said the Doctor. "If that wind would just stay with us, steady, for a full day we'd see land."

But suddenly the wind changed, swung to the east, then back to the northeast—then to the north. It came in fitful gusts, as though it hadn't made up its mind which way to blow; and I was kept busy at the wheel, swinging *The Curlew* this way and that to keep the right side of it.

Presently we heard Polynesia, who was in the rigging keeping a lookout for land or passing ships, screech down to us, "Bad weather coming. That jumpy wind is an ugly sign. And look!—over there in the east—see that black line, low down? If that isn't a storm I'm a landlubber. The gales around here are fierce, when they do blow—tear your canvas out like paper. You take the wheel, Doctor: It'll need a strong arm if it's a real storm. I'll go wake Bumpo and Chee-Chee. This looks bad to me. We'd best get all the sail down right away till we see how strong she's going to blow."

Indeed the whole sky was now beginning to take on a very

threatening look. The black line to the eastward grew blacker as it came nearer and nearer. A low, rumbly, whispering noise went moaning over the sea. The water which had been so blue and smiling turned to a ruffled ugly gray. And across the darkening sky, shreds of cloud swept like tattered witches flying from the storm.

I must confess I was frightened. You see, I had so far seen the sea only in friendly moods: sometimes quiet and lazy; sometimes laughing, venturesome and reckless; sometimes brooding and poetic, when moonbeams turned her ripples into silver threads and dreaming snowy night-clouds piled up fairy castles in the sky. But as yet I had not known, or even guessed at, the terrible strength of the sea's wild anger.

When that storm finally struck us we leaned right over, flat on our side, as though some invisible giant had slapped the poor *Curlew* on the cheek.

After that things happened so thick and so fast that—what with the wind that stopped your breath, the driving, blinding water, the deafening noise, and the rest—I haven't a very clear idea of how our shipwreck came about.

I remember seeing the sails, which we were now trying to roll up upon the deck, torn out of our hands by the wind and go overboard like a penny balloon—very nearly carrying Chee-Chee with them. And I have a dim recollection of Polynesia screeching somewhere for one of us to go downstairs and close the portholes.

In spite of our masts being bare of sail we were now scudding along to the southward at a great pace. But every once in a while huge gray-black waves would arise from under the ship's side like nightmare monsters, swell and climb, then crash down upon us, pressing us into the sea; and the poor

Curlew would come to a standstill half under water, like a gasping, drowning pig.

While I was clambering along toward the wheel to see the Doctor, clinging like a leech with hands and legs to the rails lest I be blown overboard, one of these tremendous seas tore loose my hold, filled my throat with water and swept me like a cork the full length of the deck. My head struck a door with an awful bang. And then I fainted.

· The Fourth Chapter ·
WRECKED!

WHEN I awoke I was very hazy in my head. The sky was blue and the sea was calm. At first I thought that I must have fallen asleep in the sun on the deck of *The Curlew*. And thinking that I would be late for my turn at the wheel, I tried to rise to my feet. I found I couldn't. My arms were tied to something behind me with a piece of rope. By twisting my neck around I found this to be a mast, broken off short. Then I realized that I wasn't sitting on a ship at all; I was sitting on only a piece of one. I began to feel uncomfortably scared. Screwing up my eyes, I searched the rim of the sea north, east, south, and west: no land; no ships; nothing was in sight. I was alone in the ocean!

At last, little by little, my bruised head began to remember what had happened: first, the coming of the storm; the sails going overboard; then the big wave which had banged me against the door. But what had become of the Doctor and the others? What day was this, tomorrow or the day after? And why was I sitting on only part of a ship?

Working my hand into my pocket, I found my penknife and cut the rope that tied me. This reminded me of a shipwreck story that Joe had once told me, of a captain who had tied his son to a mast in order that he shouldn't be washed overboard by the gale. So of course it must have been the Doctor who had done the same to me.

But where was he?

The awful thought came to me that the Doctor and the rest of them must be drowned, since there was no other wreckage to be seen upon the waters. I got to my feet and stared around the sea again. Nothing—nothing but water and sky!

Presently a long way off I saw the small dark shape of a bird skimming low down over the swell. When it came quite close I saw it was a stormy petrel. I tried to talk to it, to see if it could give me news. But unluckily I hadn't learned much seabird language and I couldn't even attract its attention, much less make it understand what I wanted.

Twice it circled around my raft, lazily, with hardly a flip of the wing. And I could not help wondering, in spite of the distress I was in, where it had spent last night—how it, or any other living thing, had weathered such a smashing storm. It made me realize the great big difference between different creatures, and that size and strength are not everything. To this petrel, a frail little thing of feathers, much smaller and weaker than I, the sea could do anything she liked, it seemed, and his only answer was a lazy, saucy flip of the wing! *He* was the one who should be called the *able seaman*. For, come raging gale, come sunlit calm, this wilderness of water was his home.

After swooping over the sea around me (just looking for food, I supposed) he went off in the direction from which he had come. And I was alone once more.

I found I was somewhat hungry—and a little thirsty, too. I began to think all sorts of miserable thoughts, the way one

"I was alone in the ocean!"

does when he is lonesome and has missed breakfast. What was going to become of me now, if the Doctor and the rest were drowned? I would starve to death or die of thirst. Then the sun went behind some clouds and I felt cold. How many hundreds or thousands of miles was I from any land? What if another storm should come and smash up even this poor raft on which I stood?

I went on like this for a while, growing gloomier and gloomier, when suddenly I thought of Polynesia. "You're always safe with the Doctor," she had said. "He gets there. Remember that."

I'm sure I wouldn't have minded so much if he had been here with me. It was this being all alone that made me want to weep. And yet the petrel was alone! What a baby I was, I told myself, to be scared to the verge of tears just by loneliness! I was quite safe where I was—for the present, anyhow. John Dolittle wouldn't get scared by a little thing like this. He got excited only when he made a discovery, found a new bug or something. And if what Polynesia had said was true, he couldn't be drowned and things would come out all right in the end, somehow.

I threw out my chest, buttoned up my collar, and began walking up and down the short raft to keep warm. I would be like John Dolittle. I wouldn't cry. And I wouldn't get excited.

How long I paced back and forth I don't know. But it was a long time—for I had nothing else to do.

At last I got tired and lay down to rest. And in spite of all my troubles, I soon fell fast asleep.

This time when I woke up, stars were staring down at me out of a cloudless sky. The sea was still calm, and my strange craft was rocking gently under me on an easy swell. All my fine courage left me as I gazed up into the big silent night and felt the pains of hunger and thirst set to work in my stomach harder than ever.

"Are you awake?" said a high silvery voice at my elbow.

I sprang up as though someone had stuck a pin in me. And there, perched at the very end of my raft, her beautiful golden tail glowing dimly in the starlight, sat Miranda, the purple bird of paradise!

Never have I been so glad to see anyone in my life. I almost fell into the water as I leapt to hug her.

"I didn't want to wake you," said she. "I guessed you must be tired after all you've been through. . . . Don't squash the life out of me, boy; I'm not a stuffed duck, you know."

"Oh, Miranda, you dear old thing," said I, "I'm so glad to see you. Tell me, where is the Doctor? Is he alive?"

"Of course he's alive—and it's my firm belief he always will be. He's over there, about forty miles to the westward."

"What's he doing there?"

"He's sitting on the other half of *The Curlew* shaving himself—or he was, when I left him."

"Well, thank heaven he's alive!" said I. ". . . And Bumpo . . . and the animals . . . are they all right?"

"Yes, they're with him. Your ship broke in half in the storm. The Doctor had tied you down when he found you stunned. And the part you were on got separated and floated away. Golly, it *was* a storm! One has to be a gull or an albatross to stand that sort of weather. I had been watching for the Doctor for three weeks, from a cliff top, but last night I had to take refuge in a cave to keep my tail feathers from blowing out. As soon as I found the Doctor, he sent me off with some porpoises to look for you. A stormy petrel volunteered to help us in our search. There had been quite a gathering of seabirds waiting to greet the Doctor, but the rough weather sort of broke up the arrangements that had been made to welcome him properly. It was the petrel that first gave us the tip where you were."

"Well, but how can I get to the Doctor, Miranda? I haven't any oars."

"Get to him! Why, you're going to him now. Look behind you."

I turned around. The moon was just rising on the sea's edge. And I now saw that my raft was moving through the water, but so gently that I had not noticed it before.

"What's moving us?" I asked.

"The porpoises," said Miranda.

I went to the back of the raft and looked down into the water. And just below the surface I could see the dim forms of four big porpoises, their sleek skins glinting in the moonlight, pushing at the raft with their noses.

"They're old friends of the Doctor's," said Miranda. "They'd do anything for John Dolittle. We should see his party soon now. We're pretty near the place I left them. . . . Yes, there they are! See that dark shape? . . . No, more to the right of where you're looking. Can't you make out the figure of the black man standing against the sky? Now Chee-Chee spies us. . . . He's waving. Don't you see them?"

I didn't—for my eyes were not as sharp as Miranda's. But presently from somewhere in the murky dusk I heard Bumpo singing his African songs with the full force of his enormous voice. And in a little, by peering and peering in the direction of the sound, I at last made out a dim mass of tattered, splintered wreckage—all that remained of the poor *Curlew*—floating low down upon the water.

A hulloa came through the night. And I answered it. We kept it up, calling to one another back and forth across the calm night sea. And a few minutes later the two halves of our brave little ruined ship bumped gently together again.

Now that I was nearer and the moon was higher I could see more plainly. Their half of the ship was much bigger than mine.

It lay partly upon its side, and most of them were perched upon the top munching ship's biscuit.

But close down to the edge of the water, using the sea's calm surface for a mirror and a piece of broken bottle for a razor, John Dolittle was shaving his face by the light of the moon.

· The Fifth Chapter ·

LAND!

THEY all gave me a great greeting as I clambered off my half of the ship onto theirs. Bumpo brought me a wonderful drink of fresh water which he drew from a barrel, and Chee-Chee and Polynesia stood around me feeding me ship's biscuit.

But it was the sight of the Doctor's smiling face—just knowing that I was with him once again—that cheered me more than anything else. As I watched him carefully wipe his glass razor and put it away for future use, I could not help comparing him in my mind with the stormy petrel. Indeed the vast strange knowledge which he had gained from his speech and friendship with animals had brought him the power to do things that no other human being would dare to try. Like the petrel, he could apparently play with the sea in all her moods. It was no wonder that many of the peoples among whom he passed in his voyages made statues of him showing him as half a fish, half a bird, and half a man. And ridiculous though it was, I could quite understand what Miranda meant when she said she firmly believed that he could never die.

Just to be with him gave you a wonderful feeling of comfort and safety.

Except for his appearance (his clothes were crumpled and damp and his battered high hat was stained with salt water) that storm which had so terrified me had disturbed him no more than getting stuck on the mudbank in Puddleby River.

Politely thanking Miranda for getting me so quickly, he asked her if she would now go ahead of us and show us the way to Spider Monkey Island. Next, he gave orders to the porpoises to leave my old piece of the ship and push the bigger half wherever the bird of paradise should lead us.

How much he had lost in the wreck besides his razor I did not know—everything, most likely, together with all the money he had saved up to buy the ship with. And still he was smiling as though he wanted for nothing in the world. The only things he had saved, as far as I could see—beyond the barrel of water and bag of biscuit—were his precious notebooks. These, I saw when he stood up, he had strapped around his waist with yards and yards of twine. He was, as old Matthew Mugg used to say, a great man. He was unbelievable.

And now for three days we continued our journey slowly but steadily southward.

The only inconvenience we suffered from was the cold. This seemed to increase as we went forward. The Doctor said that the island, disturbed from its usual paths by the great gale, had evidently drifted farther south than it had ever been before.

On the third night poor Miranda came back to us nearly frozen. She told the Doctor that in the morning we would find the island quite close to us, though we couldn't see it now, as it was a misty dark night. She said that she must hurry back at once to a warmer climate, and that she would visit the Doctor in Puddleby next August as usual.

"Don't forget, Miranda," said John Dolittle, "if you should hear anything of what happened to Long Arrow, to get word to me."

The bird of paradise assured him she would. And after the Doctor had thanked her again and again for all that she had done for us, she wished us good luck and disappeared into the night.

We were all awake early in the morning, long before it was light, waiting for our first glimpse of the country we had come so far to see. And as the rising sun turned the eastern sky to gray, of course it was old Polynesia who first shouted that she could see palm trees and mountain tops.

With the growing light it became plain to all of us: a long island with high rocky mountains in the middle—and so near to us that you could almost throw your hat upon the shore.

The porpoises gave us one last push and our strange-looking craft bumped gently on a low beach. Then, thanking our lucky stars for a chance to stretch our cramped legs, we all bundled off onto the land—the first land, even though it was floating land, that we had trodden for six weeks. What a thrill I felt as I realized that Spider Monkey Island, the little spot in the atlas, which my pencil had touched, lay at last beneath my feet!

When the light increased still further, we noticed that the palms and grasses of the island seemed withered and almost dead. The Doctor said that it must be on account of the cold that the island was now suffering from in its new climate. These trees and grasses, he told us, were the kind that belonged to warm, tropical weather.

The porpoises asked if we wanted them any further. And

HUGH LOFTING

"A long island with high rocky mountains in the middle"

the Doctor said that he didn't think so, not for the present—nor the raft either, he added, for it was already beginning to fall to pieces and could not float much longer.

As we were preparing to go inland and explore the island, we suddenly noticed a whole band of Indians watching us with great curiosity from among the trees. The Doctor went forward to talk to them. But he could not make them understand. He tried by signs to show them that he had come on a friendly visit. The Indians didn't seem to like us, however.

They had bows and arrows and long hunting spears, with stone points, in their hands; and they made signs back to the Doctor to tell him that if he came a step nearer they would kill us all. They evidently wanted us to leave the island at once. It was a very uncomfortable situation.

At last the Doctor made them understand that he wanted only to see the island all over and that then he would go away —though how he meant to do it, with no boat to sail in, was more than I could imagine.

While they were talking among themselves another Indian arrived—apparently with a message that they were wanted in some other part of the island. Because presently, shaking their spears threateningly at us, they went off with the new-comer.

"What discourteous pagans!" said Bumpo. "Did you ever see such inhospitability? Never even asked us if we'd had breakfast, the benighted bounders!"

"Sh! They're going off to their village," said Polynesia. "I'll bet there's a village on the other side of those mountains. If you take my advice, Doctor, you'll get away from this beach while their backs are turned. Let us go up into the higher land for the present—some place where they won't know where we are. They may grow friendlier when they see we mean no harm. They have honest, open faces and look like a decent crowd to me. They're just ignorant—probably never saw people like us before."

So, feeling a little bit discouraged by our first reception, we moved off toward the mountains in the center of the island.

· The Sixth Chapter ·
THE JABIZRI

WE found the woods at the feet of the hills thick and tangly and somewhat hard to get through. On Polynesia's advice, we kept away from all paths and trails, feeling it best to avoid meeting any Indians for the present.

But she and Chee-Chee were good guides and splendid jungle hunters, and the two of them set to work at once looking for food for us. In a very short space of time they had found quite a number of different fruits and nuts, which made excellent eating, though none of us knew the names of any of them. We discovered a nice clean stream of good water that came down from the mountains, so we were supplied with something to drink as well.

We followed the stream up toward the heights. And presently we came to parts where the woods were thinner and the ground rocky and steep. Here we could get glimpses of wonderful views all over the island, with the blue sea beyond.

While we were admiring one of these the Doctor suddenly said, "Sh! A jabizri! Don't you hear it?"

We listened and heard, somewhere in the air about us, an extraordinarily musical hum—like a bee, but not just one note. This hum rose and fell, up and down—almost like someone singing.

"No other insect but the jabizri beetle hums like that," said the Doctor. "I wonder where he is. Quite near, by the sound— flying among the trees probably. Oh, if I only had my butterfly net! Why didn't I think to strap that around my waist too. Confound the storm: I may miss the chance of a lifetime now of getting the rarest beetle in the world, Oh, look, there he goes!"

A huge beetle, easily three inches long I should say, suddenly flew by our noses. The Doctor got frightfully excited. He took off his hat to use as a net, swooped at the beetle and caught it. He nearly fell down a precipice onto the rocks below in his wild hurry, but that didn't bother him in the least. He knelt down, chortling, upon the ground with the jabizri safe under his hat. From his pocket he brought out a glass-topped box, and into this he very skillfully made the beetle walk from under the rim of the hat. Then he rose up, happy as a child, to examine his new treasure through the glass lid.

It certainly was a most beautiful insect. It was pale blue underneath, but its back was glossy black with huge red spots on it.

"There isn't an entomologist in the whole world who wouldn't give all he has to be in my shoes today," said the Doctor. "Hulloa! This jabizri's got something on his leg. . . . Doesn't look like mud. I wonder what it is."

He took the beetle carefully out of the box and held it by its back in his fingers, where it waved its six legs slowly in the air. We all crowded about him, peering at it. Rolled around the middle section of its right foreleg was something that looked like a thin dried leaf. It was bound on very neatly with strong spiderweb.

It was marvelous to see how John Dolittle with his fat, heavy fingers undid that cobweb cord and unrolled the leaf whole, without tearing it or hurting the precious beetle. The jabizri he put back into the box. Then he spread the leaf out flat and examined it.

You can imagine our surprise when we found that the inside of the leaf was covered with signs and pictures, drawn so tiny that you almost needed a magnifying glass to tell what they were. Some of the signs we couldn't make out at all, but nearly all of the pictures were quite plain—figures of men and mountains, mostly. The whole was done in a curious sort of brown ink.

For several moments there was a dead silence while we all stared at the leaf, fascinated and mystified.

"I think this is written in blood," said the Doctor at last. "It turns that color when it's dry. Somebody pricked his finger to make these pictures. It's an old dodge when you're short of ink—but highly unsanitary. What an extraordinary thing to find tied to a beetle's leg! I wish I could talk beetle language and find out where the jabizri got it from."

"But what is it?" I asked. . . . "Rows of little pictures and signs. What do you make of it, Doctor?"

"It's a letter," he said, "—a picture letter. All these little things put together mean a message. But why give a message to a beetle to carry—and to a jabizri, the rarest beetle in the world? What an extraordinary thing!"

Then he fell to muttering over the pictures.

"I wonder what it means: men walking up a mountain; men walking into a hole in a mountain; a mountain falling down—it's a good drawing, that; men pointing to their open mouths; bars—prison bars, perhaps; men praying; men lying down—they look as though they might be sick; and, last of all, just a mountain—a peculiar-shaped mountain."

All of a sudden the Doctor looked up sharply at me, a wonderful smile of delighted understanding spreading over his face.

"Long Arrow!" he cried. "Don't you see, Stubbins? Why, of course! Only a naturalist would think of doing a thing like this: giving his letter to a beetle—not to a common beetle, but to the rarest of all, one that other naturalists would try to catch. Well, well! Long Arrow! A picture-letter from Long Arrow. For pictures are the only writing that he knows."

"Yes, but who is the letter to?" I asked.

"It's to me, very likely. Miranda had told him, I know, years ago, that some day I meant to come here. But if not for me, then it's for anyone who caught the beetle and read it. It's a letter to the world."

"Well, but what does it say? It doesn't seem to me that it's much good to you now you've got it."

"Yes, it is," he said, "because, look, I can read it now. First picture: men walking up a mountain—that's Long Arrow and his party; men going into a hole in a mountain—they enter a cave looking for medicine plants or mosses; a mountain falling down—some hanging rocks must have slipped and trapped them, imprisoned them in the cave. And this was the only living creature that could carry a message for them to the outside world—a beetle, who could *burrow* his way into the open air. Of course it was only a slim chance that the beetle would ever be caught and the letter read. But it *was* a chance, and when men are in great danger they grab at any straw of hope. . . . All right, now look at the next picture: men pointing to their open mouths—they are hungry; men praying—begging anyone who finds this letter to come to their assistance; men lying down—they are sick or starving. This letter, Stubbins, is their last cry for help."

He sprang to his feet as he ended, snatched out a notebook, and put the letter between the leaves. His hands were trembling with haste and agitation.

"Come on!" he cried. "Up the mountain—all of you. There's not a moment to lose. Bumpo, bring the water and nuts with you. Heaven only knows how long they've been pining underground. Let's hope and pray we're not too late!"

"But where are you going to look?" I asked. "Miranda said the island was a hundred miles long and the mountains seem to run all the way down the center of it."

"Didn't you see the last picture?" he said, grabbing up his hat from the ground and cramming it on his head. "It was an oddly shaped mountain—looked like a hawk's head. Well, there's where he is—if he's still alive. First thing for us to do is to get up on a high peak and look around the island for a mountain shaped like a hawk's head. Just to think of it! There's a chance of my meeting Long Arrow, the son of Golden Arrow, after all! Come on! Hurry! To delay may mean death to the greatest naturalist ever born!"

· The Seventh Chapter ·
HAWK'S-HEAD MOUNTAIN

WE all agreed afterward that none of us had ever worked so hard in our lives before as we did that day. For my part, I know I was often on the point of dropping exhausted with fatigue; but I just kept on going—like a machine—determined that, whatever happened, *I* would not be the first to give up.

When we had scrambled to the top of a high peak, almost instantly we saw the strange mountain pictured in the letter. In shape it was the perfect image of a hawk's head and was, as far as we could see, the second highest summit on the island.

Although we were all out of breath from our climb, the Doctor didn't let us rest a second as soon as he had sighted it. With one look at the sun for direction, down he dashed again, breaking through thickets, splashing over brooks, taking all the short cuts. For a fat man, he was certainly the swiftest cross-country runner I ever saw.

We floundered after him as fast as we could. When I say *we*, I mean Bumpo and myself; for the animals, Jip, Chee-

Chee, and Polynesia, were a long way ahead—even beyond the Doctor—enjoying the hunt like a paper-chase.

At length we arrived at the foot of the mountain we were making for, and we found its sides very steep. Said the Doctor, "Now we will separate and search for caves. This spot where we now are will be our meeting place. If anyone finds anything like a cave or a hole where the earth and rocks have fallen in, he must shout and hulloa to the rest of us. If we find nothing we will all gather here in about an hour's time. Everybody understand?"

Then we all went off our different ways.

Each of us, you may be sure, was anxious to be the one to make a discovery. And never was a mountain searched so thoroughly. But alas! nothing could we find that looked in the least like a fallen-in cave. There were plenty of places where rocks had tumbled down to the foot of the slopes, but none of these appeared as though caves or passages could possibly lie behind them.

One by one, tired and disappointed, we straggled back to the meeting place. The Doctor seemed gloomy and impatient but by no means inclined to give up.

"Jip," he said, "couldn't you *smell* any men hiding anywhere?"

"No," said Jip. "I sniffed at every crack on the mountain-side. But I am afraid my nose will be of no use to you here, Doctor. The trouble is, the whole air is so saturated with the smell of spider monkeys that it drowns every other scent. And besides, it's too cold and dry for good smelling."

"It is certainly that," said the Doctor, "and getting colder all the time. I'm afraid the island is still drifting southward. Let's hope it stops before long or we won't be able to get even nuts and fruit to eat. Everything on the island will perish. Chee-Chee, what luck did you have?"

"None, Doctor. I climbed to every peak and pinnacle I could see. I searched every hollow and cleft. But not one place could I find where men might be hidden."

"And Polynesia," asked the Doctor, "did you see nothing that might put us on the right track?"

"Not a thing, Doctor, but I have a plan."

"Oh, good!" cried John Dolittle, full of hope renewed. "What is it? Let's hear it."

"You still have that beetle with you," she asked, "—the biz-biz, or whatever it is you call the wretched insect?"

"Yes," said the Doctor, producing the glass-topped box from his pocket, "here it is."

"All right. Now, listen," said she. "If what you have supposed is true—that is, that Long Arrow had been trapped inside the mountain by falling rock, he probably found that beetle inside the cave—perhaps many other different beetles too, eh? He wouldn't have been likely to take the biz-biz in with him, would he? He was hunting plants, you say, not beetles. Isn't that right?"

"Yes," said the Doctor, "that's probably so."

"Very well. It is fair to suppose then that the beetle's home, or his hole, is in that place—the part of the mountain where Long Arrow and his party are imprisoned, isn't it?"

"Quite, quite."

"All right. Then the thing to do is to let the beetle go—and watch him; and sooner or later he'll return to his home in Long Arrow's cave. And there we will follow him. Or at all events," she added smoothing down her wing feathers with a very superior air, "we will follow him till the miserable bug

starts nosing under the earth. But at least he will show us
what part of the mountain Long Arrow is hidden in."

"But he may fly, if I let him out," said the Doctor. "Then we
shall just lose him and be no better off than we were before."

"*Let* him fly," snorted Polynesia scornfully. "A parrot can
wing it as fast as a biz-biz, I fancy. If he takes to the air, I'll
guarantee not to let the little devil out of my sight. And if he
just crawls along the ground you can follow him yourself."

"Splendid!" cried the Doctor. "Polynesia, you have a great
brain. I'll set him to work at once and see what happens."

Again we all clustered around the Doctor as he carefully
lifted off the glass lid and let the big beetle climb out upon his
finger.

"Ladybug, ladybug, fly away home!" crooned Bumpo.
"Your house is on fire and your chil—"

"Oh, be quiet!" snapped Polynesia crossly. "Stop insulting
him! Don't you suppose he has wits enough to go home without your telling him?"

"I thought perchance he might be of a philandering disposi-
tion," said Bumpo humbly. "It could be that he is tired of his
home and needs to be encouraged. Shall I sing him 'Home,
Sweet Home,' think you?"

"No. Then he'd never go back. Your voice needs a rest.
Don't sing to him: just watch him. . . . Oh, and Doctor, why
not tie another message to the creature's leg, telling Long
Arrow that we're doing our best to reach him and that he
mustn't give up hope?"

"I will," said the Doctor. And in a minute he had pulled a
dry leaf from a bush nearby and was covering it with little
pictures in pencil.

At last, neatly fixed up with his new mailbag, Mr. Jabizri
crawled off the Doctor's finger to the ground and looked

about him. He stretched his legs, polished his nose with his front feet, and then moved off leisurely to the west.

We had expected him to walk *up* the mountain; instead, he walked *around* it. Do you know how long it takes a beetle to walk around a mountain? Well, I assure you it takes an unbelievably long time. As the hours dragged by, we hoped and hoped that he would get up and fly the rest, and let Polynesia carry on the work of following him. But he never opened his wings once. I had not realized before how hard it is for a human being to walk slowly enough to keep up with a beetle. It was the most tedious thing I have ever gone through. And as we dawdled along behind, watching him like hawks lest we lose him under a leaf or something, we all got so cross and ill-tempered we were ready to bite one another's heads off. And when he stopped to look at the scenery or polish his nose some more, I could hear Polynesia behind me letting out the most dreadful seafaring swearwords you ever heard.

After he had led us the whole way around the mountain he brought us to the exact spot where we started from and there he came to a dead stop.

"Well, " said Bumpo to Polynesia, "what you think of the beetle's sense now? You see he *doesn't* know enough to go home."

"Oh, be still!" snapped Polynesia. "Wouldn't *you* want to stretch your legs for exercise if you'd been shut up in a box all day? Probably his home is near here, and that's why he's come back."

"But why," I asked, "did he go the whole way around the mountain first?"

Then the three of us got into a violent argument. But in the middle of it all the Doctor suddenly called out, "Look, look!"

We turned and found that he was pointing to the jabizri,

who was now walking *up* the mountain at a much faster and more businesslike gait.

"Well," said Bumpo, sitting down wearily, "if he is going to walk *over* the mountain and back for more exercise, I'll wait for him here. Chee-Chee and Polynesia can follow him."

Indeed it would have taken a monkey or a bird to climb the place that the beetle was now walking up. It was a smooth, flat part of the mountain's side, steep as a wall.

But presently, when the jabizri was no more than ten feet above our heads, we all cried out together. For, even while we watched him, he had disappeared into the face of the rock like a raindrop soaking into sand.

"He's gone," cried Polynesia. "There must be a hole up there." And in a twinkling she had fluttered up the rock and was clinging to the face of it with her claws.

"Yes," she shouted down, "we've run him to earth at last. His hole is right here, behind a patch of lichen, big enough to get two fingers in."

"Ah," cried the Doctor, "this great slab of rock then must have slid down from the summit and shut off the mouth of the cave like a door. Poor fellows! What a dreadful time they must have spent in there! Oh, if we only had some picks and shovels now!"

"Picks and shovels wouldn't do much good," said Polynesia. "Look at the size of the slab: a hundred feet high and as many broad. You would need an army for a week to make any impression on it."

"I wonder how thick it is," said the Doctor, and he picked up a big stone and banged it with all his might against the face of the rock. It made a hollow booming sound, like a giant drum. We all stood still listening while the echo of it died slowly away.

"He banged it with all his might against the face of the rock"

And then a cold shiver ran down my spine. For, from within the mountain, back came three answering knocks: *Boom! . . . Boom! . . . Boom!*

Wide-eyed we looked at one another as though the earth itself had spoken. And the solemn little silence that followed was broken by the Doctor.

"Thank heaven," he said in a hushed reverent voice, "some of them at least are alive!"

PART V

· The First Chapter ·
A GREAT MOMENT

THE next part of our problem was the hardest of all: how to roll aside, pull down, or break open that gigantic slab. As we gazed up at it towering above our heads, it looked indeed a hopeless task for our tiny strength.

But the sounds of life from inside the mountain had put new heart in us. And in a moment we were all scrambling around trying to find any opening or crevice that would give us something to work on. Chee-Chee scaled up the sheer wall of the slab and examined the top of it where it leaned against the mountain's side; I uprooted bushes and stripped off hanging creepers that might conceal a weak place; the Doctor got more leaves and composed new picture-letters for the jabizri to take in if he should turn up again; whilst Polynesia carried up a handful of nuts and pushed them into the beetle's hole, one by one, for the prisoners inside to eat.

"Nuts are so nourishing," she said.

But Jip it was who, scratching at the foot of the slab like a good ratter, made the discovery which led to our final success.

"Doctor," he cried, running up to John Dolittle with his

219

nose all covered with black mud, "this slab is resting on nothing but a bed of soft earth. You never saw such easy digging. I guess the cave behind must be just too high up for the Indians to reach the earth with their hands, or they could have scraped a way out long ago. If we can only scratch the earthbed away from under, the slab might drop a little. Then maybe the Indians can climb out over the top."

The Doctor hurried to examine the place where Jip had dug.

"Why, yes," he said, "if we can get the earth away from under this front edge, the slab is standing up so straight, we might even make it fall right down in this direction. It's well worth trying. Let's get at it, quick."

We had no tools but the sticks and slivers of stone which we could find around. A strange sight we must have looked, the whole crew of us squatting down on our heels, scratching and burrowing at the foot of the mountain, like six badgers in a row.

After about an hour, during which in spite of the cold the sweat fell from our foreheads in all directions, the Doctor said, "Be ready to jump from under, clear out of the way, if she shows signs of moving. If this slab falls on anybody, it will squash him flatter than a pancake."

Presently there was a grating, grinding sound.

"Look out!" yelled John Dolittle. "Here she comes! Scatter!"

We ran for our lives, outward, toward the sides. The big rock slid gently down about a foot, into the trough that we had made beneath it. For a moment I was disappointed, for like that, it was as hopeless as before—no signs of a cave mouth showing above it. But as I looked upward, I saw the top coming very slowly away from the mountainside. We had unbalanced it below. As it moved apart from the face of the mountain, sounds of human voices, crying gladly in a strange tongue, issued from behind. Faster and faster the top swung forward, downward. Then, with a roaring crash that shook the whole mountain range beneath our feet, it struck the earth and cracked in halves.

How can I describe to anyone that first meeting between the two greatest naturalists the world ever knew, Long Arrow, the son of Golden Arrow and John Dolittle, M.D., of Puddleby-on-the-Marsh? The scene rises before me now, plain and clear in every detail, though it took place so many, many years ago. But when I come to write of it, words seem such poor things with which to tell you of that great occasion.

I know that the Doctor, whose life was surely full enough of big happenings, always counted the setting free of the Indian scientist as the greatest thing he ever did. For my part, knowing how much this meeting must mean to him, I was on pins and needles of expectation and curiosity as the great stone finally thundered down at our feet and we gazed across it to see what lay behind.

The gloomy black mouth of a tunnel, full twenty feet high, was revealed. In the center of this opening stood an enormous Indian, seven feet tall, handsome, muscular, slim, and naked but for a beaded cloth about his middle and an eagle's feather in his hair. He held one hand across his face to shield his eyes from the blinding sun, which he had not seen in many days.

"It is he!" I heard the Doctor whisper at my elbow. "I know him by his great height and the scar upon his chin."

And he stepped forward slowly across the fallen stone with his hand outstretched to the red man.

Presently the Indian uncovered his eyes. And I saw that they had a curious piercing gleam in them—like the eyes of

"It was a great moment"

an eagle, but kinder and more gentle. He slowly raised his right arm, the rest of him still and motionless like a statue, and took the Doctor's hand in his. It was a great moment. Polynesia nodded to me in a knowing, satisfied kind of way. And I heard old Bumpo sniffle sentimentally.

Then the Doctor tried to speak to Long Arrow. But the Indian knew no English, of course, and the Doctor knew no Indian. Presently, to my surprise, I heard the Doctor trying him in different animal languages.

"How do you do?" he said in dog talk; "I am glad to see you," in horse signs; "How long have you been buried?" in deer language. Still the Indian made no move but stood there, straight and stiff, understanding not a word.

The Doctor tried again, in several other animal dialects. But with no result.

Till at last he came to the language of eagles.

"Great Long Arrow," he said in the fierce screams and short grunts that the big birds use, "never have I been so glad in all my life as I am today to find you still alive."

In a flash Long Arrow's stony face lit up with a smile of understanding, and back came the answer in eagle tongue, "Mighty Friend, I owe my life to you. For the remainder of my days I am your servant to command."

Afterward Long Arrow told us that this was the only bird or animal language that he had ever been able to learn. But that he had not spoken it in a long time, for no eagles ever came to this island.

Then the Doctor signaled to Bumpo, who came forward with the nuts and water. But Long Arrow neither ate nor drank. Taking the supplies with a nod of thanks, he turned and carried them into the inner dimness of the cave. We followed him.

Inside we found nine other Indians, men, women and boys, lying on the rock floor in a dreadful state of thinness and exhaustion.

Some had their eyes closed, as if dead. Quickly the Doctor went around them all and listened to their hearts. They were all alive, but one woman was too weak even to stand upon her feet.

At a word from the Doctor, Chee-Chee and Polynesia sped off into the jungle after more fruit and water.

While Long Arrow was handing around what food we had to his starving friends, we suddenly heard a sound outside the cave. Turning about we saw, clustered at the entrance, the band of Indians who had met us so inhospitably at the beach.

They peered into the dark cave cautiously at first. But as soon as they saw Long Arrow and the other Indians with us, they came rushing in, laughing, clapping their hands with joy, and jabbering away at a tremendous rate.

Long Arrow explained to the Doctor that the nine Indians we had found in the cave with him were two families who had accompanied him into the mountains to help him gather medicine plants. And while they had been searching for a kind of moss—good for indigestion—which grows only inside of damp caves, the great rock slab had slid down and shut them in. Then for two weeks they had lived on the medicine moss and such fresh water as could be found dripping from the damp walls of the cave. The other Indians on the island had given them up for lost and mourned them as dead, and they were now very surprised and happy to find their relatives alive.

When Long Arrow turned to the newcomers and told them in their own language that it was this man who had found and freed their relatives, they gathered around John Dolittle, all talking at once and beating their breasts.

Long Arrow said they were apologizing and trying to tell the Doctor how sorry they were that they had seemed unfriendly to him at the beach. They had never seen a man like him before and had really been afraid of him—especially when they saw him conversing with the porpoises. They had thought he was the devil, they said.

Then they went outside and looked at the great stone we had thrown down, big as a meadow; and they walked around and around it, pointing to the break running through the middle and wondering how the trick of felling it was done.

Travelers who have since visited Spider Monkey Island tell me that that huge stone slab is now one of the regular sights of the island. And that the Indian guides, when showing it to visitors, always tell *their* story of how it came there. They say that when the Doctor found that the rocks had entrapped his friend, Long Arrow, he was so angry that he ripped the mountain in halves with his bare hands and let him out.

· The Second Chapter ·

"THE MEN OF THE MOVING LAND"

 ROM that time on the Indians' treatment of us was very different. We were invited to their village for a feast to celebrate the recovery of the lost families. And after we had made a litter from saplings to carry the sick woman in, we all started off down the mountain.

On the way the Indians told Long Arrow something which appeared to be sad news, for on hearing it, his face grew very grave. The Doctor asked him what was wrong. And Long Arrow said he had just been informed that the chief of the tribe, an old man of eighty, had died early that morning.

"That," Polynesia whispered in my ear, "must have been what they went back to the village for, when the messenger fetched them from the beach. Remember?"

"What did he die of?" asked the Doctor.

"He died of cold," said Long Arrow.

Indeed, now that the sun was setting, we were all shivering ourselves.

"This is a serious thing," said the Doctor to me. "The island is still in the grip of that wretched current flowing southward. We will have to look into this tomorrow. If nothing can be done about it, the Indians had better take to canoes and leave the island. The chance of being wrecked will be better than getting frozen to death in the ice floes of the Antarctic."

Presently we came over a saddle in the hills, and looking downward on the far side of the island, we saw the village—a large cluster of grass huts and gaily colored totem poles close by the edge of the sea.

"How artistic!" said the Doctor. "Delightfully situated. What is the name of the village?"

"Popsipetel," said Long Arrow. "That is the name also of the tribe. The word signifies in Indian tongue, *the men of the moving land.* There are two tribes of Indians on the island: the Popsipetels at this end and the Bag-jagderags at the other."

"Which is the larger of the two peoples?"

"The Bag-jagderags, by far. Their city covers two square leagues. But," added Long Arrow a slight frown darkening his handsome face, "for me, I would rather have one Popsipetel than a hundred Bag-jagderags."

The news of the rescue we had made had evidently gone ahead of us. For as we drew nearer to the village we saw crowds of Indians streaming out to greet the friends and relatives whom they had never thought to see again.

These good people, when they too were told how the rescue had been the work of the strange visitor to their shores, all gathered around the Doctor, shook him by the hands, patted him, and hugged him. Then they lifted him up upon their strong shoulders and carried him down the hill into the village.

There the welcome we received was even more wonderful. In spite of the cold air of the coming night, the villagers, who had all been shivering within their houses, threw open their doors and came out in hundreds. I had no idea that the little village could hold so many. They thronged about us, smiling and nodding and waving their hands; and as the details of what we had done were recited by Long Arrow, they kept shouting strange singing noises, which we supposed were words of gratitude or praise.

We were next escorted to a brand-new grass house, clean and sweet-smelling within, and informed that it was ours. Six strong Indian boys were told to be our servants.

On our way through the village we noticed a house, larger than the rest, standing at the end of the main street. Long Arrow pointed to it and told us it was the Chief's house, but that it was now empty—no new chief having yet been elected to take the place of the old one who had died.

Inside our new home a feast of fish and fruit had been prepared. Most of the more important men of the tribe were already seating themselves at the long dining table when we got there. Long Arrow invited us to sit down and eat.

This we were glad enough to do, as we were all hungry. But we were both surprised and disappointed when we found that the fish had not been cooked. The Indians did not seem to think this extraordinary in the least, but went ahead gobbling the fish with much relish the way it was, raw.

With many apologies, the Doctor explained to Long Arrow that if they had no objection we would prefer our fish cooked.

Imagine our astonishment when we found that the great Long Arrow, so learned in the natural sciences, did not know what the word *cooked* meant!

Polynesia, who was sitting on the bench between John Dolittle and myself, pulled the Doctor by the sleeve.

"I'll tell you what's wrong, Doctor," she whispered as he

leant down to listen to her: *"These people have no fires!* They don't know how to make a fire. Look outside: It's almost dark, and there isn't a light showing in the whole village. This is a fireless people."

· The Third Chapter ·
FIRE

THEN the Doctor asked Long Arrow if he knew what fire was, explaining it to him by pictures drawn on the buckskin tablecloth. Long Arrow said he had seen such a thing coming out of the tops of volcanoes, but that neither he nor any of the Popsipetels knew how it was made.

"No wonder the old chief died of cold!" muttered Bumpo.

At that moment we heard a crying sound at the door. And turning around, we saw a weeping Indian mother with a baby in her arms. She said something to the Indians that we could not understand, and Long Arrow told us the baby was sick and she wanted the doctor to try and cure it.

"Oh, Lord!" groaned Polynesia in my ear. "Just like Puddleby: Patients arriving in the middle of dinner. Well, one thing, the food's raw so nothing can get cold anyway."

The Doctor examined the baby and found at once that it was thoroughly chilled.

"Fire . . . *fire*! That's what it needs," he said, turning to Long Arrow. "That's what you all need. This child will have pneumonia if it isn't kept warm."

"Aye, truly. But how to make a fire?" said Long Arrow.

"Where to get it? That is the difficulty. All the volcanoes in this land are dead."

Then we fell to hunting through our pockets to see if any matches had survived the shipwreck. The best we could muster were two whole ones and a half—all with the heads soaked off them by salt water.

"Hark, Long Arrow," said the Doctor, "divers ways there be of making fire without the aid of matches. One: with a strong glass and the rays of the sun. That, however, since the sun has set, we cannot now employ. Another is by grinding a hard stick into a soft log. Is the daylight gone without? Alas, yes. Then I fear we must await the morrow, for besides the different woods, we need an old squirrel's nest for fuel. And that, without lamps, you could not find in your forests at this hour."

"Great are your cunning and your skill, oh, Great Doctor," Long Arrow replied. "But in this you do us an injustice. Know you not that all fireless peoples can see in the dark? Having no lamps we are forced to train ourselves to travel through the blackest night, lightless. I will despatch a messenger and you shall have your squirrel's nest within the hour."

He gave an order to two of our boy servants who promptly disappeared, running. And sure enough, in a very short space of time a squirrel's nest, together with hard and soft woods, was brought to our door.

The moon had not yet risen and within the house it was practically pitch-black. I could feel and hear, however, that the Indians were moving about comfortably as though it were daylight. The task of making fire the Doctor had to perform almost entirely by the sense of touch, asking Long Arrow and the Indians to hand him his tools when he mislaid them in the dark. And then I made a curious discovery: Now that I had to, I found that I was beginning to see a little in the dark myself. And for the first time I realized that of course there *is* no such thing as pitch-dark, so long as you have a door open or a sky above you.

Calling for the loan of a bow, the Doctor loosened the string, put the hard stick into a loop, and began grinding this stick into the soft wood of the log. Soon I smelled that the log was smoking. Then he kept feeding the part that was smoking with the inside lining of the squirrel's nest, and he asked me to blow upon it with my breath. He made the stick drill faster and faster. More smoke filled the room. And at last the darkness about us was suddenly lit up. The squirrel's nest had burst into flame.

The Indians murmured and grunted with astonishment. At first they were all for falling on their knees and worshiping the fire. Then they wanted to pick it up with their bare hands and play with it. We had to teach them how it was to be used, and they were quite fascinated when we laid our fish across it on sticks and cooked it. They sniffed the air with relish as, for the first time in history, the smell of fried fish passed through the village of Popsipetel.

Then we got them to bring us piles and stacks of dry wood, and we made an enormous bonfire in the middle of the main street. Around this, when they felt its warmth, the whole tribe gathered and smiled and wondered. It was a striking sight, one of the pictures from our voyages that I most frequently remember: that roaring jolly blaze beneath the black night sky, and all about it a vast ring of Indians, the firelight gleaming on bronze cheeks, white teeth, and flashing eyes—a whole town trying to get warm, giggling and pushing like school-children.

In a little, when we had gotten them more used to the handling of fire, the Doctor showed them how it could be taken into their houses if a hole were only made in the roof to let the smoke out. And before we turned in after that long, long, tiring day, we had fires going in every hut in the village.

The poor people were so glad to get really warm again that we thought they'd never go to bed. Well on into the early hours of the morning the little town fairly buzzed with a great low murmur: the Popsipetels sitting up talking of their wonderful pale-faced visitor and this strange good thing he had brought with him—*fire*!

· The Fourth Chapter ·
WHAT MAKES AN ISLAND FLOAT

ERY early in our experience of Popsipetel kindness we saw that if we were to get anything done at all, we would almost always have to do it secretly. The Doctor was so popular and loved by all that as soon as he showed his face at his door in the morning crowds of admirers waiting patiently outside flocked about him and followed him wherever he went. After his fire-making feat, these people expected him, I think, to be continually doing magic, and they were determined not to miss a trick.

It was only with great difficulty that we escaped from the crowd the first morning and set out with Long Arrow to explore the island at our leisure.

In the interior we found that not only the plants and trees were suffering from the cold, the animal life was in even worse straits. Everywhere shivering birds were to be seen, their feathers all fluffed out, gathering together for flight to summer lands. And many lay dead upon the ground. Going down to the shore, we watched land crabs in large numbers taking to the sea to find some better home. While away to the southeast we could see many icebergs floating—a sign that we were now not far from the terrible region of the Antarctic.

As we were looking out to sea, we noticed our friends the porpoises jumping through the waves. The Doctor hailed them and they came inshore.

He asked them how far we were from the south polar continent.

About a hundred miles, they told him. And then they asked why he wanted to know.

"Because this floating island we are on," said he, "is drifting southward all the time in a current. It's an island that ordinarily belongs somewhere in the tropic zone—real sultry weather, sunstrokes, and all that. If it doesn't stop going southward, pretty soon everything on it is going to perish."

"Well," said the porpoises, "then the thing to do is to get it back into a warmer climate, isn't it?"

"Yes, but how?" said the Doctor. "We can't *row* it back."

"No," said they, "but whales could push it—if you only got enough of them."

"What a splendid idea! Whales, the very thing!" said the Doctor. "Do you think you could get me some?"

"Why, certainly," said the porpoises. "We passed one herd of them out there, sporting about among the icebergs. We'll ask them to come over. And if they aren't enough, we'll try and hunt up some more. Better have plenty."

"Thank you," said the Doctor. "You are very kind. . . . By the way, do you happen to know how this island came to be a floating island? At least half of it, I notice, is made of stone. It is very odd that it floats at all, isn't it?"

"It is unusual," they said. "But the explanation is quite simple. It used to be a mountainous part of South America—an overhanging part—sort of an awkward corner, you might say. Way back in the glacial days, thousands of years ago, it broke off from the mainland; and by some curious accident the inside of it, which is hollow, got filled with air as it fell into the ocean. You can see only less than half of the island: the bigger half is under water. And in the middle of it, underneath, is a huge rock air chamber running right up inside the mountains. And that's what keeps it floating."

"What a pecurious phenometer!" said Bumpo.

"It is indeed," said the Doctor. "I must make a note of that." And out came the everlasting notebook.

The porpoises went bounding off toward the icebergs. And not long after, we saw the sea heaving and frothing as a big herd of whales came toward us at full speed.

They certainly were enormous creatures, and there must have been a good two hundred of them.

"Here they are," said the porpoises, poking their heads out of the water.

"Good!" said the Doctor. "Now just explain to them, will you please, that this is a very serious matter for all the living creatures in this land. And ask them if they will be so good as to go down to the far end of the island, put their noses against it, and push it back near the coast of southern Brazil."

The porpoises evidently succeeded in persuading the whales to do as the Doctor asked, for presently we saw them thrashing through the seas, going off toward the south end of the island.

Then we lay down upon the beach and waited.

After about an hour the Doctor got up and threw a stick into the water. For a while this floated motionless. But soon we saw it begin to move gently down the coast.

"Ah!" said the Doctor, "see that? The island is going north at last. Thank goodness!"

Faster and faster we left the stick behind, and smaller and dimmer grew the icebergs on the skyline.

The Doctor took out his watch, threw more sticks into the water, and made a rapid calculation.

"Humph! Fourteen and a half knots an hour," he murmured. "A very nice speed. It should take us about five days to get back near Brazil. Well, that's that. . . . Quite a load off my mind. I declare, I feel warmer already. Let's go and get something to eat."

· The Fifth Chapter ·
WAR!

ON our way back to the village the Doctor began discussing natural history with Long Arrow. But their most interesting talk, mainly about plants, had hardly begun when an Indian runner came dashing up to us with a message.

Long Arrow listened gravely to the breathless, babbled words, then turned to the Doctor and said in eagle tongue, "Great Doctor, an evil thing has befallen the Popsipetels. Our neighbors to the south, the thievish Bag-jagderags, who for so long have cast envious eyes on our stores of ripe corn, have gone upon the warpath, and even now are advancing to attack us."

"Evil news indeed," said the Doctor. "Yet let us not judge harshly. Perhaps it is that they are desperate for food, having their own crops frost-killed before harvest. For are they not even nearer the cold south than you?"

"Make no excuses for any man of the tribe of the Bagjagderags," said Long Arrow shaking his head. "They are an idle, shiftless race. They do but see a chance to get corn without the labor of husbandry. If it were not that they are a much bigger tribe and hope to defeat their neighbor by sheer force of numbers, they would not have dared to make open war upon the brave Popsipetels."

When we reached the village we found it in a great state of excitement. Everywhere men were seen putting their bows in order, sharpening spears, grinding battle-axes, and making arrows by the hundred. Women were raising a high fence of bamboo poles all around the village. Scouts and messengers kept coming and going, bringing news of the movements of the enemy. While high up in the trees and hills about the village we could see lookouts watching the mountains to the south.

Long Arrow brought another Indian, short but enormously broad, and introduced him to the Doctor as Big Teeth, the chief warrior of the Popsipetels.

The Doctor volunteered to go and see the enemy and try to argue the matter out peacefully with them instead of fighting; for war, he said, was at best a stupid, wasteful business. But the two shook their heads. Such a plan was hopeless, they said. In the last war when they had sent a messenger to do peaceful arguing, the enemy had merely hit him with an ax.

While the Doctor was asking Big Teeth how he meant to defend the village against attack, a cry of alarm was raised by the lookouts.

"They're coming! . . . the Bag-jagderags . . . swarming down the mountains in thousands!"

"Well," said the Doctor, "it's all in the day's work, I suppose. I don't believe in war, but if the village is attacked we must help defend it."

And he picked up a club from the ground and tried the heft of it against a stone.

"This," he said, "seems like a pretty good tool to me." And

he walked to the bamboo fence and took his place among the
other waiting fighters.

Then we all got hold of some kind of weapon with which to
help our friends, the gallant Popsipetels: I borrowed a bow
and a quiver full of arrows; Jip was content to rely upon his
old, but still strong teeth; Chee-Chee took a bag of rocks and
climbed a palm where he could throw them down upon the
enemies' heads; and Bumpo marched after the Doctor to the
fence armed with a young tree in one hand and a doorpost in
the other.

When the enemy drew near enough to be seen from where
we stood, we all gasped with astonishment. The hillsides
were actually covered with them—thousands upon thousands. They made our small army within the village look like
a mere handful.

"Saints alive!" muttered Polynesia. "Our little lot will stand
no chance against that swarm. This will never do. I'm going
off to get some help."

Where she was going and what kind of help she meant to
get, I had no idea. She just disappeared from my side. But
Jip, who had heard her, poked his nose between the bamboo
bars of the fence to get a better view of the enemy and said,

"Likely enough she's gone after the black parrots. Let's
hope she finds them in time. Just look at those ugly ruffians
climbing down the rocks—millions of 'em! This fight's going
to keep us all hopping."

And Jip was right. Before a quarter of an hour had gone by,
our village was completely surrounded by one huge mob of
yelling, raging Bag-jagderags.

I now come again to a part in the story of our voyages
where things happened so quickly, one upon the other, that
looking backward I see the picture only in a confused kind of

"The Terrible Three"

From an Indian rock engraving found on Hawk's-Head Mountain, Spider Monkey Island

way. I know that if it had not been for the Terrible Three—as
they came afterward to be fondly called in Popsipetel history
—Long Arrow, Bumpo, and the Doctor, the war would have
been soon over and the whole island would have belonged to
the worthless Bag-jagderags. But the Englishman, the African, and the Indian were a regiment in themselves, and between them they made that village a dangerous place for any
man to try to enter.

The bamboo fencing that had been hastily set up around
the town was not a very strong affair, and right from the start
it gave way in one place after another as the enemy thronged
and crowded against it. Then the Doctor, Long Arrow, and
Bumpo would hurry to the weak spot, a terrific hand-to-hand
fight would take place, and the enemy be thrown out. But
almost instantly a cry of alarm would come from some other
part of the village wall; and the Three would have to rush off
and do the same thing all over again.

The Popsipetels were themselves no mean fighters, but the
strength and weight of those three men of different lands,
standing close together, swinging their enormous war clubs,
was really a sight for the wonder and admiration of anyone.

Many weeks later when I was passing an Indian campfire
at night I heard this song being sung. It has since become one
of the traditional folksongs of the Popsipetels.

The Song of the Terrible Three

Oh, hear ye the song of the Terrible Three
And the fight that they fought by the edge of the sea.
Down from the mountains, the rocks and the crags,
Swarming like wasps, came the Bag-jagderags.

Surrounding our village, our walls they broke down.

Oh, sad was the plight of our men and our town!
  But Heaven determined our land to set free
And sent us the help of the Terrible Three.

  Shoulder to shoulder, they hammered and hit.
Like demons of fury they kicked and they bit.
  Like a wall of destruction they stood in a row,
Flattening enemies, six at a blow.

  And long shall we sing of the Terrible Three
And the fight that they fought by the edge of the sea.

· The Sixth Chapter ·
GENERAL POLYNESIA

UT, alas, even the Three, mighty though they were, could not last forever against an army that seemed to have no end. In one of the hottest scrimmages, when the enemy had broken a particularly wide hole through the fence, I saw Long Arrow's great figure topple and come down with a spear sticking in his broad chest.

For another half hour Bumpo and the Doctor fought on side by side. How their strength held out so long I cannot tell, for never a second were they given to get their breath or rest their arms.

The Doctor—the quiet, kindly, peaceable little Doctor!— well, you wouldn't have known him if you had seen him that day dealing out whacks you could hear a mile off, walloping and swatting in all directions.

As for Bumpo, with staring eyeballs and grim set teeth, he was a veritable demon. None dared come within yards of that wicked, wide-circling doorpost. But a stone, skillfully thrown, struck him at last in the center of the forehead. And down went the second of the Three. John Dolittle, the last of the Terribles, was left fighting alone.

Jip and I rushed to his side and tried to take the places of the fallen ones. But far too light and too small, we made but a poor exchange. Another length of the fence crashed down, and through the widened gap the Bag-jagderags poured in on us like a flood.

"To the canoes! To the sea!" shouted the Popsipetels. "Fly for your lives! All is over! The war is lost!"

But the Doctor and I never got a chance to fly for our lives. We were swept off our feet and knocked down flat by the sheer weight of the mob. And once down, we were unable to get up again. I thought we would surely be trampled to death.

But at that moment, above the din and racket of the battle, we heard the most terrifying noise that ever assaulted human ears: the sound of millions and millions of parrots all screeching with fury together.

The army, which in the nick of time Polynesia had brought to our rescue, darkened the whole sky to the west. I asked her afterward how many birds there were, and she said she didn't know exactly but that they certainly numbered somewhere between sixty and seventy million. In that extraordinarily short space of time she had brought them from the mainland of South America.

If you have ever heard a parrot screech with anger, you will know that it makes a truly frightful sound; and if you have ever been bitten by one, you will know that its bite can be a nasty and a painful thing.

The black parrots (coal-black all over, they were—except for a scarlet beak and a streak of red in wing and tail) on the word of command from Polynesia set to work upon the Bag-jagderags who were now pouring through the village looking for plunder.

And the black parrots' method of fighting was peculiar.

This is what they did: On the head of each Bag-jagderag three or four parrots settled and took a good foothold in his hair with their claws; then they leaned down over the sides of his head and began clipping snips out of his ears, for all the world as though they were punching tickets. That is all they did. They never bit them anywhere else except the ears. But it won the war for us.

With howls pitiful to hear, the Bag-jagderags fell over one another in their haste to get out of that accursed village. It was no use their trying to pull the parrots off their heads because for each head there were always four more parrots waiting impatiently to get on.

Some of the enemy were lucky, and with only a snip or two managed to get outside the fence—where the parrots immediately left them alone. But with most, before the black birds had done with them, the ears presented a very singular appearance—like the edge of a postage stamp. This treatment, very painful at the time, did not however do them any permanent harm beyond the change in looks. And it later got to be the tribal mark of the Bag-jagderags. No really smart young lady of this tribe would be seen walking with a man who did not have scalloped ears—for such was a proof that he had been in the Great War. And that (though it is not generally known to scientists) is how this people came to be called by the other Indian nations, the *Ragged-Eared Bag-jagderags*.

As soon as the village was cleared of the enemy the Doctor turned his attention to the wounded.

In spite of the length and fierceness of the struggle, there were surprisingly few serious injuries. Poor Long Arrow was the worst off. However, after the Doctor had washed his wound and got him to bed, he opened his eyes and said he already felt better. Bumpo was only badly stunned.

With this part of the business over, the Doctor called to Polynesia to have the black parrots drive the enemy right back into their own country and to wait there, guarding them all night.

Polynesia gave the short word of command, and like one bird those millions of parrots opened their red beaks and let out once more their terrifying battle scream.

The Bag-jagderags didn't wait to be bitten a second time, but fled helter-skelter over the mountains from which they had come, whilst Polynesia and her victorious army followed watchfully behind like a great threatening black cloud.

The Doctor picked up his high hat which had been knocked off in the fight, dusted it carefully, and put it on.

"Tomorrow," he said, shaking his fist toward the hills, "we will arrange the terms of peace—and we will arrange them—in the City of Bag-jagderag!"

His words were greeted with cheers of triumph from the admiring Popsipetels. The war was over.

· The Seventh Chapter ·
THE PEACE OF THE PARROTS

THE next day we set out for the far end of the island, and reaching it in canoes (for we went by sea) after a journey of twenty-five hours, we remained no longer than was necessary in the City of Bag-jagderag.

When he threw himself into that fight at Popsipetel, I saw the Doctor really angry for the first time in my life. But his anger, once aroused, was slow to die. All the way down the coast of the island he never ceased to rail against this cowardly people who had attacked his friends, the Popsipetels, for no other reason but to rob them of their corn because they were too idle to till the land themselves. And he was still angry when he reached the City of Bag-jagderag.

Long Arrow had not come with us, for he was as yet too weak from his wound. But the Doctor—always clever at languages—was already getting familiar with the Indian tongue. Besides, among the half dozen Popsipetels who accompanied us to paddle the canoes, was one boy to whom we had taught a little English. He and the Doctor between them managed to make themselves understood to the Bag-jagderags. These people—with the terrible parrots still blackening the hills about their stone town, waiting for the word to descend and attack —were, we found, in a very humble mood.

Leaving our canoes we passed up the main street to the palace of the chief. Bumpo and I couldn't help smiling with satisfaction as we saw how the waiting crowds that lined the roadway bowed their heads to the ground as the little, round, angry figure of the Doctor strutted ahead of us with his chin in the air.

At the foot of the palace steps the chief and all the more important personages of the tribe were waiting to meet him, smiling humbly and holding out their hands in friendliness. The Doctor took not the slightest notice. He marched right by them, up the steps to the door of the palace. There he turned around and at once began to address the people in a firm voice.

I never heard such a speech in my life—and I am quite sure that they never did, either. First he called them a long string of names: cowards, loafers, thieves, vagabonds, good-for-nothings, bullies, and whatnot. Then he said he was still seriously thinking of allowing the parrots to drive them on into the sea in order that this pleasant land might be rid, once for all, of their worthless carcasses.

At this a great cry for mercy went up, and the chief and all of them fell on their knees, calling out that they would submit to any conditions of peace he wished.

Then the Doctor called for one of their scribes—that is, a man who did picture-writing. And on the stone walls of the palace of Bag-jagderag he bade him write down the terms of the peace as he dictated it. This peace is known as *The Peace of the Parrots,* and—unlike most peaces—was, and is, strictly kept—even to this day.

It was quite long in words. The half of the palace front was covered with picture-writing, and fifty pots of paint were used before the weary scribe had done. But the main part of it all was that there should be no more fighting and that the two tribes should give solemn promise to help one another whenever there was corn famine or other distress in the lands belonging to either.

This greatly surprised the Bag-jagderags. They had expected from the Doctor's angry face that he would at least chop a couple of hundred heads off—and probably make the rest of them slaves for life.

But when they saw that he only meant kindly by them, their great fear of him changed to a tremendous admiration. And as he ended his long speech and walked briskly down the steps again on his way back to the canoes, the group of chieftains threw themselves at his feet and cried, "Do but stay with us, Great Lord, and all the riches of Bag-jagderag shall be poured into your lap. Gold mines we know of in the mountains and pearl beds beneath the sea. Only stay with us, that your all-powerful wisdom may lead our Council and our people in prosperity and peace."

The Doctor held up his hand for silence.

"No man," said he, "would wish to be the guest of the Bag-jagderags till they had proved by their deeds that they are an honest race. Be true to the terms of the Peace and from yourselves shall come good government and prosperity. Farewell!"

Then he turned and followed by Bumpo, the Popsipetels, and myself, walked rapidly down to the canoes.

· The Eighth Chapter ·
THE HANGING STONE

UT the change of heart in the Bag-jagderags
was really sincere. The Doctor had made a great impression
on them—a deeper one than even he himself realized at the
time. In fact, I sometimes think that that speech of his from
the palace steps had more effect upon the Indians of Spider
Monkey Island than had any of his great deeds that, great
though they were, were always magnified and exaggerated
when the news of them was passed from mouth to mouth.

A sick girl was brought to him as he reached the place
where the boats lay. She turned out to have some quite simple ailment that he quickly gave the remedy for. But this increased his popularity still more. And when he stepped into
his canoe, the people all around us actually burst into tears.
It seems (I learned this afterward) that they thought he was
going away across the sea for good, to the mysterious foreign
lands from which he had come.

Some of the chieftains spoke to the Popsipetels as we
pushed off. What they said I did not understand, but we noticed that several canoes filled with Bag-jagderags followed
us at a respectful distance all the way back to Popsipetel.

The Doctor had determined to return by the other shore, so that we should be thus able to make a complete trip round the island's shores.

Shortly after we started, while still off the lower end of the island, we sighted a steep point on the coast where the sea was in a great state of turmoil, white with soapy froth. On going nearer, we found that this was caused by our friendly whales who were still faithfully working away with their noses against the end of the island, driving us northward. We had been kept so busy with the war that we had forgotten all about them. But as we paused and watched their mighty tails lashing and churning the sea, we suddenly realized that we had not felt cold in quite a long while. Speeding up our boat lest the island be carried away from us altogether, we passed on up the coast; and here and there we noticed that the trees on the shore already looked greener and more healthy. Spider Monkey Island was getting back into her home climate.

About halfway to Popsipetel we went ashore and spent two or three days exploring the central part of the island. Our Indian paddlers took us up into the mountains, very steep and high in this region, overhanging the sea. And they showed us what they called the Whispering Rocks.

This was a very peculiar and striking piece of scenery. It was like a great vast basin, in the mountains, and out of the center of it there rose a table of rock with an ivory chair upon it. All around this the mountains went up like stairs, or theater seats, to a great height—except at one narrow end, which was open to a view of the sea. You could imagine it a council place or concert hall for giants, and the rock table in the center the stage for performers or the stand for the speaker.

We asked our guides why it was called the Whispering

"Working away with their noses against the end
of the island"

Rocks, and they said, "Go down into it and we will show you."

The great bowl was miles deep and miles wide. We scrambled down the rocks and they showed us how, even when you stood far, far apart from one another, you merely had to whisper in that great place and everyone in the theater could hear you. This was, the Doctor said, on account of the echoes which played backward and forward between the high walls of rock.

Our guides told us that it was here, in days long gone by when the Popsipetels owned the whole of Spider Monkey Island, that the kings were crowned. The ivory chair upon the table was the throne on which they sat. And so great was the big theater that all the Indians in the island were able to get seats in it to see the ceremony.

They showed us also an enormous hanging stone perched on the edge of a volcano's crater—the highest summit in the whole island. Although it was very far below us, we could see it quite plainly, and it looked wobbly enough to be pushed off its perch with the hand. There was a legend among the people, they said, that when the greatest of all Popsipetel kings should be crowned in the ivory chair, this hanging stone would tumble into the volcano's mouth and go straight down to the center of the earth.

The Doctor said he would like to go and examine it closer.

And when we had come to the lip of the volcano (it took us half a day to get up to it), we found the stone was unbelievably large—big as a cathedral. Underneath it we could look right down into a black hole that seemed to have no bottom. The Doctor explained to us that volcanoes sometimes spurted up fire from these holes in their tops, but that those on floating islands were always cold and dead.

"The Whispering Rocks"

"Stubbins," he said, looking up at the great stone towering above us, "do you know what would most likely happen if that boulder should fall in?"

"No," said I, "what?"

"You remember the air chamber which the porpoises told us lies under the center of the island?"

"Yes."

"Well, this stone is heavy enough, if it fell into the volcano, to break through into that air chamber from above. And once it did, the air would escape and the floating island would float no more. It would sink."

"But then everybody on it would be drowned, wouldn't they?" said Bumpo.

"Oh, no, not necessarily. That would depend on the depth of the sea where the sinking took place. The island might touch bottom when it had only gone down, say, a hundred feet. But there would be lots of it still sticking up above the water then, wouldn't there?"

"Yes," said Bumpo, "I suppose there would. Well, let us hope that the ponderous fragment does *not* lose its equilibriosity, for I don't believe it would stop at the center of the earth. More likely, it would fall right through the world and come out the other side."

Many other wonders there were that these men showed us in the central regions of their island. But I have not time or space to tell you of them now.

Descending toward the shore again, we noticed that we were still being watched, even here among the highlands, by the Bag-jagderags who had followed us. And when we put to sea once more a boatload of them proceeded to go ahead of us in the direction of Popsipetel. Having lighter canoes, they traveled faster than our party, and we judged that they should reach the village—if that was where they were going —many hours before we could.

The Doctor was now becoming anxious to see how Long Arrow was getting on, so we all took turns at the paddles and went on traveling by moonlight through the whole night.

We reached Popsipetel just as the dawn was breaking.

To our great surprise we found that not only we, but the whole village also, had been up all night. A great crowd was gathered about the dead chief's house. And as we landed our canoes upon the beach we saw a large number of old men, the seniors of the tribe, coming out at the main door.

We inquired what was the meaning of all this and were told that the election of a new chief had been going on all through the whole night. Bumpo asked the name of the new chief, but this, it seemed, had not yet been given out. It would be announced at midday.

As soon as the Doctor had paid a visit to Long Arrow and seen that he was doing nicely, we proceeded to our own house at the far end of the village. Here we ate some breakfast and then lay down to take a good rest.

Rest, indeed, we needed, for life had been strenuous and busy for us ever since we had landed on the island. And it wasn't many minutes after our weary heads struck the pillows that the whole crew of us were sound asleep.

· The Ninth Chapter ·
THE ELECTION

WE were awakened by music. The glaring noonday sunlight was streaming in at our door, outside of which some kind of a band appeared to be playing.

We got up and looked out. Our house was surrounded by the whole population of Popsipetel. We were used to having quite a number of curious and admiring Indians waiting at our door at all hours, but this was quite different. The vast crowd was dressed in its best clothes. Bright beads, gaudy feathers, and gay blankets gave cheerful color to the scene. Everyone seemed in very good humor, singing or playing on musical instruments—mostly painted wooden whistles or drums made from skins.

We found Polynesia—who while we slept had arrived back from Bag-jagderag—sitting on our doorpost watching the show. We asked her what all the holiday-making was about.

"The result of the election has just been announced," said she. "The name of the new chief was given out at noon."

"And who is the new chief?" asked the Doctor.

"You are," said Polynesia quietly.

"*I!*" gasped the Doctor— "Well, of all things!"

258

"Yes," said she. "You're the one— And what's more, they've changed your surname for you. They didn't think that Dolittle was a proper or respectful name for a man who had done so much. So you are now to be known as Jong Thinkalot. How do you like it?"

"But I don't *want* to be a chief," said the Doctor in an irritable voice.

"I'm afraid you'll have hard work to get out of it now," said she, "—unless you're willing to put to sea again in one of their rickety canoes. You see you've been elected not merely the Chief of the Popsipetels, you're to be a king—the King of the whole of Spider Monkey Island. The Bag-jagderags, who were so anxious to have you govern them, sent spies and messengers ahead of you; and when they found that you had been elected Chief of the Popsipetels overnight they were bitterly disappointed. However, rather than lose you altogether, the Bag-jagderags were willing to give up their independence and insisted that they and their lands be united to the Popsipetels in order that you could be made king of both. So now you're in for it."

"Oh, Lord!" groaned the Doctor, "I do wish they wouldn't be so enthusiastic! Bother it, I don't *want* to be a king!"

"I should think, Doctor," said I, "you'd feel rather proud and glad. I wish *I* had a chance to be a king."

"Oh, I know it sounds grand," said he, pulling on his boots miserably. "But the trouble is, you can't take up responsibilities and then just drop them again when you feel like it. I have my own work to do. Scarcely one moment have I had to give to natural history since I landed on this island. I've been doing someone else's business all the time. And now they want me to go on doing it! Why, once I'm made King of the Popsipetels, that's the end of me as a useful naturalist. I'd be

too busy for anything. All I'd be then is just a . . . er . . . er
. . . just a king."

"Well, that's something!" said Bumpo. "My father is a king
and has a hundred and twenty wives."

"That would make it worse," said the Doctor, "—a hundred
and twenty times worse. I have my work to do. I don't want
to be a king."

"Look," said Polynesia, "here come the head men to an-
nounce your election. Hurry up and get your boots laced."

The throng before our door had suddenly parted asunder,
making a long lane, and down this we now saw a group of
personages coming toward us. The man in front, a handsome
old Indian with a wrinkled face, carried in his hands a
wooden crown—a truly beautiful and gorgeous crown, even
though of wood. Wonderfully carved and painted, it had two
lovely blue feathers springing from the front of it. Behind the
old man came eight strong Indians bearing a litter, a sort of
chair with long handles underneath to carry it by.

Kneeling down on one knee, bending his head almost to
the ground, the old man addressed the Doctor, who now
stood in the doorway putting on his collar and tie.

"Oh, Mighty One," said he, "we bring you word from the
Popsipetel people. Great are your deeds beyond belief, kind is
your heart and your wisdom, deeper than the sea. Our chief
is dead. The people clamor for a worthy leader. Our old enemies, the Bag-jagderags are become, through you, our brothers and good friends. They too desire to bask beneath the
sunshine of your smile. Behold then, I bring to you the Sacred Crown of Popsipetel that, since ancient days when this
island and its peoples were one, beneath one monarch, has
rested on no kingly brow. Oh, Kindly One, we are bidden by
the united voices of the peoples of this land to carry you to

the Whispering Rocks, that there, with all respect and majesty, you may be crowned our king—King of all the Moving Land."

The good Indians did not seem to have even considered the possibility of John Dolittle's refusing. As for the poor Doctor, I never saw him so upset by anything. It was in fact the only time I have known him to get thoroughly fussed.

"Oh, dear!" I heard him murmur, looking around wildly for some escape. "What *shall* I do? . . . Did any of you see where I laid that stud of mine? . . . How on earth can I get this collar on without a stud? What a day this is, to be sure! . . . Maybe it rolled under the bed, Bumpo. . . . I do think they might have given me a day or so to think it over in. Who ever heard of waking a man right out of his sleep and telling him he's got to be a king, before he has even washed his face? . . . Can't any of you find it? Maybe you're standing on it, Bumpo. Move your feet."

"Oh don't bother about your stud," said Polynesia. "You will have to be crowned without a collar. They won't know the difference."

"I tell you I'm not going to be crowned," cried the Doctor, "—not if I can help it. I'll make them a speech. Perhaps that will satisfy them."

He turned back to the Indians at the door.

"My friends," he said, "I am not worthy of this great honor you would do me. Little or no skill have I in the arts of kingcraft. Assuredly among your own brave men you will find many better fitted to lead you. For this compliment, this confidence, and trust, I thank you. But, I pray you, do not think of me for such high duties which I could not possibly fulfill."

The old man repeated his words to the people behind him

in a louder voice. Stolidly they shook their heads, moving not an inch. The old man turned back to the Doctor.

"You are the chosen one," said he. "They will have none but you."

Into the Doctor's perplexed face suddenly there came a flash of hope.

"I'll go and see Long Arrow," he whispered to me. "Perhaps he will know of some way to get me out of this."

And asking the personages to excuse him a moment, he left them there, standing at his door, and hurried off in the direction of Long Arrow's house. I followed him.

We found our big friend lying on a grass bed outside his home, where he had been moved so that he might witness the holiday-making.

"Long Arrow," said the Doctor speaking quickly in eagle tongue so that the bystanders should not overhear, "in dire peril I come to you for help. These men would make me their king. If such a thing befall me, all the great work I hoped to do must go undone, for who is there unfreer than a king? I pray you speak with them and persuade their kind well-meaning hearts that what they plan to do would be unwise."

Long Arrow raised himself upon his elbow.

"Oh, Kindly One," said he (this seemed now to have become the usual manner of address when speaking to the Doctor), "sorely it grieves me that the first wish you ask of me I should be unable to grant. Alas! I can do nothing. These people have so set their hearts on keeping you for king that if I tried to interfere they would drive me from their land and likely crown you in the end in any case. A king you must be, if only for a while. We must so arrange the business of governing that you may have time to give to nature's secrets. Later we may be able to hit upon some plan to relieve you of the burden of the crown. But for now you must be king. These people are a headstrong tribe and they will have their way. There is no other course."

Sadly the Doctor turned away from the bed and faced about. And there behind him stood the old man again, the crown still held in his wrinkled hands and the royal litter waiting at his elbow. With a deep reverence the bearers motioned toward the seat of the chair, inviting the man to get in.

Once more the poor Doctor looked wildly, hopelessly about him for some means of escape. For a moment I thought he was going to take to his heels and run for it. But the crowd around us was far too thick and densely packed for anyone to break through it. A band of whistles and drums nearby suddenly started the music of a solemn processional march. He turned back pleadingly again to Long Arrow in a last appeal for help. But the big Indian merely shook his head and pointed, like the bearers, to the waiting chair.

At last, almost in tears, John Dolittle stepped slowly into the litter and sat down. As he was hoisted onto the broad shoulders of the bearers I heard him still feebly muttering beneath his breath, "Botheration take it! I don't *want* to be a king!"

"Farewell!" called Long Arrow from his bed, "and may good fortune ever stand within the shadow of your throne!"

"He comes! He comes!" murmured the crowd. "Away! Away! To the Whispering Rocks!"

And as the procession formed up to leave the village, the crowd about us began hurrying off in the direction of the mountains to make sure of good seats in the giant theater where the crowning ceremony would take place.

· The Tenth Chapter ·

THE CORONATION OF
KING JONG

IN my long lifetime I have seen many grand and inspiring things, but never anything that impressed me half as much as the sight of the Whispering Rocks as they looked on the day King Jong was crowned. As Bumpo, Chee-Chee, Polynesia, Jip, and I finally reached the dizzy edge of the great bowl and looked down inside it, it was like gazing over a never-ending ocean of copper-colored faces, for every seat in the theater was filled; every man, woman and child in the island—including Long Arrow who had been carried up on his sickbed—was there to see the show.

Yet not a sound, not a pin-drop, disturbed the solemn silence of the Whispering Rocks. It was quite creepy and sent chills running up and down your spine. Bumpo told me afterward that it took his breath away too much for him to speak, but that he hadn't known before that there were that many people in the world.

Away down by the Table of the Throne stood a brand-new, brightly colored totem pole. All the Indian families had totem poles and kept them set up before the doors of their houses. The idea of a totem pole is something like a doorplate or a

visiting card. It represents in its carvings the deeds and qualities of the family to which it belongs. This one, beautifully
decorated and much higher than any other, was the Dolittle
or, as it was to be henceforth called, the Royal Thinkalot
totem. It had nothing but animals on it, to signify the Doctor's great knowledge of creatures. And the animals chosen to
be shown were those that to the Indians were supposed to
represent good qualities of character, such as the deer for
speed, the ox for perseverance, the fish for discretion, and so
on. But at the top of the totem is always placed the sign or
animal by which the family is most proud to be known. This,
on the Thinkalot pole, was an enormous parrot, in memory
of the famous Peace of the Parrots.

The Ivory Throne had been all polished with scented oil
and it glistened whitely in the strong sunlight. At the foot of it
there had been strewn great quantities of branches of flower-
ing trees, which with the new warmth of milder climates
were now blossoming in the valleys of the island.

Soon we saw the royal litter, with the Doctor seated in it,
slowly ascending the winding steps of the Table. Reaching
the flat top at last, it halted and the Doctor stepped out upon
the flowery carpet. So still and perfect was the silence that
even at that distance above I distinctly heard a twig snap
beneath his tread.

Walking to the throne accompanied by the old man, the
Doctor got up upon the stand and sat down. How tiny his
little round figure looked when seen from that tremendous
height! The throne had been made for longer-legged kings,
and when he was seated, his feet did not reach the ground but
dangled six inches from the top step.

Then the old man turned around and looking up at the
people began to speak in a quiet, even voice, but every word

he said was easily heard in the farthest corner of the Whispering Rocks.

First he recited the names of all the great Popsipetel kings who in days long ago had been crowned in this ivory chair. He spoke of the greatness of the Popsipetel people, of their triumphs, of their hardships. Then waving his hand toward the Doctor he began recounting the things which this king-to-be had done. And I am bound to say that they easily outmatched the deeds of those who had gone before him.

As soon as he started to speak of what the Doctor had achieved for the tribe, the people, still strictly silent, all began waving their right hands toward the throne. This gave to the vast theater a very singular appearance: acres and acres of something moving—with never a sound.

At last the old man finished his speech and stepping up to the chair, very respectfully removed the Doctor's battered high hat. He was about to put it upon the ground, but the Doctor took it from him hastily and kept it on his lap. Then taking up the Sacred Crown he placed it upon John Dolittle's head. It did not fit very well (for it had been made for smaller-headed kings), and when the wind blew in freshly from the sunlit sea the Doctor had some difficulty in keeping it on. But it looked very splendid.

Turning once more to the people, the old man said,

"Men of Popsipetel, behold your elected king! . . . Are you content?"

And then at last the voice of the people broke loose.

"JONG! JONG!" they shouted, "LONG LIVE KING JONG!"

The sound burst upon the solemn silence with the crash of a hundred cannons. There, where even a whisper carried miles, the shock of it was like a blow in the face. Back and forth the mountains threw it to one another. I thought the echoes of it would never die away as it passed rumbling through the whole island, jangling among the lower valleys, booming in the distant sea caves.

Suddenly I saw the old man point upward, to the highest mountain in the island; and looking over my shoulder, I was just in time to see the Hanging Stone topple slowly out of sight—down into the heart of the volcano.

"See ye, Men of the Moving Land!" the old man cried. "The stone has fallen and our legend has come true: The King of Kings is crowned this day!"

The Doctor too had seen the stone fall and he was now standing up looking at the sea expectantly.

"He's thinking of the air chamber," said Bumpo in my ear. "Let us hope that the sea isn't very deep in these parts."

After a full minute (so long did it take the stone to fall that depth) we heard a muffled, distant, crunching thud—and then, immediately after, a great hissing of escaping air. The Doctor, his face tense with anxiety, sat down in the throne again still watching the blue water of the ocean with staring eyes.

Soon we felt the island slowly sinking beneath us. We saw the sea creep inland over the beaches as the shores went down—one foot, three feet, ten feet, twenty, fifty, a hundred. And then, thank goodness, gently as a butterfly alighting on a rose, it stopped! Spider Monkey Island had come to rest on the sandy bottom of the Atlantic, and earth was joined to earth once more.

Of course many of the houses near the shores were now under water. Popsipetel Village itself had entirely disappeared. But it didn't matter. No one was drowned, for every soul in the island was high up in the hills watching the coronation of King Jong.

The Indians themselves did not realize at the time what was taking place, though of course they had felt the land sinking beneath them. The Doctor told us afterward that it must have been the shock of that tremendous shout, coming from a million throats at once, which had toppled the Hanging Stone off its perch. But in Popsipetel history the story was handed down (and it is firmly believed to this day) that when King Jong sat upon the throne, so great was his mighty weight that the very island itself sank down to do him honor and never moved again.

PART VI

· The First Chapter ·
NEW POPSIPETEL

JONG THINKALOT had not ruled over his new kingdom for more than a couple of days before my notions about kings and the kind of lives they led changed very considerably. I had thought that all that kings had to do was to sit on a throne and have people bow down before them several times a day. I now saw that a king can be the hardest-working man in the world—if he attends properly to his business.

From the moment that he got up early in the morning till the time he went to bed late at night—seven days in the week —John Dolittle was busy, busy, busy. First of all, there was the new town to be built. The village of Popsipetel had disappeared: the City of New Popsipetel must be made. With great care a place was chosen for it—and a very beautiful position it was, at the mouth of a large river. The shores of the island at this point formed a lovely wide bay where canoes—and ships too, if they should ever come—could lie peacefully at anchor without danger from storms.

In building this town the Doctor gave the Indians a lot of new ideas. He showed them what town sewers were and how garbage should be collected each day and burned. High up in the hills he made a large lake by damming a stream. This was the water supply for the town. None of these things had the Indians ever seen, and many of the sicknesses that they had suffered from before were now entirely prevented by proper drainage and pure drinking water.

Peoples who don't use fire do not, of course, have metals either because without fire it is almost impossible to shape iron and steel. One of the first things that John Dolittle did was to search the mountains till he found iron and copper mines. Then he set to work to teach the Indians how these metals could be melted and made into knives and plows and water pipes and all manner of things.

In his kingdom the Doctor tried his hardest to do away with most of the old-fashioned pomp and grandeur of a royal court. As he said to Bumpo and me, if he must be a king he meant to be a thoroughly democratic one, that is, a king who is chummy and friendly with his subjects and doesn't put on airs. And when he drew up the plans for the City of New Popsipetel he had no palace shown of any kind. A little cottage in a back street was all that he had provided for himself.

But this the Indians would not permit on any account. They had been used to having their kings rule in a truly grand and kingly manner, and they insisted that he have built for himself the most magnificent palace ever seen. In all else they let him have his own way absolutely, but they wouldn't allow him to wriggle out of any of the ceremony or show that goes with being a king. A thousand servants he had to keep in his palace, night and day, to wait on him. The Royal Canoe had to be kept up—a gorgeous, polished mahogany boat, seventy feet long, inlaid with mother-of-pearl and paddled by the hundred strongest men in the island. The palace gardens covered a square mile and employed a hundred and sixty gardeners.

Even in his dress the poor man was compelled always to be grand and elegant and uncomfortable. The beloved and battered high hat was put away in a closet and only looked at secretly. State robes had to be worn on all occasions. And when the Doctor did once in a while manage to sneak off for a short natural-history expedition he never dared to wear his old clothes, but had to chase his butterflies with a crown upon his head and a scarlet cloak flying behind him in the wind.

There was no end to the kinds of duties the Doctor had to perform and the questions he had to decide upon—everything from settling disputes about lands and boundaries to making peace between husband and wife who had been throwing shoes at one another. In the east wing of the Royal Palace was the Hall of Justice. And here King Jong sat every morning from nine to eleven passing judgment on all cases that were brought before him.

Then in the afternoon he taught school. The sort of things he taught were not always those you find in ordinary schools. Grown-ups as well as children came to learn.

Bumpo and I helped with the teaching as far as we could—simple arithmetic and easy things like that. But the classes in astronomy, farming science, the proper care of babies, with a host of other subjects, the Doctor had to teach himself. The Indians were tremendously keen about the schooling and they came in droves and crowds, so that even with the open-air classes (a schoolhouse was impossible of course) the Doctor had to take them in relays and batches of five or six thousand at a time and used a big megaphone or trumpet to make himself heard.

"Had to chase his butterflies with a crown upon his head"

The rest of his day was more than filled with road making, building water mills, attending the sick, and a million other things.

In spite of his being so unwilling to become a king, John Dolittle made a very good one—once he got started. He may not have been as dignified as many kings in history, who were always running off to war and getting themselves into romantic situations, but since I have grown up and seen something of foreign lands and governments I have often thought that Popsipetel under the reign of Jong Thinkalot was perhaps the best-ruled state in the history of the world.

The Doctor's birthday came around after we had been on the island six months and a half. The people made a great public holiday of it and there was much feasting, dancing, fireworks, speechmaking, and jollification.

Toward the close of the day the chief men of the two tribes formed a procession and passed through the streets of the town, carrying a very gorgeously painted tablet of ebony wood, ten feet high. This was a picture history, such as they preserved for all of the ancient kings of Popsipetel to record their deeds.

With great and solemn ceremony it was set up over the door of the new palace and everybody then clustered around to look at it. It had six pictures on it commemorating the six great events in the life of King Jong and beneath were written the verses that explained them. They were composed by the Court Poet, and this is a translation:

I

His Landing on the Island

Heaven-sent,
In his dolphin-drawn canoe

From worlds unknown
He landed on our shores.
The very palms
Bowed down their heads
In welcome to the coming King.

II
His Meeting with the Beetle

By moonlight in the mountains
He communed with beasts.
The shy jabizri brings him picture-words
Of great distress.

III
He Liberates the Lost Families

Big was his heart with pity;
Big were his hands with strength.
See how he tears the mountain like a yam!
See how the lost ones
Dance forth to greet the day!

IV
He Makes Fire

Our land was cold and dying.
He waved his hand, and lo!
Lightning leapt from cloudless skies;
The sun leaned down;
And fire was born!
Then while we crowded around
The grateful glow, pushed he
Our wayward, floating land

Back to peaceful anchorage
In sunny seas.

V
He Leads the People to Victory in War

Once only
Was his kindly countenance
Darkened by a deadly frown.
Woe to the wicked enemy
That dares attack
The tribe with Thinkalot for Chief!

VI
He Is Crowned King

The birds of the air rejoiced;
The sea laughed and gamboled with her shores;
All men wept for joy
The day we crowned him King.
He is the Builder, the Healer, the Teacher, and the Prince;
He is the greatest of them all.
May he live a thousand thousand years,
Happy in his heart,
To bless our land with peace.

· The Second Chapter ·
THOUGHTS OF HOME

IN the Royal Palace Bumpo and I had a beautiful suite of rooms of our very own—which Polynesia, Jip, and Chee-Chee shared with us. Officially, Bumpo was Minister of the Interior, while I was First Lord of the Treasury. Long Arrow also had quarters there, but at present he was absent, traveling abroad.

One night after supper when the Doctor was away in the town somewhere visiting a newborn baby, we were all sitting around the big table in Bumpo's reception room. This we did every evening, to talk over the plans for the following day and various affairs of state. It was a kind of cabinet meeting.

Tonight however we were talking about England—and also about things to eat. We had gotten a little tired of Indian food. You see, none of the natives knew how to cook, and we had the most discouraging time training a chef for the Royal Kitchen. Most of them were champions at spoiling good food. Often we got so hungry that the Doctor would sneak downstairs with us into the palace basement, after all the cooks were safe in bed, and fry pancakes secretly over the dying embers of the fire. The Doctor himself was the finest cook that ever lived. But he used to make a terrible mess of the kitchen, and of course we had to be awfully careful that we didn't get caught.

Well, as I was saying, tonight food was the subject of discussion at the cabinet meeting, and I had just been reminding Bumpo of the nice dishes we had had at the bed maker's house in Monteverde.

"I tell you what I would like now," said Bumpo, "a large cup of cocoa with whipped cream on the top of it. In Oxford we used to be able to get the most wonderful cocoa. It is really too bad they haven't any cocoa trees in this island, or cows to give cream."

"When do you suppose," asked Jip, "the Doctor intends to move on from here?"

"I was talking to him about that only yesterday," said Polynesia. "But I couldn't get any satisfactory answer out of him. He didn't seem to want to speak about it."

There was a pause in the conversation.

"Do you know what I believe?" she added presently. "I believe the Doctor has given up even thinking of going home."

"Good Lord!" cried Bumpo. "You don't say!"

"Sh!" said Polynesia. "What's that noise?"

We listened, and away off in the distant corridors of the palace we heard the sentries crying, "The King! Make way! The King!"

"It's he—at last," whispered Polynesia. "Late, as usual. Poor man, how he does work! Chee-Chee, get the pipe and tobacco out of the cupboard and lay the dressing gown ready on his chair."

When the Doctor came into the room he looked serious and thoughtful. Wearily he took off his crown and hung it on a peg behind the door. Then he exchanged the royal cloak for the dressing gown, dropped into his chair at the head of the table with a deep sigh, and started to fill his pipe.

"Well," asked Polynesia quietly, "how did you find the baby?"

"The baby?" he murmured—his thoughts still seemed to be very far away. "Ah, yes. The baby was much better, thank you. It has cut its second tooth."

Then he was silent again, staring dreamily at the ceiling through a cloud of tobacco smoke, while we all sat around quite still, waiting.

"We were wondering, Doctor," said I at last, "—just before you came in—when you would be starting home again. We will have been on this island seven months tomorrow."

The Doctor sat forward in his chair looking rather uncomfortable.

"Well, as a matter of fact," said he after a moment, "I meant to speak to you myself this evening on that very subject. But it's—er—a little hard to make anyone exactly understand the situation. I am afraid that it would be impossible for me to leave the work I am now engaged on. . . . You remember, when they first insisted on making me king, I told you it was not easy to shake off responsibilities once you had taken them up. These people have come to rely on me for a great number of things. We have, one might say, changed the current of their lives considerably. Now it is a very ticklish business, to change the lives of other people. And whether the changes we have made will be, in the end, for good or for bad, is our lookout."

He thought a moment—then went on in a quieter, sadder voice: "I would like to continue my voyages and my natural history work, and I would like to go back to Puddleby—as much as any of you. This is March, and the crocuses will be showing in the lawn. . . . But that which I feared has come true: I cannot close my eyes to what might happen if I should leave these people and run away. They would probably go back to their old habits and customs: wars, superstitions, devil worship, and whatnot; and many of the new things we have taught them might be put to improper use and make their condition, then, worse by far than that in which we found them. . . . They like me; they trust me; they have come to look to me for help in all their problems and troubles. And no man wants to do unfair things to them who trust him. . . . And then again, *I* like *them*. They are, as it were, my children—I never had any children of my own—and I am terribly interested in how they will grow up. Don't you see what I mean? How can I possibly run away and leave them in the lurch? . . . No. I have thought it over a good deal and tried to decide what was best. And I am afraid that the work I took up when I assumed the crown I must stick to. I'm afraid —I've got to stay."

"For good—for your whole life?" asked Bumpo in a low voice.

For some moments the Doctor, frowning, made no answer.

"I don't know," he said at last. "Anyhow, for the present there is certainly no hope of my leaving. It wouldn't be right."

The sad silence that followed was broken finally by a knock upon the door.

With a patient sigh the Doctor got up and put on his crown and cloak again.

"Come in," he called, sitting down in his chair once more.

The door opened and a footman—one of the hundred and forty-three who were always on night duty—stood bowing in the entrance.

"Oh, Kindly One," said he, "there is a traveler at the palace gate who would have speech with Your Majesty."

"Another baby's been born, I'll bet a shilling," muttered Polynesia.

"Did you ask the traveler's name?" inquired the Doctor.

"Yes, Your Majesty," said the footman. "It is Long Arrow, the son of Golden Arrow."

· The Third Chapter ·
THE RED MAN'S SCIENCE

L ONG ARROW!" cried the Doctor. "How splendid! Show him in—show him in at once.

"I'm so glad," he continued, turning to us as soon as the footman had gone. "I've missed Long Arrow terribly. He's an awfully good man to have around—even if he doesn't talk much. Let me see: It's five months now since he went off to Brazil. I'm so glad he's back safe. He does take such tremendous chances with that canoe of his—clever as he is. It's no joke, crossing a hundred miles of open sea in a twelve-foot canoe. I wouldn't care to try it."

Another knock, and when the door swung open in answer to the Doctor's call, there stood our big friend on the threshold, a smile upon his strong, bronzed face. Behind him appeared two porters carrying loads done up in Indian palm matting. These, when the first salutations were over, Long Arrow ordered to lay their burdens down.

"Behold, oh, Kindly One," said he, "I bring you, as I promised, my collection of plants that I had hidden in a cave in the Andes. These treasures represent the labors of my life."

The packages were opened, and inside were many smaller

283

packages and bundles. Carefully they were laid out in rows upon the table.

It appeared at first a large but disappointing display. There were plants, flowers, fruits, leaves, roots, nuts, beans, honeys, gums, bark, seeds, bees, and a few kinds of insects.

The study of plants—or botany, as it is called—was a kind of natural history that had never interested me very much. I had considered it, compared with the study of animals, a dull science. But as Long Arrow began taking up the various things in his collection and explaining their qualities to us, I became more and more fascinated. And before he had done, I was completely absorbed by the wonders of the Vegetable Kingdom that he had brought so far.

"These," said he, taking up a little packet of big seeds, "are what I have called 'laughing-beans.'"

"What are they for?" asked Bumpo.

"To cause mirth," said the Indian.

Bumpo, while Long Arrow's back was turned, took three of the beans and swallowed them.

"Alas!" said the Indian when he discovered what Bumpo had done. "If he wished to try the powers of these seeds he should have eaten no more than a quarter of one. Let us hope that he does not die of laughter."

The beans' effect upon Bumpo was most extraordinary. First he broke into a broad smile; then he began to giggle; finally he burst into such prolonged roars of hearty laughter that we had to carry him into the next room and put him to bed. The Doctor said afterward that he probably would have died laughing if he had not had such a strong constitution. All through the night he gurgled happily in his sleep. And even when we woke him up the next morning he rolled out of bed still chuckling.

Returning to the Reception Room, we were shown some red roots that Long Arrow told us had the property, when made into a soup with sugar and salt, of causing people to dance with extraordinary speed and endurance. He asked us to try them but we refused, thanking him. After Bumpo's exhibition we were a little afraid of any more experiments for the present.

There was no end to the curious and useful things that Long Arrow had collected: an oil from a vine that would make hair grow in one night; an orange as big as a pumpkin that he had raised in his own mountain garden in Peru; a black honey (he had brought the bees that made it too and the seeds of the flowers they fed on) that would put you to sleep, just with a teaspoonful, and make you wake up fresh in the morning; a nut that made the voice beautiful for singing; a waterweed that stopped cuts from bleeding; a moss that cured snakebite; a lichen that prevented seasickness.

The Doctor of course was tremendously interested. Well into the early hours of the morning he was busy going over the articles on the table one by one, listing their names and writing their properties and descriptions into a notebook as Long Arrow dictated.

"There are things here, Stubbins," he said as he ended, "that in the hands of skilled druggists will make a vast difference to the medicine and chemistry of the world. I suspect that this sleeping-honey by itself will take the place of half the bad drugs we have had to use so far. Long Arrow has discovered a pharmacopoeia of his own. Miranda was right: He is a great naturalist. His name deserves to be placed beside Linnaeus. Someday I must get all these things to England. But when," he added sadly. "Yes, that's the problem: **When?**"

· The Fourth Chapter ·
THE SEA SERPENT

FOR a long time after that cabinet meeting of which I have just told you we did not ask the Doctor anything further about going home. Life in Spider Monkey Island went forward—month in, month out—busily and pleasantly. The winter with Christmas celebrations came and went, and summer was with us once again before we knew it.

As time passed the Doctor became more and more taken up with the care of his big family, and the hours he could spare for his natural history work grew fewer and fewer. I knew that he often still thought of his house and garden in Puddleby and of his old plans and ambitions because once in a while we would notice his face grow thoughtful and a little sad, when something reminded him of England or his old life. But he never spoke of these things. And I truly believe he would have spent the remainder of his days on Spider Monkey Island if it hadn't been for an accident—and for Polynesia.

The old parrot had grown very tired of the Indians and she made no secret of it.

"The very idea," she said to me one day as we were walking

on the seashore, "—the idea of the famous John Dolittle spending his valuable life waiting on these people! Why, it's preposterous!"

All that morning we had been watching the Doctor superintend the building of the new theater in Popsipetel—there was already an opera house and a concert hall—and finally she had got so grouchy and annoyed at the sight that I had suggested her taking a walk with me.

"Do you really think," I asked as we sat down on the sands, "that he will never go back to Puddleby again?"

"I don't know," said she. "At one time I felt sure that the thought of the pets he had left behind at the house would take him home soon. But since Miranda brought him word last August that everything was all right there, that hope's gone. For months and months I've been racking my brains to think up a plan. If we could only hit upon something that would turn his thoughts back to natural history again . . . I mean something big enough to get him really excited . . . we might manage it. But how?"—she shrugged her shoulders in disgust— "How? . . . when all he thinks of now is paving streets and teaching papooses that twice one is two!"

It was a perfect Popsipetel day, bright and hot, blue and yellow. Drowsily I looked out to sea thinking of my mother and father. I wondered if they were getting anxious over my long absence. Beside me old Polynesia went on grumbling away in low, steady tones, and her words began to mingle and mix with the gentle lapping of the waves upon the shore. It may have been the even murmur of her voice, helped by the soft and balmy air, that lulled me to sleep. I don't know. Anyhow, I presently dreamed that the island had moved again—not floatingly as before, but suddenly, jerkily, as though something enormously powerful had heaved it up from its bed just once and let it down.

How long I slept after that I have no idea. I was awakened by a gentle pecking on the nose.

"Tommy! Tommy!" It was Polynesia's voice. "Wake up! Gosh, what a boy, to sleep through an earthquake and never notice it! Tommy, listen: Here's our chance now. Wake *up*, for goodness' sake!"

"What's the matter?" I asked, sitting up with a yawn.

"Sh! Look!" whispered Polynesia, pointing out to sea.

Still only half awake, I stared before me with bleary, sleep-laden eyes. And in the shallow water, not more than thirty yards from shore I saw an enormous pale pink shell. Dome-shaped, it towered up in a graceful rainbow curve to a tremendous height, and around its base the surf broke gently in little waves of white. It could have belonged to the wildest dream.

"What in the world is it?" I asked.

"That," whispered Polynesia, "is what sailors for hundreds of years have called the *sea serpent*. I've seen it myself more than once from the decks of ships, at long range, curving in and out of the water. But now that I see it close and still, I very strongly suspect that the sea serpent of history is no other than the great glass sea snail that the fidgit told us of. If that isn't the only fish of its kind in the seven seas, call me a carrion crow—Tommy, we're in luck. Our job is to get the Doctor down here to look at that prize specimen before it moves off to the Deep Hole. If we can, then, trust me, we may leave this blessed island yet. You stay here and keep an eye on it while I go after the Doctor. Don't move or speak—don't even breathe heavy: he might get scared—awful timid things, snails. Just watch him, and I'll be back in two shakes."

Stealthily creeping up the sands till she could get behind the cover of some bushes before she took to her wings, Polynesia went off in the direction of the town, while I remained alone upon the shore fascinatedly watching this unbelievable monster wallowing in the shallow sea.

It moved very little. From time to time it lifted its head out of the water showing its enormously long neck and horns. Occasionally it would try and draw itself up, the way a snail does when he goes to move, but almost at once it would sink down again as if exhausted. It seemed to me to act as though it were hurt underneath, but the lower part of it, which was below the level of the water, I could not see.

I was still absorbed in watching the great beast when Polynesia returned with the Doctor. They approached so silently and so cautiously that I neither saw nor heard them coming till I found them crouching beside me on the sand.

One sight of the snail changed the Doctor completely. His eyes just sparkled with delight. I had not seen him so thrilled and happy since the time we caught the jabizri beetle when we first landed on the island.

"It is he!" he whispered, "—the great glass sea snail himself . . . not a doubt of it. Polynesia, go down the shore a way and see if you can find any of the porpoises for me. Perhaps they can tell us what the snail is doing here. It's very unusual for him to be in shallow water like this. And Stubbins, you go over to the harbor and bring me a small canoe. But be most careful how you paddle it around into this bay. If the snail should take fright and go out into the deeper water, we may never get a chance to see him again."

"And don't tell any of the Indians," Polynesia added in a whisper as I moved to go. "We must keep this a secret or we'll have a crowd of sightseers around here in five minutes. It's mighty lucky we found the snail in a quiet bay."

Reaching the harbor, I picked out a small light canoe from among the number that were lying there and without telling anyone what I wanted it for, got in and started off to paddle it down the shore.

I was mortally afraid that the snail might have left before I got back. And you can imagine how delighted I was, when I rounded a rocky cape and came in sight of the bay, to find he was still there.

Polynesia, I saw, had gotten her errand done and returned ahead of me, bringing with her a pair of porpoises. These were already conversing in low tones with John Dolittle. I beached the canoe and went up to listen.

"What I want to know," the Doctor was saying, "is how the snail comes to be here. I was given to understand that he usually stayed in the Deep Hole, and that when he did come to the surface it was always in mid-ocean."

"Oh, didn't you know? . . . Haven't you heard?" the porpoises replied: "You covered up the Deep Hole when you sank the island. Why, yes, you let it down right on top of the mouth of the Hole—sort of put the lid on, as it were. The fishes that were in it at the time have been trying to get out ever since. The great snail had the worst luck of all: the island nipped him by the tail just as he was leaving the Hole for a quiet evening stroll. And he was held there for six months trying to wriggle himself free. Finally he had to heave the whole island up at one end to get his tail loose. Didn't you feel a sort of an earthquake shock about an hour ago?"

"Yes I did," said the Doctor. "It shook down part of the theater I was building."

"Well, that was the snail heaving up the island to get out of the Hole," they said. "All the other fishes saw their chance and escaped when he raised the lid. It was lucky for them he's so big and strong. But the strain of that terrific heave told on him: he sprained a muscle in his tail and it started swelling rather badly. He wanted some quiet place to rest up, and seeing this soft beach handy he crawled in here."

"Dear me!" said the Doctor. "I'm terribly sorry. I suppose I should have given some sort of notice that the island was going to be let down. But, to tell the truth, we didn't know it ourselves; it happened by a kind of an accident. Do you imagine the poor fellow is hurt very badly?"

"We're not sure," said the porpoises, "because none of us can speak his language. But we swam right around him on our way in here, and he did not seem to be really seriously injured."

"Can't any of your people speak shellfish?" the Doctor asked.

"Not a word," said they. "It's a most frightfully difficult language."

"Do you think that you might be able to find me some kind of a fish that could?"

"We don't know," said the porpoises. "We might try."

"I should be extremely grateful to you if you would," said the Doctor. "There are many important questions I want to ask this snail. . . . And besides, I would like to do my best to cure his tail for him. It's the least I can do. After all, it was my fault, indirectly, that he got hurt."

"Well, if you wait here," said the porpoises, "we'll see what can be done."

· The Fifth Chapter ·

THE SHELLFISH RIDDLE
SOLVED AT LAST

SO Doctor Dolittle with a crown on his head sat down upon the shore like King Knut, and waited. And for a whole hour the porpoises kept going and coming, bringing up different kinds of sea beasts from the deep to see if they could help him.

Many and curious were the creatures they produced. It would seem, however, that there were very few things that spoke shellfish except the shellfish themselves. Still, the porpoises grew a little more hopeful when they discovered a very old sea urchin (a funny, ball-like little fellow with long whiskers all over him) who said he could not speak pure shellfish, but he used to understand starfish—enough to get along—when he was young. This was coming nearer, even if it wasn't anything to go crazy about. Leaving the urchin with us, the porpoises went off once more to hunt up a starfish.

They were not long getting one, for they were quite common in those parts. Then, using the sea urchin as an interpreter, they questioned the starfish. He was a rather stupid sort of creature, but he tried his best to be helpful. And after a little patient examination we found to our delight that he could speak shellfish moderately well.

Feeling quite encouraged, the Doctor and I now got into the canoe; and, with the porpoises, the urchin, and the starfish swimming alongside, we paddled very gently out till we were close under the towering shell of the great snail.

And then began the most curious conversation I have ever witnessed. First the starfish would ask the snail something; and whatever answer the snail gave, the starfish would tell it to the sea urchin; the urchin would tell it to the porpoises; and the porpoises would tell it to the Doctor.

In this way we obtained considerable information, mostly about the very ancient history of the Animal Kingdom, but we missed a good many of the finer points in the snail's longer speeches on account of the stupidity of the starfish and all this translating from one language to another.

While the snail was speaking, the Doctor and I put our ears against the wall of his shell and found that we could in this way hear the sound of his voice quite plainly. It was, as the fidgit had described, deep and bell-like. But of course we could not understand a single word he said. However the Doctor was by this time terrifically excited about getting near to learning the language he had sought so long. And presently by making the other fishes repeat over and over again short phrases that the snail used, he began to put words together for himself. You see, he was already familiar with one or two fish languages, and that helped him quite a little. After he had practiced for a while like this he leaned over the side of the canoe and, putting his face below the water, tried speaking to the snail directly.

It was hard and difficult work, and hours went by before he

got any results. But presently I could tell by the happy look on his face that, little by little, he was succeeding.

The sun was low in the west and the cool evening breeze was beginning to rustle softly through the bamboo groves when the Doctor finally turned from his work and said to me, "Stubbins, I have persuaded the snail to come in onto the dry part of the beach and let me examine his tail. Will you please go back to the town and tell the workmen to stop working on the theater for today? Then go on to the palace and get my medicine bag. I think I left it under the throne in the Audience Chamber."

"And remember," Polynesia whispered as I turned away, "not a word to a soul. If you get asked questions, keep your mouth shut. Pretend you have a toothache or something."

This time when I got back to the shore—with the medicine bag—I found the snail high and dry on the beach. Seeing him at his full length like this, it wås easy to understand how old-time superstitious sailors had called him the sea serpent. He certainly was a most gigantic and, in his way, a graceful, beautiful creature. John Dolittle was examining a swelling on his tail.

From the bag that I had brought the Doctor took a large bottle of embrocation and began rubbing the sprain. Next he took all the bandages he had in the bag and fastened them end to end. But even like that, they were not long enough to go more than halfway around the enormous tail. The Doctor insisted that he must get the swelling strapped tight, somehow. So he sent me off to the palace once more to get all the sheets from the Royal Linen Closet. These Polynesia and I tore into bandages for him. And at last, after terrific exertions, we got the sprain strapped to his satisfaction.

The snail really seemed to be quite pleased with the

attention he had received, and he stretched himself in lazy comfort when the Doctor was done. In this position, when the shell on his back was empty, you could look right through it and see the palm trees on the other side.

"I think one of us had better sit up with him all night," said the Doctor. "We might put Bumpo on that duty; he's been napping all day, I know—in the summerhouse. It's a pretty bad sprain, that; and if the snail shouldn't be able to sleep, he'll be happier with someone with him for company. He'll get all right, though—in a few days I should judge. If I wasn't so confoundedly busy I'd sit up with him myself. I wish I could because I still have a lot of things to talk over with him."

"But, Doctor," said Polynesia as we prepared to go back to the town, "you ought to take a holiday. All kings take holidays once in the while—every one of them. And you haven't taken one since you were crowned, have you now?"

"No," said the Doctor, "I suppose that's true."

"Well, now, I tell you what you do," said she: "As soon as you get back to the palace you publish a royal proclamation that you are going away for a week into the country for your health. And you're going *without any servants*, you understand—just like a plain person. It's called traveling incognito, when kings go off like that. They all do it. . . . It's the only way they can ever have a good time. Then the week you're away you can spend lolling on the beach back there with the snail. How's that?"

"I'd like to," said the Doctor. "It sounds most attractive. But there's that new theater to be built; none of our carpenters would know how to get those rafters on without me to show them. And then there are the babies: these native mothers need my help."

"Oh, bother the theater—and the babies, too," snapped Polynesia. "The theater can wait a week. And as for babies, they never have anything more than colic. How do you suppose babies got along before you came here, for heaven's sake? Take a holiday. . . . You need it."

· The Sixth Chapter ·
THE LAST CABINET MEETING

FROM the way Polynesia talked, I guessed that this idea of a holiday was part of her plan.

The Doctor made no reply, and we walked on silently toward the town. I could see, nevertheless, that her words had made an impression on him.

After supper he disappeared from the palace without saying where he was going—a thing he had never done before. Of course we all knew where he had gone: back to the beach to sit up with the snail. We were sure of it because he had said nothing to Bumpo about attending to the matter.

As soon as the doors were closed upon the cabinet meeting that night, Polynesia addressed the ministry: "Look here, you fellows," said she, "we've simply got to get the Doctor to take this holiday somehow—unless we're willing to stay on this blessed island for the rest of our lives."

"But what difference," Bumpo asked, "is his taking a holiday going to make?"

Impatiently Polynesia turned upon the Minister of the Interior.

"Don't you see? If he has a clear week to get thoroughly

interested in his natural history again—marine stuff, his
dream of seeing the floor of the ocean, and all that—there
may be some chance of his consenting to leave this pesky
place. But while he is here on duty as king he never gets a
moment to think of anything outside of the business of government."

"Yes, that's true. He's far too consententious," Bumpo
agreed.

"And besides," Polynesia went on, "his only hope of ever
getting away from here would be to escape secretly. He's got
to leave while he is holiday-making, incognito—when no one
knows where he is or what he's doing but us. If he built a ship
big enough to cross the sea in, all the Indians would see it
and hear it being built, and they'd ask what it was for. They
would interfere. They'd sooner have anything happen than
lose the Doctor. Why, I believe if they thought he had any
idea of escaping, they would put chains on him."

"Yes, I really think they would," I agreed. "Yet without a
ship of some kind I don't see how the Doctor is going to get
away, even secretly."

"Well, I'll tell you," said Polynesia. "If we do succeed in
making him take this holiday, our next step will be to get the
sea snail to promise to take us all in his shell and carry us to
the mouth of Puddleby River. If we can once get the snail
willing, the temptation will be too much for John Dolittle
and he'll come, I know—especially as he'll be able to take
those new plants and drugs of Long Arrow's to the English
doctors, as well as see the floor of the ocean on the way."

"How thrilling!" I cried. "Do you mean the snail could take
us under the sea all the way back to Puddleby?"

"Certainly," said Polynesia. "A little trip like that is nothing
to him. He would crawl along the floor of the ocean and the

Doctor could see all the sights. Perfectly simple. Oh, John Dolittle will come all right, if we can only get him to take that holiday—*and* if the snail will consent to give us the ride."

"Golly, I hope he does!" sighed Jip. "I'm sick of these beastly tropics—they make you feel so lazy and good-for-nothing. And there are no rats or anything here—not that a fellow would have the energy to chase 'em even if there were. My, wouldn't I be glad to see old Puddleby and the garden again! And won't Dab-Dab be glad to have us back!"

"By the end of next month," said I, "it will be two whole years since we left England—since we pulled up the anchor at Kingsbridge and bumped our way out into the river."

"And got stuck on the mudbank," added Chee-Chee in a dreamy, faraway voice.

"Do you remember how all the people waved to us from the river wall?" I asked.

"Yes. And I suppose they've often talked about us in the town since," said Jip, "—wondering whether we're dead or alive."

"Cease," said Bumpo. "I feel I am about to weep from sediment."

· The Seventh Chapter ·
THE DOCTOR'S DECISION

WELL, you can guess how glad we were
when the next morning the Doctor, after his all-night conversation with the snail, told us that he had made up his mind to
take the holiday. A proclamation was published right away
by the Town Crier that His Majesty was going into the country for a seven-day rest, but that during his absence the palace and the government offices would be kept open as usual.

Polynesia was immensely pleased. She at once set quietly
to work making arrangements for our departure—taking
good care the while that no one should get an inkling of
where we were going, what we were taking with us, the hour
of our leaving, or which of the palace gates we would go out
by.

Cunning old schemer that she was, she forgot nothing. And
not even we, who were of the Doctor's party, could imagine
what reasons she had for some of her preparations. She took
me inside and told me that the one thing I must remember to
bring with me was *all* of the Doctor's notebooks. Long Arrow,
who was the only Indian let into the secret of our destination,
said he would like to come with us as far as the beach to see

300

the great snail, and him Polynesia told to be sure and bring his collection of plants. Bumpo she ordered to carry the Doctor's high hat—carefully hidden under his coat. She sent off nearly all the footmen who were on night duty to do errands in the town, so that there should be as few servants as possible to see us leave. And midnight, the hour when most of the townspeople would be asleep, she finally chose for our departure.

We had to take a week's food supply with us for the royal holiday. So, with our other packages, we were heavy laden when on the stroke of twelve we opened the west door of the palace and stepped cautiously and quietly into the moonlit garden.

"Tiptoe incognito," whispered Bumpo as we gently closed the heavy doors behind us.

No one had seen us leave.

At the foot of the stone steps leading from the Peacock Terrace to the Sunken Rosary, something made me pause and look back at the magnificent palace which we had built in this strange, far-off land. Somehow, I felt it in my bones that we were leaving it tonight never to return again. And I wondered what other kings and ministers would dwell in its splendid halls when we were gone. The air was hot, and everything was deadly still but for the gentle splashing of the tame flamingoes paddling in the lily pond. Suddenly the twinkling lantern of a night watchman appeared around the corner of a cypress hedge. Polynesia plucked at my stocking and, in an impatient whisper, bade me hurry before our flight be discovered.

On our arrival at the beach we found the snail already feeling much better and now able to move his tail without pain.

The porpoises (who are by nature inquisitive creatures)

"The porpoises were still hanging about"

were still hanging about in the offing to see if anything of interest was going to happen. Polynesia, the plotter, while the Doctor was occupied with his new patient, signaled to them and drew them aside for a little private chat.

"Now, see here, my friends," said she speaking low, "you know how much John Dolittle has done for the animals— given his whole life up to them, one might say. Well, here is your chance to do something for him. Listen, he got made king of this island against his will, see? And now that he has taken the job on, he feels that he can't leave it—thinks the Indians won't be able to get along without him and all that—which is nonsense, as you and I very well know. All right. Then here's the point: If this snail were only willing to take him and us—and a little baggage—not very much, thirty or forty pieces, say—inside his shell and carry us to England, we feel sure that the Doctor would go because he's just crazy to mess about on the floor of the ocean. What's more, this would be his one and only chance of escape from the island. Now it is highly important that the Doctor return to his own country to carry on his proper work, which means such a lot to the animals of the world. So what we want you to do is to tell the sea urchin to tell the starfish to tell the snail to take us in his shell and carry us to Puddleby River. Is that plain?"

"Quite, quite," said the porpoises. "And we will willingly do our very best to persuade him, for it is, as you say, a perfect shame for the great man to be wasting his time here when he is so much needed by the animals."

"And don't let the Doctor know what you're about," said Polynesia as they started to move off. "He might balk if he thought we had any hand in it. Get the snail to offer on his own account to take us. See?"

John Dolittle, unaware of anything save the work he was engaged on, was standing knee-deep in the shallow water, helping the snail try out his mended tail to see if it was well enough to travel on. Bumpo and Long Arrow, with Chee-Chee and Jip, were lolling at the foot of a palm a little way up the beach. Polynesia and I now went and joined them.

Half an hour passed.

What success the porpoises had met with, we did not know

304 THE VOYAGES OF DOCTOR DOLITTLE

till suddenly the Doctor left the snail's side and came splashing out to us, quite breathless.

"What *do* you think?" he cried. "While I was talking to the snail just now he offered, of his own accord, to take us all back to England inside his shell. He says he has got to go on a voyage of discovery anyway, to hunt up a new home, now that the Deep Hole is closed. Said it wouldn't be much out of his way to drop us at Puddleby River, if we cared to come along. . . . Goodness, what a chance! I'd love to go. To examine the floor of the ocean all the way from Brazil to Europe! No man ever did it before. What a glorious trip! . . . Oh, that I had never allowed myself to be made king! Now I must see the chance of a lifetime slip by."

He turned from us and moved down the sands again to the middle beach, gazing wistfully, longingly out at the snail. There was something peculiarly sad and forlorn about him as he stood there on the lonely, moonlit shore, the crown upon his head, his figure showing sharply black against the glittering sea behind.

Out of the darkness at my elbow Polynesia rose and quietly moved down to his side.

"Now, Doctor," said she in a soft persuasive voice as though she were talking to a wayward child, "you know this king business is not your real work in life. These natives will be able to get along without you—not so well as they do with you, of course—but they'll manage—the same as they did before you came. Nobody can say you haven't done your duty by them. It was their fault they made you king. Why not accept the snail's offer, and just drop everything now, and go? The work you'll do, the information you'll carry home, will be of far more value than what you're doing here."

"Good friend," said the Doctor turning to her sadly, "I

cannot. They would go back to their old unsanitary ways: bad water, uncooked fish, no drainage, enteric fever, and the rest. . . . No, I must think of their health, their welfare. I began life as a people's doctor: I seem to have come back to it in the end. I cannot desert them. Later perhaps something will turn up. But I cannot leave them now."

"That's where you're wrong, Doctor," said she. "Now is when you should go. Nothing will 'turn up.' The longer you stay, the harder it will be to leave. Go now. Go tonight."

"What, steal away without even saying good-bye to them! Why, Polynesia, what a thing to suggest!"

"A fat chance they would give you to say good-bye!" snorted Polynesia, growing impatient at last. "I tell you, Doctor, if you go back to that palace tonight, for good-byes or anything else, you will stay there. Now—this moment—is the time for you to go."

The truth of the old parrot's words seemed to be striking home, for the Doctor stood silent a minute, thinking.

"But there are the notebooks," he said presently. "I would have to go back to fetch them."

"I have them here, Doctor," said I, speaking up, "—all of them."

Again he pondered.

"And Long Arrow's collection," he said. "I would have to take that with me also."

"It is here, Oh, Kindly One," came the Indian's deep voice from the shadow beneath the palm.

"But what about provisions," asked the Doctor, "—food for the journey?"

"We have a week's supply with us, for our holiday," said Polynesia, "—that's more than we will need."

For a third time the Doctor was silent and thoughtful.

"And then there's my hat," he said fretfully at last. "That settles it: I'll *have* to go back to the palace. I can't leave without my hat. How could I appear in Puddleby with this crown on my head?"

"Here it is, Doctor," said Bumpo producing the hat, old, battered, and beloved, from under his coat.

Polynesia had indeed thought of everything.

Yet even now we could see the Doctor was still trying to think up further excuses.

"Oh, Kindly One," said Long Arrow, "why tempt ill fortune? Your way is clear. Your future and your work beckon you back to your foreign home beyond the sea. With you will go also what lore I too have gathered for mankind—to lands where it will be of wider use than it can ever here. I see the glimmerings of dawn in the eastern heaven. Day is at hand. Go before your subjects are abroad. Go before your project is discovered. For truly I believe that if you go not now you will linger the remainder of your days a captive king in Popsipetel."

Great decisions often take no more than a moment in the making. Against the now paling sky I saw the Doctor's figure suddenly stiffen. Slowly he lifted the Sacred Crown from off his head and laid it on the sands.

And when he spoke his voice was choked with tears.

"They will find it here," he murmured, "when they come to search for me. And they will know that I have gone. . . . My children, my poor children! I wonder, will they ever understand why it was I left them. . . . I wonder, will they ever understand—and forgive."

He took his old hat from Bumpo; then facing Long Arrow, gripped his outstretched hand in silence.

"You decide aright, oh, Kindly One," said the Indian,

"—though none will miss and mourn you more than Long Arrow, the son of Golden Arrow. Farewell, and may good fortune ever lead you by the hand!"

It was the first and only time I ever saw the Doctor weep. Without a word to any of us, he turned and moved down the beach into the shallow water of the sea.

The snail humped up its back and made an opening between its shoulders and the edge of its shell. The Doctor clambered up and passed within. We followed him, after handing up the baggage. The opening shut tight with a whistling suction noise.

Then turning in the direction of the east, the great creature began moving smoothly forward, down the slope into the deeper waters.

Just as the swirling dark green surf was closing in above our heads, the big morning sun popped his rim up over the edge of the ocean. And through our transparent walls of pearl we saw the watery world about us suddenly light up with that most wondrously colorful of visions, a daybreak beneath the sea.

The rest of the story of our homeward voyage is soon told.

Our new quarters we found very satisfactory. Inside the spacious shell, the snail's wide back was extremely comfortable to sit and lounge on—better than a sofa when you once got accustomed to the damp and clammy feeling of it. He asked us, shortly after we started, if we wouldn't mind taking off our boots, as the hobnails in them hurt his back as we ran excitedly from one side to another to see the different sights.

The motion was not unpleasant, very smooth and even; in fact, but for the landscape passing outside, you would not know, on the level going, that you were moving at all.

I had always thought, for some reason or other, that the bottom of the sea was flat. I found that it was just as irregular and changeful as the surface of the dry land. We climbed over great mountain ranges, with peaks towering above peaks. We threaded our way through dense forests of tall sea plants. We crossed wide empty stretches of sandy mud, like deserts—so vast that you went on for a whole day with nothing ahead of you but a dim horizon. Sometimes the scene was moss-covered rolling country, green and restful to the eye like rich pastures, so that you almost looked to see sheep cropping on these underwater downs. And sometimes the snail would roll us forward inside him like peas, when he suddenly dipped downward to descend into some deep secluded valley with steeply sloping sides.

In these lower levels we often came upon the shadowy shapes of dead ships, wrecked and sunk heaven only knows how many years ago, and passing them we would speak in hushed whispers like children seeing monuments in churches.

Here too, in the deeper, darker waters, monstrous fishes, feeding quietly in caves and hollows would suddenly spring up, alarmed at our approach, and flash away into the gloom with the speed of an arrow. While other bolder ones, all sorts of unearthly shapes and colors, would come right up and peer in at us through the shell.

"I suppose they think we are a sort of sanaquarium," said Bumpo, "—I'd hate to be a fish."

It was a thrilling and ever-changing show. The Doctor wrote or sketched incessantly. Before long, we had filled all the blank notebooks we had left. Then we searched our pockets for any odd scraps of paper on which to jot down still

more observations. We even went through the used books a
second time, writing in between the lines, scribbling all over
the covers, back and front.

Our greatest difficulty was getting enough light to see by. In
the lower waters it was very dim. On the third day we passed
a band of fire eels, a sort of large marine glowworm, and the
Doctor asked the snail to get them to come with us for a way.
This they did, swimming alongside, and their light was very
helpful, though not brilliant.

How our giant shellfish found his way across that vast and
gloomy world was a great puzzle to us. John Dolittle asked
him by what means he navigated—how he knew he was on
the right road to Puddleby River. And what the snail said in
reply got the Doctor so excited that, having no paper left, he
tore out the lining of his precious hat and covered it with
notes.

By night of course it was impossible to see anything, and
during the hours of darkness the snail used to swim instead
of crawl. When he did so he could travel at a terrific speed,
just by waggling that long tail of his. This was the reason we
completed the trip in so short a time—five and a half days.

The air of our chamber, not having a change in the whole
voyage, got very close and stuffy, and for the first two days
we all had headaches. But after that we got used to it and
didn't mind it in the least.

Early in the afternoon of the sixth day, we noticed we were
climbing a long, gentle slope. As we went upward it grew
lighter. Finally we saw that the snail had crawled right out of
the water altogether and had now come to a dead stop on a
long strip of gray sand.

Behind us we saw the surface of the sea rippled by the

wind. On our left was the mouth of a river with the tide running out. While in front, the low flat land stretched away into the mist—which prevented one from seeing very far in any direction. A pair of wild ducks with craning necks and whirring wings passed over us and disappeared like shadows, seaward.

As a landscape, it was a great change from the hot, brilliant sunshine of Popsipetel.

With the same whistling suction sound, the snail made the opening for us to crawl out by. As we stepped down upon the marshy land we noticed that a fine, drizzling autumn rain was falling.

"Can this be Merrie England?" asked Bumpo, peering into the fog. "Doesn't look like any place in particular. Maybe the snail hasn't brought us right, after all."

"Yes," sighed Polynesia, shaking the rain off her feathers, "this is England, all right. . . . You can tell it by the beastly climate."

"Oh, but fellows," cried Jip, as he sniffed up the air in great gulps, "it has a *smell*—a good and glorious smell! Excuse me a minute: I see a water rat."

"Sh! Listen!" said Chee-Chee through teeth that chattered with the cold. "There's Puddleby church-clock striking four. Why don't we divide up the baggage and get moving. We've got a long way to foot it home across the marshes."

"Let's hope," I put in, "that Dab-Dab has a nice fire burning in the kitchen."

"I'm sure she will," said the Doctor as he picked out his old handbag from among the bundles— "With this wind from the east she'll need it to keep the animals in the house warm. Come on. Let's hug the riverbank so we don't miss our way in the fog. You know, there's something rather attractive in the bad weather of England—when you've got a kitchen fire to look forward to. . . . Four o'clock! Come along—we'll just be in nice time for tea."

· Afterword ·

IT has been some time since the Doctor Dolittle books have been published in this country. While they continued to sell millions of copies in more than a dozen languages around the world, ironically in the United States, where this world-renowned story of the doctor who learned to speak the animal languages was first published, the books have been out of print for more than a decade.

It was, therefore, particularly gratifying when Dell announced plans to bring back the Doctor Dolittle books. Once more Doctor Dolittle, Tommy Stubbins, Matthew Mugg, and the Doctor's animal family from Puddleby-on-the-Marsh—Polynesia the parrot, Dab-Dab the duck, Jip the dog, Too-Too the owl, Chee-Chee the monkey—will be sharing their adventures with a whole new generation of young readers.

When it was decided to reissue the Doctor Dolittle books, we were faced with a challenging opportunity and decision. In some of the books there were certain incidents depicted that, in light of today's sensitivities, were considered by some to be disrespectful to ethnic minorities and, therefore, per-

haps inappropriate for today's young reader. In these centenary editions, this issue is addressed.

The problem that the editors at Dell faced was whether or
not to delete or rewrite portions of the Doctor Dolittle stories.
Publishers rightfully believe that it is their job to publish a
writer's work, not to act as censors. Because the author is no
longer living, it was impossible to obtain his permission to
make changes. The Doctor Dolittle stories are, moreover,
classics of children's literature, and on principle one can
make a strong argument that one should not tamper with the
classics.

Yet times have changed. Is it appropriate to reissue the
Doctor Dolittle books exactly as written and stand on principle at the expense of our obligation to respect the feelings of
others? Should future generations of children be denied the
opportunity to read the Doctor Dolittle stories because of a
few minor references in one or two of the books which were
never intended by the author to comment on any ethnic
group, particularly when the references are not an integral or
important part of the story? What should our response be
when there is widespread disagreement among well-meaning
parents, librarians, and teachers as to the proper action to
take?

Book banning or censorship is not an American tradition!
To change the original could be interpreted as censorship.
Then again, so could a decision to deny children access to an
entire series of classics on the basis of isolated passing references. These were the difficulties we faced when trying to
decide whether or not to reissue the Doctor Dolittle books
and, if we did, whether or not it was appropriate to make
changes in the original version.

After much soul-searching the consensus was that changes

should be made. The deciding factor was the strong belief that the author himself would have immediately approved of making the alterations. Hugh Lofting would have been appalled at the suggestion that any part of his work could give offense and would have been the first to have made the changes himself. In any case, the alterations are minor enough not to interfere with the style and spirit of the original.

In addition, some of the original illustrations from the book have been deleted and others—also original Hugh Lofting illustrations never before published in book form—have been added.

The message that Hugh Lofting conveyed throughout his work was one of respect for life and the rights of all who share the common destiny of our world. That theme permeates the entire Doctor Dolittle series. I would like to acknowledge the following editors whose faith in the literary value of these children's classics was invaluable in the publication of the new editions: Janet Chenery, consulting editor; Olga Fricker, Hugh Lofting's sister-in-law, who worked closely with the author and edited the last four original books; Lori Mack, associate editor at Dell; and Lois Myller, whose special love for Doctor Dolittle helped make this project possible. If our alterations help to refocus Hugh Lofting's intended lessons to his young audience, we will know our decision was the right one.

Christopher Lofting

· About the Author ·

HUGH LOFTING was born in Maidenhead, England, in 1886 and was educated at home with his brothers and sister until he was eight. He studied engineering in London and at the Massachusetts Institute of Technology. After his marriage in 1912 he settled in the United States.

During World War One he left his job as a civil engineer, was commissioned a lieutenant in the Irish Guards, and found that writing illustrated letters to his children eased the strain of war. "There seemed to be very little to write to youngsters from the front; the news was either too horrible or too dull. One thing that kept forcing itself more and more upon my attention was the very considerable part the animals were playing in the war. That was the beginning of an idea: an eccentric country physician with a bent for natural history and a great love of pets. . . ."

These letters became *The Story of Doctor Dolittle*, published in 1920. Children all over the world have read this book and the eleven that followed, for they have been translated into almost every language. *The Voyages of Doctor Dolittle* won the Newbery Medal in 1923. Drawing from the twelve *Doctor Dolittle* volumes,

Hugh Lofting's sister-in-law, Olga Fricker, later compiled *Doctor Dolittle: A Treasury,* which was published by Dell in 1986 as a Yearling Classic.

Hugh Lofting died in 1947 at his home in Topanga, California.